Wild
Daisies
Bloom

Books by

PEGGY TROTTER

Year of Jubilee
Reviving Jules

~Unchained Souls Series~
The Secret Things
The Secret Storm

~Society of Outcasts~
The Misfit Bride
The Lowborn Lady
The Spellbound Schoolmarm

~Up from the Miry Clay~
Tattered Blossoms Rise
Wild Daisies Bloom
Flawed Roses Flourish (Releasing 2023-2024)

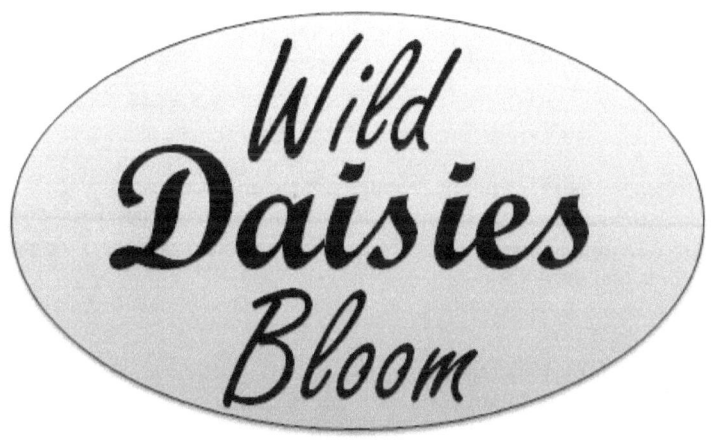

Up From the Miry Clay
Book Two

PEGGY TROTTER

Wild Daisies Bloom

Visit the author's website at: www.peggytrotter.com

Published by Ransomed-Ever-After Books

This novel is a work of fiction. Names, characters, businesses, places, events, and incidents are either the products of the author's imagination or used in a fictitious manner. Any resemblance to actual persons, living or dead, or actual events is purely coincidental.

First Edition, 2023
ISBN: 979-8-218-31429-3
Library of Congress Control Number: 2023922021
Printed in Columbus, SC, United States of America

All Scriptures used with this work are from the King James Version (KJV).

Cover Illustration © 2023 by Zanne Davis
Edited by Nancy Clark

[1]I waited patiently for the Lord: and He inclined unto me, and heard my cry.

[2]He brought me up also out of an horrible pit,

out of the miry clay...

...and set my feet upon a rock, and established my goings.

[2]And he hath put a new song in my mouth,

even praise unto our God: many shall see it, and fear, and shall trust in

the LORD.

Psalm 40:1-2

Chapter One

Cairo, Illinois—August, 1889

Their best customer lay dead.

Tyne Daisy Ciders took the lantern shoved at her. Then she stepped back into the room, past the huge bald man standing at the doorway and several scantily-dressed ladies. Most of them drew their filmy gowns across their bodies, shook their heads and, one by one, griping and swearing, abandoned the hallway. After all, it'd look more innocent if they were startled from their boudoirs by the sheriff.

Circling the foot of the bed, Tyne lifted the light. Ervy Gumpers lay dead in a pool of his own blood on the puncheon floor. She repressed the vomit surging up her throat and focused on practical matters. "You know what we gotta do, Kerth."

The broad-shouldered man grunted and entered. They hadn't much time. Tyne plopped the gun and lantern on the end table. Then she clasped the dead man's legs while Kerth clutched the fat motionless wrists. This would be no easy task. But Kerth tossed the body onto the mattress, nearly knocking Tyne to the floor in the process.

"How many times I gotta tell you to let me do it?"

The grumpy bald man grabbed the gun from the man's holster and transferred it to the dead man's hand.

"Dang, Miss Sapphire. Couldn't ya have shot him where's it looked like he'd done it himself?"

Miss Sapphire. She'd give a gold nugget to never be called that again. Not that she had one. Tyne shrugged and grabbed a nearby silk robe to mop up the blood. "Sorry. Didn't have time."

Kerth shoved the man's hand down and just laid the weapon under his chest. "Never do. Now get."

Tyne jerked up at the distant pounding. They were here. Already.

"Like I said…" He swiped his hand to indicate her exit.

Shaking from head to foot, she swiped up the gun and scurried from the room, rolling the soiled robe in her hand. Would there be any telltale wetness between the floorboards? She could only hope the dark night and the dim lantern light would hide it. Pansy Jo was safe, and that's all that counted.

With distaste, Tyne dropped the offending gun back into the cigar box. The stockings that had kept her footsteps discrete only minutes before she'd pulled the trigger, now muffled her scurrying feet up the stairway. She hung right and slipped through the last door. The dark room soothed her jangled nerves.

Thumps and heavy footsteps filtered up the stairway. What was she waiting for? She stood, frozen, gripping the blood-soaked robe. It was only a matter of minutes before they'd find her. Kerth could not protect her this time.

With a strangled squeak, she rushed to her wardrobe and pulled an old brown skirt and stained white shirtwaist from behind the showy satin gowns. It was what she'd arrived in three years ago. And it was what she'd leave in. Monitoring the noise on the first level to determine the deputies' whereabouts, she dressed and then shoved a few essentials in a small bag. Lastly, she stuffed the bloodied robe inside.

Then she gripped the carpet bag handle and raised the sill. Ten feet below lay the roof of the tobacco shop. She'd done this before, though the drop brought sweat to her palms. The dark night would shield her, yet the obscure hush of just past midnight would broadcast every noise.

Footsteps up the stairs forced her leg upon the sill. It was now or never. It was time to run.

❧

Glennis Bluff, Texas—August, 1893

It was time to hide. Again. Above all else, she had to remember her adjusted name Clementyne Bowlanders, not Tyne Ciders. And if things went to plan, in just two days, her name would change once more. Another desperate jump into obscurity. She hoped it was the final one.

A woman in a glowing blue dress swept in front of her, her ruffled hoop banging against Tyne's pitifully worn boot. The sheen of the fashionable dress could only be called sapphire. Like fire on a blanket of dark sky. *Sapphire.* Tyne's lashes swept closed for just a moment. How she had tried to bury that color in the last four years. If she never heard that name—word again, she might just find a shred of happiness.

Her first glance from the coal dust-covered Gulf, Colorado, and Santa Fe Railroad car conveyed a new train station plopped in a midst of a brown, dusty landscape. The platform wood underneath still smelled new. At least something was. The buildings that dotted the margins of the road ahead, with their false fronts, couldn't have been very old, yet their tumble-down construction gave the impression of a long history of Glennis Bluff.

Texas. The last place she'd ever thought to be. To her, it was the end of the world, nearly, and the end of the rail line. But that served her purpose. Perhaps here, she could finally put away the past and start anew. Yet, even her fresh start was stained with lies. She was...Mrs. Clementyne Bowlanders, widow. After all, that label sounded better than runaway prostitute.

"Can we ride in a wagon?" Daisy chirped.

Correction. Widow and single mother. Well, at least one was true.

How could the three-year-old have any energy left after the exhausting two day train ride from Kansas City? Tyne wanted nothing more than to collapse beneath the nearest shade tree.

She squatted to eye-level and gave her daughter her brightest smile. "We'll see about that. But first, we must find Mr. Hendricks."

Daisy nodded soulfully, her blue eyes widening in anticipation.

Sapphire eyes, the Almighty's blight upon Tyne. It was an everyday reminder of who she really was.

"And I'll have a new papa!" Daisy squealed as mischief leaped into those color-condemning eyes.

Tyne gave the imp a firm look and shushed her. Amid the sizable crowd on the modest loading platform, Tyne clasped the carpetbag in one hand and the small palm in her other. She maneuvered to the edge and stepped beneath an imposing live oak. After cutting through the collected bunches of people, she paused to rest next to the ticket office. There she pulled her daughter into her arms.

"You mustn't say that," Tyne breathed into the toddler's ear. "Remember, it's our secret."

Daisy continued to stare at her mother as she swung her head from side to side, rebelliousness boiling just below the surface. Tyne placed her hand firmly into Daisy's and lowered her to the ground.

The girl burned energy by skipping and leaping, nearly separating Tyne's arm from its shoulder socket. They strode around the building to the dusty road. It'd been a grave mistake to let her daughter in on the whole point of the trip. After all, Mr. Oliver Hendricks knew nothing about a child.

And, fortunately, he knew nothing about her, or at least anything important. Roxie had assured her a whole new identity in the most unconventional way, God rest her Aunt Clementine's soul. Now, Tyne would masquerade as her aunt, a mail-promised bride. Nevertheless, she'd arrived two weeks early hoping to speed the process. Her daughter remained silent only for a few steps.

"Will he be big, Mama?"

"I don't know."

"Will he have a beard?"

"I'm not sure."

"Will he wear big ol' boots?"

I have no idea."

"Will he have chickens?"

"I wish I knew."

"Will he like me?"

Tyne sighed audibly, warning Daisy who'd already asked this set of questions numerous times on the journey.

"Daisy," Tyne began, stopping to bend over, "I want you to be a very good girl. You understand? Don't ask Mr. Hendricks a lot of questions. Since we came early, it may take him a while to get used to us."

Daisy bobbed her head in perfect understanding, those innocent eyes wide and so very…sapphire. The familiar twinge of shame and disgrace smote Tyne to the very core. She breathed a soft humph and clawed her right pointer finger into the hollow of her right thumb. A rough patchy scab lay there from her continuous scraping, a nervous fidget that plagued her when life spun out of control. Which was always. Tyne let out a soft, short groan. "Let's just wait and see, okay?"

Tyne grabbed up the bag once more. The upward slope to the town proper somehow made the carpet bag pick up ten pounds each time she'd set it down. Daisy wiggled and bounced as they strolled, and Tyne's sore arm felt every jerk.

They walked exactly one minute.

"Do you think he has a horse?" Daisy questioned before coming to a full stop.

Tyne, grateful for the rest, set the carpetbag down once more. Perspiration trickled from her forehead. She tugged the lacy hanky from her sleeve and patted the moisture, gathering the patience and courage to address her daughter again. Glory, she would not make it.

Amid a prance, her daughter froze. In the bright sunlight Tyne realized the reason for Daisy's unusual immobile stance. Tyne pivoted at the sound of a horse and wagon, and she snagged the collar of Daisy's dress.

The conveyance tossed up dry dust as it moved. As the driver came abreast, he slowed to a stop. Her stray gaze met his. Tyne encountered two very blue eyes in the hairiest face she'd ever seen. Those eyes were not sapphire, thank the Creator, but lighter…somehow.

His beard hung long and shaggy, a fuzzy mess, and his hair nearly stood on end. Or perhaps it was in tangles. Anyway, he appeared ragged and unkempt. What little skin that showed glowed darkly tanned, making his eyes, squinted against the full sun, bright as the sky. Yet, not sapphire. Sky blue. Tyne took a step back. For several agonizing seconds, he eyed them up and down.

"You looking for someone?" His deep voice had a soft edge.

She cleared her throat and tried to squelch the hopelessness surging within her.

"I'm looking for Mr. Oliver Hendricks," she replied, putting her hand to her forehead to block the sun.

The man's face elongated as if he had just raised his brows beneath the rat's nest hair. Then he turned his gaze ahead. She took advantage to assess the rest of him and his wagon. He wore dusty jeans, nearly in threads, tattered boots, and a stained, stretched-out white collared shirt.

From the rolled-up sleeves, his thick arms emerged, sun-darkened, covered in a mass of dark hair, and bulged with muscle. His hands were dirty and work-swollen. She lowered her eyes and realized her five foot frame had never made her feel quite so small. Well, maybe once or twice. But that was buried deep.

She tucked a stray hair behind her ear before glancing back to the man. Had she only known what a waif-like figure she presented to him with her ragged dress and bonnet, sunken cheeks and huge eyes, she would've fled without an answer.

"Mr. Oliver Hendricks?"

"Yes, sir," she answered, slipping back into her scullery maid replies.

"You kin?" He eyeballed her, glancing from carpetbag to

Daisy and then back to her.

She shuffled her weight from foot to foot feeling increasingly guarded under his gaze.

"He's gonna be my new papa!" Daisy exclaimed, tugging from Tyne's grip with a squeal. With pure joy, the toddler spun and giggled.

Tyne pressed her eyes closed for a moment. Would this day never end? The sun beating down on her already exhausted body made her sway. She sidestepped and reached for the wagon wheel. Then, he was there. That hairy stranger with his enormous hands on her shoulders, steadied her. She should pull away. This wasn't the Fleabag Saloon anymore. But low on funds, she hadn't eaten in nearly two days. His strength was almost…welcomed.

The man grabbed her carpetbag from the dust and tossed it in the back of the wagon. He shuffled Tyne closer to the wagon. Daisy giggled and launched a hug against his leg. Oh, dear. This was getting out of hand. With a surprised grunt, he swept Daisy up and set her high in the wagon seat.

"Please, I couldn't…"

"Yes, ma'am, you can. You ain't been much in the sun have you?" he murmured as he lifted her with ease to the seat.

She shrugged. Never had she been one to take to the heat. And since the birth of Daisy, she'd been even more so inclined to grow faint, much to her consternation. For Tyne had been formed hard in the forge of her brief life. Swooning was out of the question.

He climbed up and took the reins. "Oliver Hendricks is a

neighbor of mine."

The blood returned to Tyne's head as the wagon gave a gentle pitch forward. Aware a stranger now drove Daisy and her away from town, far from the safety of the sparse crowd, she whispered her last, weak protest. "Please, we can't accept a ride. It just wouldn't be right."

Zeph appraised the petite woman with the pale green eyes. A hint of yellow encircled the center like cat's eyes. Her hair, a soft brown, so fine and unruly, framed her face much like her daughter's of a darker shade.

"Maybe not, but the shape you're in, it won't hurt."

Never in his finest dreams would he have predicted sitting next to such a lovely woman when he woke this morning. Nope, he figured just another jaunt into town, same ol', same ol'. Not that it mattered.

"What's your name?"

The slip of a girl asked in sing-song tones, her tiny body wedged between him and the woman. The child patted her hand on his thigh which made him a bit nervous of her carefree familiarity.

"Zeph Rowley."

"My name's Daisy. Actually, Daisy Belle. The Belle's after my 'dopted aunt. She sneaked Mama food when she hid in the barn."

"Daisy!"

"Yes, Mama?" The girl lifted her angelic face.

16

"You mustn't talk so much." The woman's whisper resembled a hiss.

The child nodded.

Little Daisy now rested her tiny hand on Zeph's forearm, legs swinging back and forth under the seat. "You gots hairy arms. Zeph. You live in a barn?"

"Daisy," her mother burst. "You must address him as Mr. and please, shush."

But the tot eyed her mother with her head cocked.

"Mama, I don't like that name, mister. Mr. Greely's name was mister and he was mean."

A decidedly charming blush rose up the woman's neck. If she'd been near to a faint before, from the look on her face, she'd likely keel from the wagon seat about now. She flicked him a glance and then leaned down to pull her daughter close.

"Stop talking about barns and Mr. Greely, you understand?"

Daisy nodded solemnly.

"As a matter of fact I don't live in a barn," Zeph felt obliged to answer.

But from the defeated look that came to the woman's green eyes, he knew he should've kept still.

"We did," Daisy chirped, "For a long time."

His cheeks widened slowly into a smile, which quite surprised him. He couldn't remember the last time he'd taken such pains.

"I'm terribly sorry. Daisy sometimes doesn't hush when she should." The woman shot meaningful eyes at the little chatterbox.

The girl merely edged closer to driver.

The man shrugged, still grinning. This was one unusual day. He couldn't resist a little dig. "Actually, she's more informative than her mother."

The woman's mouth popped opened as she stared at him, her flush deepening. Then she clasped her hands in her lap and seemed to collect herself. "I'm sorry. I didn't properly introduce myself."

Zeph almost yanked on the reins. Nope, he didn't need to know her name. He didn't want to know. Why he'd stopped to begin with was pure mystery. Well, not a true puzzlement given the woman had nearly fainted dead away in the dirt. No, his best bet was to merely drop them and run. And run fast.

'Cause the only thing worse than abandoning them to that mean old cuss Mr. Hendricks was getting involved. And he could not afford that.

Chapter Two

But the blamed woman didn't stop.

"I'm…" her lashes fluttered which did crazy things to the pit of his stomach. "Clementyne Bowlanders."

Daisy bounced on the seat. "Only—

Mrs. Bowlanders pressed a hand to the tyke's mouth. "No more talking."

The child squirmed away and clutched at him. "I know a song, Mr. Zeph Row—Leeeeee."

In her high-pitched, childish voice, she launched into "Oh, My Darling Clementine." This did not seem to settle well with Clem—daggum, her name leapt into his mind—Miss? Mrs? Bowlanders. The woman exhaled a long breath and turned her face away. But he found himself wondering at the status of her title and hating himself all the more.

Next to him Daisy continued to caterwaul. To his surprise, the girl knew several verses in a row. But when she belted out, "wooby wips above da water"...he nearly thought he might laugh aloud. Odd. Laughter hadn't been part of his life for a good long while now. But he swallowed it. Likely the handsome woman wouldn't appreciate his small bit of mirth.

But, at least the child wasn't talking, pouring out the woman's secrets one after another. The less he knew, the better.

He hung a left and the shack came within sight. Daisy continued each verse in a voice just a notch above too loud. The closer they came to the shack, the more apparent its run-down condition appeared. Guilt made Zeph's Adam's apple toggle.

Stumps littered the small yard and various animals nosed the bare ground. A broken plow, an old wagon leaning precariously to the side, and several broken chairs littered the area among the stumps. Grass grew in tall clumps.

Yep. This was the place in all its glory. Why the attractive woman had an interest in the tumbledown shack was beyond him. He eased back on the leather leads in his hands to pull May and Tay to a stop. Mr. Hendricks's huge pink sow lazed on the porch, nursing a mass of wiggly piglets. At least he assumed they were feeding. From the violent gyrations, they almost appeared to be eating the huge pig. Several hens waddled freely onto the porch unperturbed by the greedy piglets.

The sow rose and eyed the wagon before hauling her huge body up and along with her brood, squealing and complaining, stepped off the porch to settle beneath the broken wagon that lacked a wheel.

"Well, this is it," Zeph announced.

At the complete silence, he swung his gaze to his passenger. The petite woman's face had turned a sickly shade of buttermilk. Then her lips parted, emitting a strange, strangled cry.

He scurried down from the wagon. 'Twould be easier to catch her from the ground. Because from the looks of it, this wasn't quite what she'd expected.

Tears stabbed Tyne's eyes. This was her deliverance? Her final destination of never running again? A forever home that'd blot out her painful, haunting past? That strangled sound wedged out her throat once more. She clenched the seat to ease the wobble running down her legs. Then the driver appeared at her right, ready to aid her from the wagon seat.

"Are you sure this is Mr. Hendricks's place?" she choked out.

"Yes, ma'am." Zeph cocked his head, while his big, worn hands straddled the wagon sideboard below her.

Was he expecting her to pitch from the wagon in a swoon? She sucked in a long breath through her nostrils. Come to think of it, considering the long journey, the hovel, and her dashed dreams, that might not be too far off the mark.

"Catch me, Mr. Zeph Row—leeeeee."

Before Tyne could stop the precocious toddler, Daisy launched into a leap, and Tyne's heart jettisoned to her throat. But the man's more-than-capable hands locked about Daisy's waist in mid-air. Then he gave a grunt that was almost a chuckle, and set her safely to the ground. He tugged the tail of her dress down over her fluffy petticoat before the giggling child scrambled away on her next adventure.

Tyne's hot cheeks pounded in tune with her runaway heart. This couldn't be happening. Roxie hadn't been kidding when she said the end of the line. Stuck in an overgrown pigsty in the wilderness, living with a stranger was rock bottom. Literally. Could anything be worse?

The Fleabag Saloon.

She slumped at the unwanted thought. Well, this hovel was preferable to that. She stood. The hairy man, Mr. Zeph Rowley— the name Daisy had so readily latched onto—lifted his strong hands, nearly encircling her waist, and lowered her to the ground. His steadiness soothed her for a moment until she glanced up and found her scrappy three-year- old setting chase after a particularly small piglet who'd broken away from the pack.

"Daisy." The name came in a wisp of breath. My, how she missed Roxie. That woman could tame the wild beast that was Daisy. And now she wasn't here. Tyne had to handle this on her own. She opened her mouth to chastise the child and then changed her mind. Why bother? If they ended up living here, it'd soon be their normal life.

She set her chin and pulled the carpet bag from the bearded stranger. Her tattered skirt swirled as she spun and strode to the doorstep. Roxie had assured her that God had orchestrated this plan to marry Mr. Oliver Hendricks. Bless it, even. Oh, how Tyne wished the merry cook were here to see dear Mr. Hendricks's home. Tears pricked behind her eyes and bile rose in her throat.

She had no more reached the porch when the door exploded open. A short grizzled man in his mid-seventies, or thereabouts, thundered out in oversized boots, laces dragging and one leather tongue flapping wildly. A shotgun flashed in his left hand. Perhaps even the Fleabag Saloon would be preferable to this old goat?

"Whatcha business?" he demanded in a gravelly voice.

Tyne froze, all her rehearsed speeches fleeing. She cleared her throat. "I'm...Clementyne Bowlanders."

"Who?"

The man scrubbed his spindly gray beard all the while keeping one side of his face all scrunched up and his eye closed. "Don't know no one named Clementyne."

He all but yelled the reply. A deaf mute could've heard each syllable clearly from the train station. Tyne's throat dried up like mud in July. Things were sliding further south each moment.

Tyne cleared her throat. "We've...been writing to one another for some months now."

Roxie had made her memorize every detail of the letters, but, at the moment, she couldn't think straight. Only one thought hammered in her brain. *He's old. Much, much too old.*

"I don't write to nobody nowheres. Cain't read," he declared. "Now, get off my land."

He swiveled and stomped back to the door.

"Howdy, Ollie." Mr. Rowley hollered from his location back at the wagon.

The door stopped in mid-motion. The old man peeked through the opening. Then he stepped through once more. Tyne scuttled backwards. All she could do was stare as he waddled toward Mr. Rowley. The old man eyed Daisy prancing about the yard, chattering to anything that presented itself.

"Zeph, that you?"

"Yep."

"Who're these people?"

Mr. Rowley shrugged. "Here to see you."

The old man snorted. "Well, I ain't got no business with them. Tote 'em on back to town."

Daisy took her cue and raced to Mr. Rowley and held up her petite arms.

"Make me go high."

Tyne pivoted, reality squeezing her line of sight into a tight tunnel vision. Zeph swung Daisy up to the seat as the child squealed at the great height of the lift. Tyne snapped from her frozen state, tugged her carpetbag from the dirt, and marched on trembling legs back to the wagon.

"There's no need to help…" Her protest trailed to a stop. She didn't even know the way back to town.

Mr. Rowley's light blue eyes mocked her soft protest. My, when had it become so hard to breathe? Was it stress from disappointment? Or the knowing gaze of her companion? With a nod, he lifted her to the seat. She sighed in frustration and clenched her sweaty hands in her lap as the big man swung her carpetbag into the back of the wagon.

"Sorry to have troubled ya." Mr. Rowley waved to Mr. Oliver Hendricks and rocked the seat as he boarded. "Good day to ya."

"Bye-Bye, Mr. Pig Man." Daisy gyrated in the seat, waving both hands.

Tyne clamped her bottom lip between her teeth. Dear Lord. She was paying her penance for past sins to the full.

The old man snorted, spun, and muttered all the way back to the shack. Meanwhile, the bearded man in the wagon seat wasted little time turning the two bays around to head back in town. Tyne sat in miserable silence while Daisy repetitively hummed the first line of *Three Blind Mice* ad nauseam.

How had Tyne actually allowed her imagination to dream a comfortable life on the Texas frontier with a hard-working husband? Silly enough to picture the unknown Oliver Hendricks as embracing Daisy as his own and providing a decent home and a promising future.

Sure, she'd known he'd be older. After all, her aunt was the one who'd corresponded with him. But she'd entertained no idea he'd be an irate, grizzled old man.

To make matters worse, Daisy smoothed the hair on Mr. Rowley's arm like a long lost uncle. Tyne wanted to jump in a hole. She tugged the child's hands into her own.

How could she have been so stupid? Nothing in her life had ever worked out in her favor. Why would she think it'd start now? Maybe love had never been in the cards for this mail-ordained marriage, but she'd hoped for a keen friendship and a stout smokescreen from her past. At least, that's what she and Roxie had planned. How wrong they'd been.

Bitterness filled her mouth and tears threatened to appear. She kept her head turned to the right to avoid the curious stare of the driver. Tyne Ciders had never cried before. She wouldn't start now.

"Mama?"

"Yes," she whispered.

"My belly's growling."

Daisy leaned against her and stilled her slight hands in her mother's. Tyne leaned toward Daisy to kiss her head and found a dingy, but clean hanky being handed to her.

"Thank you." After wiping the grime from her daughter's face, she refolded it and patted the sweat on her forehead. "I thank you for the ride and the handkerchief. I'll be glad to pay you for all your trouble."

"No trouble. I just realized I forgot nails."

Their eyes met and Tyne felt as if she looked in a mirror. His eyes were wooden with dashed hopes. This man understood grief first hand. He knew the pain.

She tugged her gaze away. "I don't suppose there might be an inexpensive safe place to spend the night in town?"

Her anxious fingers smoothed Daisy's fine hair behind the child's ear as she rested in Tyne's lap. At least her little magpie wasn't chattering.

"The hotel isn't the place for you," Mr. Rowley spoke lowly, almost hypnotically, and Tyne suddenly felt exhausted. "But I know of someone who occasionally rents out a room now and again."

"Thank you," she murmured.

They plodded back to town in silence. Passing through on Main Street held little appeal. Tyne only wanted a place to hole up and heal. They passed the train station and a small collection of businesses. At the far side of town, Mr. Rowley stopped in front of a large, white two-storied house with an inviting front porch. It was in want of a good coat of paint, but at least the front wasn't littered with hogs and chickens.

Mr. Rowley leaped down and assisted Tyne, and now a sleeping Daisy, whom he carefully laid in her mother's arms. He collected the carpetbag and led the way to the door. Once there, he deposited his load and turned to Tyne and removed his hat.

"I won't be welcomed. But it's a good place for you and Daisy. Name's Annabelle Hutchens."

He placed his hat back on all that hair.

"Ma'am," he nodded a farewell and strode to the wagon, climbed aboard, and disappeared down the street.

Zeph cursed himself for stopping for that woman and child. It'd been the oversized carpetbag that seemed to pull the woman in one direction while the child had pulled in another. If only he'd looked away or urged May and Tay to pick up the pace.

But no, he'd stupidly stepped up and almost dropped them

on old man Hendricks and left. He shook his head. Had the woman come to town to marry that old coot? He'd heard of men sending off for mail-order brides but he'd never come upon it happening.

It smacked downright amusing to imagine the two of them walking the aisle. No, on second thought, it wasn't amusing. It was pathetic. A young woman yoked to a decrepit broken-down man, a man who clearly wanted no company.

Why, the very notion was a shame, but then life never gave to one fairly. If it did, Noreen would be beside him in the wagon with a little girl like Daisy between them, not to mention a few other imps in the back of the wagon. Zeph gritted his teeth. No, life wasn't that right.

He passed Hendricks's turn off on the left, bringing to mind green eyes filled with pain and tears. He wasn't going to dwell on it. He'd done more than most would, and he'd settle on that and not think on it again. And Zeph, who'd become quite experienced in excluding other important things from his mind, did just that.

Annabelle Hutchens squinted through sun-bleached lace curtains as her mouth curled into an ugly line. Zephaniah Rowley had pulled up and now stood on her porch. He seldom, if ever, dared to venture past her house since Noreen's death four years ago, and only did so then because her body had been shown in this very house. She closed her eyes and brought the memory into focus, Noreen so yellow and thin, Zeph so still, so quiet, so unmoved. She opened her eyes only to see the object of her hatred drive away. What was that hairy monster up to now?

Annabelle gave a start when she heard a knock echoing up the stairs. Putting on her usual stern expression, she ambled downstairs to greet what Zephaniah Rowley had deposited on her doorstep. As she descended, she glimpsed a woman through the screen door with her arms full of a sleeping child. Annabelle cracked the door open.

"Yes?" she inquired stiffly through the screen.

"I was told you had rooms?"

The woman's voice sounded desperate. Annabelle took in her slender, ragged appearance. She examined the narrow face with large eyes and sunken cheeks. She took in the small wide forehead where wisps of golden carmel hair framed her flushed, tired face.

"Very well." Money was money. Even if it came from a cast-off of Zephaniah Rowley. Annabelle nodded and pushed open the screen.

The young woman all but fell through the doorway.

"I am Mrs. Hutchens. Take the third room on the right at the top of the stairs. You can deposit your child and we'll settle the financial arrangement."

The young woman nodded. "I'm...Clementyne Bowlanders. This is my daughter, Daisy."

Loaded with the small girl and her carpet bag, the woman stumbled to the second floor. Annabelle sat in her wing chair for some twenty minutes, her receipt book in her lap and her mind calculating how much she could overcharge Zeph's guest without giving them the knowledge of her plan. In the end, she set aside the receipt book and climbed the stairs to see what was keeping her new boarder.

The door hung wide open and, being as it was Annabelle's home, she entered without knocking. There on the bed lay mother and child, asleep. The mother, little more than a child herself, bore tracks of grime across her dusty cheeks. Suddenly, Annabelle's own eyes filled with tears. The pair appeared completely defenseless, completely in need. Uncharacteristically, Annabelle pushed the issue of money from her mind and closed the door softly.

She would allow this stranger and her child in...for now. But nothing would deter Annabelle from getting to the bottom of who this "friend" of Zephaniah Rowley really was.

Chapter Three

Zeph rolled over and groaned at the early hour. Green eyes had haunted his dreams and roused him. The sun hadn't even bothered to rise yet. He blinked at the moon-illuminated window, noticing for the hundredth time the stark square of glinting pane, wondering why he'd torn down the curtains. But then...the reason was painfully clear. Noreen's hands had labored over them and he couldn't bear to look upon the happy print with the uneven hem. Guilt lay too heavy. But he wouldn't kick around that dead horse now.

He'd fallen asleep at such a late hour, he'd counted on sleeping clear to noon. Instead, here he lay, at a bit after four, some two hours earlier than time to rise. Disgusted with himself, he rose. His last thought before sleep and his first thought this morning had been of Clementyne Bowlanders, despite his resolve to put both the woman and the meeting from his mind.

At the dry sink in the corner, he splashed tepid water over his face. His heavy hair flopped forward, and with an angry thrust he flung it over his head. The heavy wad of hair, his penance, was always there to remind him of Noreen. If he'd kept the mirror his wife had prized, he would've long stared at himself over his jumbled thoughts. He would've glared at his beastly face to try to read some answers.

He shook his wooly head and cursed himself once again as he realized that instead, Mrs. Bowlanders's image had invaded his mind. It only brought a knife to his gut. The only thing worse than thinking of Noreen was replacing her with the green-eyed lovely.

He groaned. Had folks not assured him God would lessen his pain? That good, old fashioned time would take away the sting of loss? That life would continue, and he'd move forward into a brighter future? But God and time had not healed the blinding pain, but rather increased it until he cried out in physical agony. He gripped his abdomen and dreamed, prayed for it really, of the many deadly diseases it could be that would slowly, painfully rake him from this world. It would be Zeph's only blessing from God.

But the stab of pain passed and Zeph dressed. *The nails.* Blame. The green-eyed woman probably assumed he'd simply lied about the forgotten item. How he wished it were true. In his haste to put distance between himself and the woman he'd dropped at Mrs. Hutchens's, the nails had been forgotten twice over. A fool, he was. Snatching his hat, he stormed out to the barn to saddle the horse for another unwanted journey into town.

Once aboard Tay, he let the animal amble. He wasn't much of a saddle horse, rather more suited to the wagon. But Zeph had sold most everything that didn't need kept and that included his bay saddlehorse.

The comforting plod brought the drowsiness he'd sought only an hour ago. Zeph's eyes blinked closed and then opened. He needed his wits. Tay had a mind of his own when it came to meandering the countryside. If he wasn't careful, he'd find himself a county over. Yet, his eyelids grew heavy, and he slumped forward.

Zeph dozed in the saddle until the jerk of Tay stopping roused him. The poor excuse for a saddle horse dropped his neck and chomped the lush green grass in the sheltered valley. Zeph groaned aloud when he saw where the horse had taken him. The blamed animal had gone the complete opposite direction, taking the worn trail to the far pasture. The big, lone oak on the rise kept sentry over a small fenced area nestled in its shade.

"Dad burn it, Tay." Zeph gave a low growl. "I ought to call you Jonah, running off like a dang fool."

The reference that came so readily didn't sit well in his gut. That Bible stuff was behind him. Why those thoughts continued to plague him, he could only blame on the cesspool of his own sins. In short, he deserved every bit of torture.

33

He gritted his teeth and raised his eyes. The spread-eagled tree seemed to reach out and embrace not only the early morning mist and anticipate the sun, but also the small graveyard below its branches. Zeph buzzed a reluctant sound low in his throat. And thinking of torture, here lay the perfect place to chastise him. The enclosure both drew and repelled him.

He should've taken May. The mare couldn't wait to head to town toward the famous Mexican plum tree, planted by one of the town's forefathers beside the stream just outside of town. In recent years its popularity had diminished, given that most folks had propagated their own plums from that very tree. But May still counted it as a worthy landmark. Mostly her stomach did. Zeph had a time keeping that mare from stopping and chawing on the fallen fruits this time of the year. But, at least, the path would be headed in the right direction.

He sighed and swung out of the saddle. Tay seemed unaware of the emotion roiling in Zeph's gut as the horse manicured the grass surrounding the grave enclosure. Zeph leaned forward and set his hands on the picket fence he'd built. The roughness of the wood and worn whitewash smote his heart as his Adam's apple bobbed. It'd been long enough to show signs of neglect, and that nearly stole his breath. The cross he'd carved stood accusingly in the center surrounded by three other smaller ones. The overwhelming sense of what he'd lost nearly choked him, and he lowered his head a moment to suck in a gulp of air. Then he peeked up, staring at the name he'd burned into the cross.

"Noreen." His voice came rough and gruff, like it needed

using. "Shouldn't have never brought you here. You were a delicate rose bush in the desert in this place."

He let his head drop and clenched his eyes closed. Why Annabelle Hutchens hadn't strung him from a tree yet was beyond him. The woman had planned bigger things for her daughter Noreen. She'd hoped to install Noreen in a Chicago mansion with a well-to-do gentleman husband and had almost managed. If only Noreen hadn't moved here, she might be safely running an estate and planning socialite teas.

Instead, she'd come to Texas and tried to learn how to use a thimble, a hand pump, and the big black iron stove. His eyes roved the other three crosses, marking infant-sized graves. Here rested his children who'd never seen the light of day, nor even been named, and agony seared his scarred soul.

Zeph groaned and turned away. Swear words rose up the back of his throat, but he wouldn't mutter them here. He wouldn't dare desecrate the final resting place of his dear ones. The mournful cry of a dove echoed through the vale, flaring more sadness in his chest for the sound bespoke his grief so aptly. He swung aboard Tay who was reluctant to be pulled from his grazing, and lumbered off. Maybe Zeph would purchase a bottle of whiskey with that box of nails.

Being stone drunk beneath his kitchen table sounded pretty good about now.

৩০৫

Annabelle rose at her usual early hour and went about the same meticulous routine she'd started since Elmer had passed eight years ago. His death proved too early to stop the irreparable liaison of his only daughter. At sixty-five, Annabelle's hair was liberally streaked with gray but still sported her shining black strands which she was particularly proud of.

Although the small braids she worked and proceeded to wrap around her head like a halo cramped her fingers so and often ached for hours afterwards, Annabelle gave no thought to changing the style. Reaching for the white powder that gave her skin a dry pale look, she puffed a generous amount across her paper-thin cheeks. A lady's skin should always remain untouched by the sun.

She patted the top of her head with grim satisfaction, her hands throbbing, and then reached for the large straw hat she wore every morning. She fluffed the feathered bird's nest perched there. The headdress had seen better days, but she wouldn't part with it. It was as much a part of her day as breathing.

Annabelle, whose grandparents had emigrated from London, preferred to call her early jaunt her morning constitutional and used the expression as often as possible.

Only yesterday Mr. Olinski, the town dry goods merchant, complimented her on her dedication to her faithful morning walk. Annabelle lost no time informing him she was about her morning constitutional. Mr. Olinski had nodded his perfect understanding, having heard Annabelle's Londonese for several years. As a matter of fact, the townspeople had heard it so many times, it'd long become a private joke among the townsfolk.

Annabelle collected her filmy wrap, which was unnecessary

on a beautiful July morning. But it, too, like the braids in her hair, was simply part of her daily routine. She picked up her paper fan that sat on a small table near the door and slid it into her left sleeve. It'd been a gift from her sister some thirty years past and always accompanied Annabelle on warm, close days. She checked her face in the oval mirror next to the door and, with a nod of satisfaction, opened the screen door.

Already, the sun was hot and bright as Annabelle retrieved the tucked-away fan. She looked about, especially at the flowers, to see whose landscaping had changed from the year before. Mr. Porter's climbing rose looked as if it needed watering as it clung to the leaning picket fence. It certainly didn't have as many blossoms. She would have to speak to him about the need to faithfully water his precious bushes.

So this was the sum of her life. Elmer was gone. Noreen was gone. She, now a lost soul, wandered a small, dilapidated town in Texas, examining the floral progression in the neighbors's yards. Annabelle allowed one small sigh, but only one. It was too late to mend now. But it'd help to be back in the bustling city of Chicago. She'd often longed for it. And her sister's account of the World's Fair had her almost scurrying to sell the aging two-story house Elmer had paid for in cash just before Noreen's eleventh birthday.

But how could she return? A Naomi in the modern sense. She'd lost everything. Perhaps she'd ask the local folk to call her Mara. But that would be too inane…and too painfully accurate. No, she would never return. It wouldn't be the same without

Elmer and Noreen.

Instead, she would hail Mr. Porter and lecture him on the proper care of climbers.

ᏉᎾᏉ

Tyne felt the tug of the quilt, and still clinging to the hope of just a few minutes of sleep, she pressed her face against the cotton. Her daughter would waddle down the back staircase into the spacious kitchen. And Roxie would watch Daisy and take care of her morning needs.

Her bones ached and Tyne just needed a minute or two more. Then she'd arise and bury herself within the bowels of the basement and scrape the dirt from the Wiseforths' linens and underthings. Yes, she'd slumber just a moment more. With a deep breath, she floated back into a deep sleep.

But the sunshine tickled her cheek in such an unfamiliar way that Tyne rolled over. The sun-bleached white room caused her to take a startled breath and bounce to the end of the mattress. Oh, dear. Oh…dear. She was not ensconced in the Wiseforths' servants' quarters.

Instead, she lay inside a weathered boarding house, on the cusp of the end of the world. That's where she was. She'd remembered taking the stairs, barely able to lug both Daisy and her carpet bag to the second floor. And then…she hadn't returned to settle with the proprietor. She jumped to her feet.

Why, it was morning. Her feet, a bit worse for wear having spent the night in her boots, carried her to the window covered by a filmy curtain. Tyne swiped it away. Yes, it was truly morning, and…Daisy. Roxie still resided in Kansas City, no doubt tending to the Wiseforths' breakfast eggs, which left her daughter unattended.

Oh, gracious heavens. What mother lost track of her own daughter?

Tyne bustled from the room, whispering her child's name. "Daisy?"

Tyne walked softly from room to room of the big house, peeking in each as she went. This was not good. If Daisy was up to her usual shenanigans, the landlady would toss them out on their ears faster than you could say jumping jackrabbits. And then where would they be?

Early sunshine washed each room in light and airiness making Tyne pause to study each, leaf shadows dancing on the walls. But no small toddler pranced about the rooms. Making her way back to the long hall, Tyne fixed her eyes on the only closed door at the end. Could Daisy have managed to turn the door knob?

A horrible dread washed up her throat. Of course, she could. Not two weeks ago, she'd found the child in the Wiseforths' master suite, fingering the missus's silver brush. Thank goodness, the family had been on a picnic outing and hadn't been the wiser. Roxie had lectured Tyne on keeping her eyes on the lass.

Eyeing the doorknob, Tyne hoped beyond hope it wasn't the landlady's boudoir, for nothing could be worse. She gripped the marble handle and turned.

Tyne's eyes took in the lavish room, so at odds in the simple whitewashed home. Pink paper, wreathed in delicate flowers, covered the walls, giving the room a lavish flair. In every corner, the space gushed with dolls and stuffed animals, books arranged carefully on a gorgeous ornate bookcase next to a custom handcrafted rocking horse. The name Noreen was stitched onto the saddle blanket.

Under the window, an exquisite miniature baby doll bed beckoned, complete with quilt and pillow, and resting under the covers, a porcelain doll, bright spots of pink painted on her cheeks, and topped with curly dark hair. To the left, swathed in a beautiful pink quilt and sporting a lacy canopy, stood the bed covered with a silky plethora of pillows of varying shapes.

The dream bedroom of every young girl.

Tyne's mouth plopped open, and for a moment, she stood stunned by the luxuries in the room. But, then, her gaze snagged on the child smack dab on the luscious pink carpet. In the center of the blocks, tops, and animals on wheels scattered about her, sat Daisy. Oblivious, she chattered to an elephant figurine plucked from the assortment of animals from the huge wooden replica of Noah's ark which was artfully displayed on the hearth of the fireplace.

A small squeak slipped from Tyne's throat. She pushed the door shut behind her and rushed forward.

"Look, Mama. A big fat pig."

Tyne swiped the wooden toy from her daughter's hand and snatched the elephant figurine from the plush carpet. "Daisy Belle Ciders—I mean—drat."

"But, Mama…" A long wail punctuated the child's protest.

Tyne had neither time to hush her nor sort the newest name she'd bestowed on her offspring. For she spun this way and that, too busy trying to return the tumbled toys to their rightful place. With shaking hands, she stacked the blocks on the other side of the hearth, hoping to heaven that's where they originated. Then she twirled, laying a hand over her daughter's mouth to stifle the unhappy yowl.

What if this woman had other boarders? What if the woman herself heard Daisy's cries? Why, she'd come to investigate, of course. The woman hadn't even been paid for the previous night.

They had to get out of here. *Right now.*

Chapter Four

Annabelle chastised Mr. Porter, circumvented town, and strode on her way back, filled with a bit of satisfaction that Mrs. Leatha Fontain's flower garden had certainly come up lacking. It was usually the display of the circuit, but it was obvious that it no longer deserved that crown this year. She set her lips against the thought that perhaps Leatha's poor health had caused the disarray in her garden. Annabelle merely tilted her head a bit higher. It served her right, giving her so much trouble in past years.

She climbed the porch and swung open the screen door and had just set her foot inside the parlor when she heard a long, drawn-out cry. For a moment, it made her catch her breath and remember a time long ago. Then, the door at the top of the stairway flung open, and her new boarder stepped out, shushing the child in her arms. The girl wiggled from the woman's grip and raced down the hallway, wailing as she went.

It startled Annabelle so that she swayed to the right against the stairway newel. The young woman spun to tiptoe down the hall but froze and gasped at sight of Annabelle. The audacity of the young sprite, gallivanting into Noreen's private room. Steadying herself against small table perched in the stairway alcove, Annabelle's fingers clipped a tall white vase holding a single red rose. The vessel teetered, but Annabelle managed to grasp it before it shattered to the floor. The water and rose, however, flew across the spotless wooden planks.

Ignoring the mess, Annabelle stumbled to the landing at the top of the stairs clutching the white vase to her bosom, feeling a bit dizzy. Zephaniah's castaway covered her mouth with her hand and her startling eyes widened. Annabelle scowled and took a fortifying breath.

"No one runs in this establishment. It's forbidden." Annabelle could feel her body swell with heated anger. "And no one, absolutely no one, enters that doorway. Under any circumstances. Have I made myself abundantly clear?"

She was caught. Perhaps not by the sheriff of Cairo, but nabbed nonetheless. Daisy meandered toward her, still sniffing and whining.

"Yes, ma'am, of course," Tyne drew Daisy in her arms, not just to leash her in, but as a protective barrier from the angry woman in front of her. At least the woman's appearance had

43

calmed Daisy's tantrum.

"Present yourself in the parlor in fifteen minutes, young woman," Mrs. Hutchens gritted through her teeth before spinning and stalking to the door at the end of the hall. The door shut with a decisive click.

She'd just as well fetch her carpet bag. For sure, the woman would throw Daisy and her out. With a groan Tyne returned to her room. Well, at least she wouldn't have to pack. She stumbled in the doorway and collapsed on the side of the bed. Daisy, who'd been clinging to her, pulled her head back and set her frightened eyes on her mother's.

"I'm sorry I bad, Mama," she whimpered.

Letting her mind spin, Tyne swallowed and pressed the child against her shoulder. Had her past deeds, her own wicked choices caused Daisy to be so naughty? She shook her head. No, the three-year-old had been curious. It'd been Tyne's fault. Keeping an eye on Daisy alone was wearing. Perhaps she should've never become a mother.

As if she'd had a choice. Months had passed after she'd fled from the Fleabag Saloon's second floor window before she'd realized she was in the family way. No doubt the bad seed of the very man she'd gunned down that dreaded night, or some other wayward lout with a solid buck. She squeezed her eyes closed and clenched her jaw. The past had to stay in the past. Daisy was here, and Tyne loved her. She'd do anything to make sure her daughter would never have to suffer through what Tyne had faced growing up.

But what was she going to do now? Hide in a barn again like she had before her aunt had finally secured a launderer's position for her? Hiding out in the huge carriage house had been a tad easier before Daisy had arrived and while she remained an immobile young infant. After that, it was an absolute nightmare keeping tabs on the toddler while she wore her hands to a frazzle, soaking, scrubbing, and bleaching the Wiseforths' unmentionables.

The horrible basement was full of spiders, grime, and darkness, steam and fumes rising to stifle her lungs. The job had been a drudgery beyond comprehension, but she'd happily step up to the washboard again to avoid homelessness or, worse yet, consider returning to her former occupation. No, homelessness was preferred to going back to the Fleabag Saloon. Carefully, she detached Daisy from her arms and laid her on the bed.

"I have to freshen up, and then we have to leave," she said as she stepped to the blue flowered bowl and mirror.

"Huh come we not staying? And what about my new papa? Can't we go there?"

Tyne stared in the mirror, trying to slow her breathing as she smoothed her hair. After splashing some cold water on her face and drying away the dust, Tyne stepped to her daughter and settled on the edge of the bed.

"If you only knew how much I love you, Daisy," she whispered, wishing she could somehow make it abundantly clear how much she'd sacrificed for her. But she couldn't. She was a child—her child.

Daisy drew Tyne's face nose to nose.

"I love you, Mama."

Tyne closed her eyes. The child had a way of balming her heart. She blinked her eyes open and eyed her daughter with intensity. "You must listen, Daisy. You must never run in Mrs. Hutchens's house. So, when we go downstairs, you will apologize. Do you understand?"

Daisy nodded with big swings of her head and leaped into her mother's arms. Tyne pressed her back to the bed and brought her head close to her daughter's again.

"And you must never touch her things."

"Like at the Big House?"

Tyne closed her eyes for a second to stem the wash of unwelcome memories.

"Yes."

"Huh come Mrs. Hutchens has toys?"

Tyne sighed. "Daisy, you are not to mention that room again. Do you understand? If you do I will…spank you."

Tyne seldom resorted to physical punishment for Daisy, so with its mention, the child's eyes became very serious, and she nodded solemnly. Tyne stood and collected Daisy into her arms. She dearly hoped and prayed that Mrs. Hutchens would be able to forgive the incident. Otherwise, they were in a heap of trouble. There was no Roxie to pull her iron from the fire. And Aunt Clementine was gone.

She was on her own. She and Daisy.

Quietly, she trailed to the door and then padded softly down the stairs. She chose a tattered rose armchair to settle in, Daisy firmly in her lap, as she waited for Mrs. Hutchens. The frayed carpet bag rested at her feet. Tyne couldn't help but compare the furnishings to the extravagant child's room at the top of the stairs. But she couldn't focus on that right now.

Tyne whispered directions into her daughter's ear until Mrs. Hutchens appeared at the top of the stairs. The stern woman navigated the steps in regal fashion, and Tyne scooted to the edge of the seat. Tyne's face drained of color as Mrs. Hutchens sat directly across from her. Taking advantage of Tyne's loose grip, Daisy popped up. The toddler romped over to the woman and laid her hand on Mrs. Hutchens's lap.

"I sorry, Ma'am. I naughty. You spank me." Daisy turned around and presented her bottom to Mrs. Hutchens.

Tyne gasped, rose, and snatched her up. She mumbled a quick apology and returned to her chair, Daisy in her arms. The elder woman cocked her head and raised one brow.

"Well," Mrs. Hutchens began, "at least she shows some remorse."

Tyne had seen a hard light in the woman's eyes as she had seated herself. But oddly, it softened a bit since Daisy's most sincere apology, and, of course, her backside offering as payment. Tyne's pointer finger scratched furiously at the side of her thumb.

"I'm horrified at my behavior. And my daughter's, Mrs. Hutchens. I…can give no other explanation except the exhaustion of the trip. It won't happen again, I promise. I…mean if you allow us to have another chance, that is."

Mrs. Hutchens's chin elevated.

"Are you from London?" she demanded. "Your accent leans that way."

Tyne swallowed. "I…lived there as a young child."

"I see," Mrs. Hutchens sniffed, eyed her new boarders, and reached for a receipt book on the small side table covered with a crocheted doily. "Well, I suppose as long as you can keep the child detained from anymore chaos, you may stay."

Tyne kept her lips sealed. For how could she promise that? The older woman named the monthly rent that was, thankfully, quite low, and Tyne could feel her chest fill with a smidgeon of thankfulness. She'd been given a second chance. For now, they had a room. Beyond that, well, she'd deal with that later.

How Tyne wished Roxie's loving arms would encircle Daisy and her and murmur the absolute assurance how God would take care of them. For she so needed her friend. But she squashed the childish desire and negotiated a week's stay, much to the consternation of her future landlady who much preferred a monthly arrangement. Tyne dug the proper amount for rent from her meager savings. She had a whole week. Surely, she could find a paying position in the next few days.

Tyne unpacked in her room with the door closed, Daisy corralled inside with her corncob doll. Then they made their way to the parlor.

"First, the rules." Annabelle stood quite stiffly, centered in the cherry arch leading to the dining room. Her hands clenched together in front of her chest like a prima donna soprano ready to trill scales before the opening scene of an opera. Tyne cleared her throat, pulled herself up straight, and parked herself subserviently in front of the woman, Daisy's hand firmly in hers.

"No food or dishes in rooms, no lights after nine. No coarse language, no spirits or tobacco, and certainly, no gentleman callers beyond the parlor and that, only with permission. You shall be here for meals, on time. No tardiness is tolerated. If you must miss, you shall alert me the night before. You shall not wander the house and there is…"

Here she affixed a stern gaze upon the unsuspecting Daisy, who now stood on tiptoes, leaning sideways to peer around the woman, tempted only by the aroma of bacon in the air.

"No running inside the house or on the veranda. Hot water shall be supplied for bathing twice a week. However, you shall be responsible for transporting it to your room and dumping the used water at the back fence. Should any other circumstance arise, more rules may be added at my discretion and will be announced at the dinner hour. Do you understand, Mrs. Bowlanders?"

And thus the life of polite society's confinement tightened Tyne's throat. The one thing she missed about the Fleabag Saloon was a sense of freedom. "Of course."

"Breakfast will now be served." With a brisk nod, Mrs. Hutchens flicked a hand. "You may be seated in the dining salon."

Tyne nodded, clenched Daisy's hand, and trailed obediently behind the matron of the house into the dining room. The elder woman disappeared through a far door for only a moment and reappeared with a large tray. With great decorum, Mrs. Hutchens transferred the eggs, bacon, a stack of biscuits, a teapot covered in a knitted cozy, a milk jar, jelly and a crock of butter to the table. Tyne's belly squeezed at the delicious aroma. Tyne slid into a seat and lifted Daisy to the chair next to her with a firm hand

"Oh, goody!" Daisy clapped her tiny hands and grinned.

Annabelle's stern face put a damper on the toddler's ecstasy as she set the tray down.

"My tummy's so grumbly."

Tyne shushed her daughter. No doubt at this very moment, Mrs. Hutchens devised a no talking before meals rule.

"Little girls are to be seen and not to be heard," Annabelle announced.

Daisy sat up on her knees and reached for a piece of bacon. Tyne caught her arm as it made its way back to her plate.

"Filling plates will begin after grace."

Apparently, amending the rules could happen at any meal.

"'Kay." Daisy clenched her eyes closed. "Thank you God, amen."

The child's arm tugged within Tyne's grasp. Daisy turned her eyes, giant sapphire pools, upon her mother.

"God said it was okay 'cause I so hungry."

"Ahem."

Tyne glanced at Annabelle whose features had frozen in disapproval.

"Since that was hardly adequate, I shall say the blessing over this bounty." Annabelle swept a hand beneath her backside to confine her skirt into the stiff-back chair. Then she bowed her head behind her pale clenched hands. "Great Lord, we beseech thee…"

With Mrs. Hutchens's attention upon the elaborate words of thanksgiving, Tyne squeezed Daisy's wrist until the piece of bacon fell to her plate.

"…and Lord, for those who are misfortunate, who haven't a crumb to call their own, we ask by your divine graciousness, rain sustenance down upon them, that they, too, as miserable, wretched souls might feed upon your goodness and see their own sordidness in their carnal needs as well as their blemished hearts…

The shuffle beside her had Tyne peeking at Daisy who'd leaned forward in an attempt to stab at the toast with the fork she now sported. Gritting her teeth, Tyne nabbed the utensil and tugged the child into her lap.

"…so for this magnificent bounty, our heavenly Guider, Creator, and Begetter of all things good and blessed, ordained for building our faith and strength to carry on in this arduous life, this burdensome journey of perpetually serving You and looking toward our final resting place into your ever-loving arms, we give our sincere thanksgiving for this glorious repast, evermore. And amen."

Tyne had to stifle a sigh of relief as Annabelle finally raised her regal head and grasped the teapot before her. Oh, dear. A proper serving of beverages much like the Wiseforths' rigid course succession. If that were any indicator, Tyne, herself would soon begin to feel faint from lack of food. But thankfully, Annabelle had no servants to laud out servings, collect plates, and return with the next course. Soon Daisy's and her plates were filled.

Silence reigned around the table. Even Daisy who usually chattered like a magpie remained silent. The child shoved the crunchy bacon into her mouth. Tyne shot a quick prayer of thankfulness at the hunger which kept her daughter from blurting out every known secret to her new landlady. And even though Tyne's stomach churned with nervousness, she managed to put away enough food to stave off hunger. After all, future meals hovered in uncertainty.

Tyne gathered Daisy's empty plate on hers and corralled all the silverware.

"Just leave it on the table."

Annabelle's dismissive tone screamed in capital letters that Tyne's help was not needed nor wanted. With a sigh, she thanked the woman for the meal. Perhaps the best plan was to get Daisy out of the house.

"I think Daisy and I will take a walk through town."

The woman froze as she rose, an almost approving sparkle in her eye. "Why, that is an excellent idea. A morning constitutional does wonders for one's health."

Well, it might do wonders for a body's vigor, but there were more pressing matters. Tyne had to find a job. Now.

Chapter Five

The breath of fresh air didn't contain the relief Tyne hoped it would. The sun glared hot enough to fry an egg on a shingle. She strolled and fanned, following the shade as much as possible. What businesses existed in town? At this point, without becoming Mrs. Oliver Hendricks, she'd need some other plan to sustain a roof over their heads.

Daisy pranced merrily along, singing one tune and then another, making up the words she didn't remember and then breaking away to encircle the trees and jump out at her mother on the other side. Tyne smiled at her antics, envying her childish ignorance of their dire situation and tainted past.

By the good grace of a hairy stranger, they'd managed a ride to safety, a place to stay, and food to eat for a week. Beyond that, Tyne shook her head. She didn't even have enough money left for one train ticket, let alone two. And marrying Mr. Hendricks couldn't even be considered, even if the old man had been willing. And there was even less to go back to. Here they had one precious week.

Yet, hadn't she been kept safe for almost four years now? Why, Roxie would tap her under the chin and tell her, 'to pick her chin up off the floor and make it work.'

She scanned downtown businesses as they approached the mercantile, parcel post, dressmakers, livery, church, the school, and in the middle of it all, the Swank Hotel obviously not seeing much business this early. Viney's Victuals, an establishment dedicated to slacking the appetites of the town, bubbled with late breakfasters. Not much to offer a job to a young woman toting a small child.

A man hailed her from the livery, and Tyne felt panic rise in her throat. Of course, there was always her former occupation. And, for a moment, the panic that rose made her want to flee. For she'd might choose to die rather than entertain that sort of employment again.

But the man headed straight for her, a curious expression on his face. He paused, noted Daisy, and looked even more uncertain.

"You are Clementine Bowlanders?" he asked as he pulled his round derby from his head.

His suit appeared frayed but still useful for everyday wear. He appeared older than she but not by much. But he was clean cut with clear brown eyes. A smile broke out across his features when she answered.

"Yesss…" She drew the word out, glancing about.

A smile broke out on his pleasant face. "Ah, Homer the ticket master was correct. He told me you'd arrived by train yesterday. I'm afraid I pictured you much older."

Tyne stepped back, her face puckering as she drew Daisy to her side.

"Oh, dear," he shook his head slightly, his dandy smile still in place, "Where's my manners? You'll have to excuse me, you see. I find myself in a most awkward position."

He hesitated and then shot his hand out with confidence. "I'm Hershel Hendricks."

Tyne swallowed and tilted her head to the side, barely brushing his outstretched hand. He was a small man, not much taller than Tyne's five foot frame.

"Hendricks?" This did not bode well.

"Uh…yes." His face lost a bit of its shine and turned a bit sheepish. "I'm Oliver Hendricks's great nephew."

Tyne blinked. Was that statement intended to make her feel more comfortable? For it'd failed miserably. He cleared his throat, tucked a finger in his tight collar, and glanced around the street.

"Actually, it's quite a long story, and one I certainly owe you." He hesitated and swept her up and down. "Perhaps we could step into VV's and refresh ourselves with a beverage."

She widened her eyes. "VV's?

"Oh, sorry. Of course. Viney's Victuals, local non-alcoholic watering and feeding hole. A lovely alternative to the Swank Hotel Saloon. Quite an unsavory place. Despite its downfalls, I can't say I won't miss this town. VV's is the perfect place for a lady and child. Then, we can get down to the business of…explaining the situation."

Tyne shook her head. How easily the man seemed to change subjects. "Situation? I don't understand. You said Mr. Hendricks was…"

"Yes, I'm sure it's all a muddle. Please, if you would?" He gestured for her to proceed toward the café.

Scraping at her lip with her teeth, she saw no other way to discover why this man knew of her schedule of arrival. Slowly, she turned, keeping a firm grip on her daughter, and headed to VV's. All the while, the man at her right, much like her daughter, only in manly tones, kept jabbering small talk of the pleasant day, the lovely sunshine, the town improvements. She half expected him to burst into song, perhaps "Oh, My Darling Clementine?"

The diner, still crowded, forced them to work their way to a table on the far left, in front of the window. Tyne placed her daughter in a chair and pointed her finger at her for emphasis.

"You will not talk," she commanded in low tones toward the squirmy child.

Daisy slunk down in her chair, mumbled, yes, Mama, and settled her too large head on her tiny arms. Tyne glanced around as the man held the chair and then seated himself across from her. A waitress encumbered with a heavy tray, passed by. People seemed to have an unusual interest in their particular table, Tyne noticed, and thought perhaps the gentleman across from her was well known.

The waitress then scurried back and took their order for three lemonades and disappeared amongst the crowd.

Her companion cleared his throat and then graced her again with his well-practiced smile.

"I apologize for this abrupt meeting. It just caught me by surprise since you'd indicated earlier that your arrival wouldn't occur for at least another two weeks. I thought sure I'd whisked the letter off early enough to stop you."

Tyne's furrowed brow deepened. She wasn't sure which was more distressing, the man's words or the stares.

"I'm not sure what you mean. Are you saying you sent a letter?"

Had Mr. Oliver Hendricks changed his mind and asked his great nephew to scrawl a note to cancel? That seemed to make sense as the elder Mr. Hendricks had denied being able to read. Perhaps this man had assisted him with the letters? "I believe the letters came from Mr. Oliver Hendricks."

"Yes." Again the throat clearing, and now fidgeting started from the fully grown man. "Well, I'm afraid you being here is all a big…mistake."

Mr. Hendricks's jaunty smile slipped a little and a fine sheen of perspiration broke out on his upper lip.

"A…mistake?" Had the chair just developed a huge hole? She felt as if she were sinking.

"Yes…uh. Well, you see…" His eyes darted to Daisy who

now tugged on her mother's dress.

"I'm tired, Mama," she mumbled.

Tyne woodenly pulled the child into her lap. When Tyne's gaze met Mr. Hershel Hendricks's, he had the good grace to let the smile slide from his face and dart a nervous glance out the window.

"I find myself at a loss for words, which," Mr. Hendricks gave a nervous laugh here, "is unusual given I've just accepted a position at the Louisville Courier Journal."

He gave a prideful grin that didn't quite finish as he flicked his eyes over her and her daughter. Somehow, she couldn't find it in her heart to congratulate him.

"All right, here goes." He procured a hanky from his pocket and rubbed the perspiration from his lip and brow.

The waitress bellied up to the table and delivered the lemonade glasses with loud clunks, sloshing some to the worn tabletop.

"Yum." Daisy grinned and reached for one.

With Tyne's help, the child took a long drink of the clouded goodness. Tyne took a short swig of hers as well. Prickly sensations grabbed her neck as she could literally feel the stares of the many patrons.

"Well," he repeated after he took a long drink. "I guess the best way to explain is from the beginning."

At this point, he grabbed at the bow tie at his neck and flicked his eyes again to the glass window.

"You see," he cleared his throat, "apparently, a number of

young men from the surrounding areas have been getting mail-order brides."

Tyne helped Daisy take another drink and almost spilled it at the topic he broached.

An uncomfortable laugh hiccupped from the man before he continued. "Yes. Anyway. It's become a bit of an interesting oddity, so to speak." He eyed her uneasily as he gave a small smile. "I've been reporting here locally at the Glennis Bluff Gazette, and my editor approached me a year or so back to do a personal interest story."

A strange buzzing began in Tyne's head.

"Wait." She shook her head in an attempt to clear it. "What does this all have to do with me being here?"

"Ah!" He pointed a finger into the air and gave another weak jaunty smile. "It's actually become quite a captivating story. I mean, you've become quite a local hero."

"Excuse me?" The lemonade soured in her throat.

"The entire romance has been…published, word for word, in my column, letter by letter."

"What…romance?" Her voice came in a rasp.

His chuckle came out like a strangled gag, and he yanked at the bowtie again.

"Everyone knows Clementine and Ollie's long distance relationship. From top to bottom. Each week a new letter was posted in the gazette. Like a running series. Every week. Why, you'll be proud to know it proved to be our most well-read column."

The man's face tinged a bit pink, but he forced another laugh, gesturing to the patrons taking a keen interest in their meeting. Tyne's jaw dropped. With dismay, her eyes swept the room once more. Most surveyed her with great interest. Oh, my. These people already knew...Clementine Bowlanders. She'd launched into her worst nightmare. Instead of disappearing into anonymity and shielding her true identity, she'd become a local celebrity.

Tyne felt the blood fade from her face.

Mr. Hendricks held up his hands to her. "Don't get the wrong idea. I never intended for you to actually travel here to Glennis Bluff."

He slurped a bit more of his lemonade. "And as you have no doubt well figured out by now, I used my great uncle's name simply because he never reads the newspapers, well, he can't even read, and he's a bit of a recluse."

Mr. Hendricks's face looked a bit like she felt hers did, like she was strangling. How long would it be before the local law figured out Clementine Bowlanders, mail-order bride was actually Clementyne Ciders, woman wanted for murder? Tyne could only huff a few breaths. But the blasted man wasn't finished talking.

"I wrote in his name. I thought perhaps I'd find a match for him if it came to that, but I was really looking for a good human interest story that would propel me to a bigger market. And it did do that." The horrible man had the audacity to try to laugh at this point.

"Drink, Mama," Daisy begged.

Tyne complied, feeling anger, desperation, and fear clash in her stomach.

"I must admit," he gave a smile, "that your letters portrayed you much older. And," he paused and tried to admonish her a bit, "you made no mention of a child."

He drifted off as she turned a sweltering gaze on him. The slow burn made its way up her throat as his revelation washed over her. How dare he chastise her for withholding information from letters she never wrote when he'd made the entire affair up from his imagination. And, even more appalling, he'd published them. He'd simply dallied with her aunt and her emotions for his own selfish ambitions.

Tyne opened her mouth, wanting, yearning to blurt the whole mess, how he'd carelessly exposed her aunt to the world for a pathetic promotion. Her dear aunt had believed all this was real, going to her grave believing Oliver Hendricks loved her and was her dream match come true. The woman had scraped and saved for months to buy the very tickets Tyne had used. But this journey had only put Tyne in the second most hopeless situation of her life.

But, she couldn't. To say all of those things, confess her real name, reveal the switch in brides, would only put the law on her trail all the quicker. She couldn't do that. It was bad enough that these people, all staring with mouths wide, waiting for the next installment of the gazette's mail-order bride column, thought they knew her. Instead, she took a deep breath and almost wished for the colt she'd held in her hands four years ago.

"You are a repulsive man, Mr. Hendricks," she hissed. "To play with people's emotions and lives to fill space in your newspaper column. Simply to further your career? How could you? How could anyone stoop so low?"

What little confidence that remained on the reporter's face slid away, and now he sat stammering at her words. Tyne jumped up, slapping the stiff ladder back chair against the wall behind her. Gathering Daisy into her arms, she fed that anger—anger for her dead aunt, anger for her impetuous choices, anger at having believed this trip was the answer to all her troubles. What a fool she was.

Tyne stuffed her bonnet between their two bodies. Then, chin high, she strode through the crowd, powered by her anger, disappointment, and despair. Daisy's head bobbled against her shoulder, and untouched by the bizarre meeting, drifted off to sleep. Sweat nearly sizzled from Tyne's hot face as she made her way back to Mrs. Hutchens's house.

Not only was she not going to be married, her former name buried and never to be resurrected, but every person on the street recognized her in her carefully conceived alias. She was the laughing stock of the entire town. She cut behind the buildings to avoid walking in front of the sheriff's office. This was not the time to be matched with a sketched drawing of herself hanging behind the lawman's desk.

৩∞৩

Something white hot surged in Zeph's gut as he watched

Mrs. Bowlanders scurry down the sidewalk and slip behind the buildings on Main. Something had happened. The crowd pulsated from the front door of VV's with Hershel Hendricks breaking to the front, staring at the departing woman and small child until they slipped down the alley. A strange sort of envy worked its way up his spine. Had she come to meet Hershel instead of old man Hendricks?

The newspaper man ran his hand through his oily hair, shaking his head. Zeph, a self-proclaimed hermit, avoided most folks and certainly didn't care to know much about any news in general. But he'd heard people talking about Hendricks's popular column.

Could it be that this woman was somehow involved? It didn't make sense she'd show up out of the blue, asking for old man Hendricks with the intent of hitching up. At least, little Daisy had claimed her desire to latch onto a new papa. But that old muleskinner didn't care much about anything except drinking and shooting. As a matter of fact, old Ollie was a bit of an embarrassment for Hershel.

Zeph rubbed his hairy chin. Hershel tried to put on the ruse of being a big-time reporter bound for the nitty-gritty avenues of politics and had, if rumors were correct, secured a new job, now on his way to a big city in a week or so. Zeph wouldn't miss him strutting around town in his fancy suits grinning and tipping his hat to all the ladies in the street.

Tay stomped his white hoof, bringing Zeph's mind to a stop. He forced the anger to drain from his body. In its place, the familiar bitterness rose up. What did he care about the woman—a woman with cat's eyes? With a jerk, he pulled the horse around and, with a kick, sent Tay bounding out of town, nails safely in the pouch behind the saddle. There would be no whiskey today.

Chapter Six

Roxie Hadasher whipped the eggs with violent strokes, the fat flaps under her arm slapping her plump body. She added the ham chunks, onions, peppers, cheese, and a few dashes of her secret spices to the omelets. It'd been the omelets that had saved her, she mused as she always did when she made them. She would've been gone two years ago except for these fine fluffy eggs that the Wiseforths insisted they couldn't live without.

But it had been worth it. Tyne had appeared to appeal to her Aunt Clementine, for the girl had nowhere to go. Of course, the whole story had come out in the months to come—that and her condition. My, she and Tyne's Aunt Clementine, Clemmy to Roxie, had a terrible time keeping the girl sequestered away in the barn loft, Tyne all swollen and pregnant. Then the baby arrived, and the elder Clementine fought her final demise to consumption.

Roxie knew it was her God-given right to adopt the young woman and her child, to feed and clothe her even if the child had been fathered in a brothel house. If not for the loose lips of a stable hand, the Wiseforths would've never found out. Roxie harrumphed. Why, Tyne deserved more than a leftover mail-order bride situation. But what else could be done?

Roxie shook her head to clear out the depressing thoughts. It'd do a Christian woman no good to dredge up unpleasant memories, she reasoned as she poured the egg mixture into the hot lard. And Tyne had gone to a new place with a new life. Roxie sighed. If only Tyne had found the Lord before she left. Tears smarted the woman's weathered eyes. And that baby, Roxie kept her eye on the omelets and began to pray for her dear young friend. My, that toddler was a handful, sure enough.

The thing that stayed on her mind was Oliver Hendricks. What she hadn't told Tyne was her suspicion that the man might be a bit older in years than what Tyne was prepared for. After all, Clemmy had pushed past fifty.

But, she supposed, as good as the man appeared to be in his letter, a few years wouldn't make much of a difference between Tyne and Mr. Hendricks. Still…Tyne and Daisy lay on her mind quite heavily. Roxie flipped the bacon to the plates. Best spend her day praying. No telling why the Lord laid the pair on her mind. Hopefully, 'twas nothing. Nothing…but a sweet wedding.

౸

Never had a wedding been in the works. Tyne chewed the

simple chicken salad sandwich. Quite good, she supposed. But lunch was nothing more than another silent meal at Mrs. Hutchens's. Tyne made a concentrated effort to eat all she could, knowing her meals would soon be much harder to come by. Daisy, for the most part, had eaten her meal in silence also with her huge blue eyes fixed on her mother's face.

After a nap in the afternoon, Mrs. Hutchens served soup promptly at five, another meal wrought in the stifling silence. Tyne rose, thanked her host, fetched some writing supplies, and drifted to the back door. Here, in the expansive yard, Daisy could play and chatter to her heart's content.

Tyne sat with her back against a sturdy willow and propped the pad of paper in her lap. Dear Roxie… That was the easy part. Now to explain. Daisy chattered happily to herself, her hands reaching out to brush the undersides of the long hanging willow branches. But words wouldn't come. Tyne couldn't say what she really wanted…that she was trapped and everything that Roxie had promised had fallen through. Complete homelessness loomed just a few days away.

Why, how could she even part with the money to buy the stamp? Tyne crumbled the paper in her hands, slapped the journal closed, and thrust it to the scratchy, burnt-up grass. There was no use making Roxie as hopeless as she felt.

Tomorrow she'd find a job, despite the pall of Hershel Hendricks's horrible account of her aunt's very public relationship by mail. Well, actually, it was her relationship, at least to everyone in town. Ugh. How long would it be before the authorities connected the strange mail-order bride failure with the on the lam murdering prostitute from Cairo?

Although the summer night still promised plenty more evening sunlight, Tyne called to Daisy and trudged up the stairs. Once the child fell fast asleep, she could mourn…mourn all that'd been taken away before it'd truly been given.

ॐॐ

After a fitful night upon the quilt in her sweltering second-story room, Tyne rose and dressed, ready to find a position, almost any positon save one, which would allow her to lug Daisy alongside.

The meal of French toast and sausage lay heavily as Tyne headed for town. Mrs. Hutchens might be prickly, but she laid out decent meals. She paused a moment to eye the downtown layout. Well, in the best of worlds, she wanted to work alone, away from prying eyes, away from those who might discover who she really was. With a nod of her head, she headed straight for the dressmaker's shop.

Miss E.O. Bridgetta's~Couturier of Fancy Ladies' Fashions. Just the name gave her pause. Couturier? Quite the dandified term for a dressmaker. And the defined flip of the painted script across the large pained glass gave Tyne even further pause. Nevertheless, she scraped her pointer finger across the raw place at the base of her thumb and tightened her grip on Daisy's hand. With a sniff of courage-inducing air, she turned the doorknob.

Drapes of fabric nearly blocked her line of sight. Bolts of cloth, their flowing beauty tumbling to the meticulously shined plank floor, stood upright on several tables. Like colorful waterfalls, the cascading tables presented the shopper with a multitude of selections with just a glance. Even the air smelled of newly-pressed linen and starch. Tyne scratched harder at the peeling, painful spot near her thumb.

Her shoulder jerked when Daisy grabbed a wad of shimmery white organza flowing from a bolt to the floor.

"No." Tyne pried out the costly material from the child's tight grip, hoping desperately no syrupy residue still clung to her daughter's tiny hands.

"May I help you?"

One look was all it took. The elder queenly woman, dressed in a mustard taffeta, the gown perfectly manicured to fit her slim body, wore a look tainted only slightly with pretension and suspicion. Her eyes narrowed as her gaze snapped to Daisy. One look and Tyne knew this was not the place for Daisy and her. Yet, desperation made her take a step or two toward the ruling seamstress matriarch.

"Hello. I'm Clemetyne Bowlanders. I've come…"

"I know exactly who you are, Mrs. Bowlanders. What is your business here?" The woman's pale brows rose a fraction.

Tyne banished the scratching hand behind her back. "I've come to inquire after a…position."

If possible, the aging blond woman's expression chilled even more, like scraggy grass blades after a hard frost. "There's nothing for you here, Mrs. Bowlanders."

The woman placed a hand on the high countertop, behind

which hung a plethora of plain silky dresses next to a sign proclaiming, *tailored and accessorized to your exacting specifications.*

Tyne cleared her throat. "I can do any type of work."

"Indeed? Stitch? Tat? Alter?" The disbelief nearly blocked the earlier condescension in her gaze.

"Well…no, but I could—"

"I already have three girls. One is busy tatting, another altering, and the third is sweeping the shop to rid us of stray threads and scraps of fabric. I've no other need for an unskilled girl." She blinked. "Especially one with a child. Good day, Mrs. Bowlanders."

Like wax from a hot candle, Tyne melted toward the door, towing a questioning Daisy. On the wooden walk, Tyne worked the hanky out of the neckline of her dress to dab the moisture on her brow. That had been an abject failure. If Miss Bridgetta's greeting and disdain were an example of the fairer sex in Glennis Bluff, Tyne may as well drift out of town.

Why had she ever thought she could start again by shedding her scandalous past and slipping on a new persona? With her mythical romance turned out for all to see, even the seamstress scorned her. She shook her head. There were plenty more businesses.

Tyne bypassed the small parcel post and headed straight into the mercantile. The sun glared hot enough to roast any stray chicken trotting about. Tyne set a good pace and dabbed the moisture that collected on her brow. It took precisely three minutes for the stocky mustachioed man at the mercantile to eyeball Daisy, prancing near the shelf of ladies' soaps, to reject Tyne's job request.

Much the same happened at W.T. Chattingham's Shoes and Bootery, Miss Shady's Millinery, VV's, and the Swank Hotel and Saloon. Thankfully, each local had dismissed her with less disdain but still displayed plenty of reluctance with Daisy prancing about their wares.

By Friday, Tyne scraped the barrel at the cigar store and the stable. The heat and the disappointment wrung out the last bit of energy in her body. The only saving grace was that Mr. Hershel Hendricks had left enough money with Mrs. Hutchens to buy a train ticket back to Kansas City. One. She'd pondered over the matter, knowing that returning wouldn't solve anything. So, with much trepidation, she cashed out the ticket and laid out the money for yet another week at Mrs. Hutchens. Surely, the extra time would allow her to find a place to work.

But by the following Friday, after checking at each house that appeared the owners could afford household help, she knew she was stuck between a rock and a hard place. She could either stay at Mrs. Hutchens's another week, or buy food for almost three weeks.

This decision weighed on her mind for the next couple of days. By Sunday evening, she knew she'd reached the end of her rope. She led Daisy to the back yard. She must choose the option that gave them the most time. They had to leave. Tonight would be their last night in the tidy boarding house. And then, they would be homeless and wandering once more. Worse yet, no Roxie would be around to sneak her food and supplies. She and Daisy were indeed beyond desperate.

Tyne sank to the ground beside the willow tree that had become her thinking spot. The cool shade made Daisy stay close as she pranced beneath the branches. Tyne felt a sob rise in her throat. Daisy circled a few more times before coming and settling on her mother's skirt stretched on the grass. The child grew still, her songs echoing softer and softer until she drifted asleep. Tyne envied her peaceful, blessed nap but turned her face skyward. She had nowhere else to go. Never having spoken to God before, she only murmured two words.

"Help us."

Nothing changed. The heat of the July day almost cooked the browned crispy grass. She closed her eyes. It was over. She was truly abandoned. Moisture licked at her lids and a tiny drop squeezed through. She swiped it away. Somehow she had to survive. But she'd never, never sink as low as she had at the age of fourteen. Mother gone, she'd allowed herself to be talked into doing things so base they turned her stomach.

Now, Tyne had more invested than ever before. She had Daisy. Her child deserved more than a corner in a brothel, waiting for her mother to finish up with her next customer. Sobs snuffled up her throat but she gritted her teeth. No. She would do whatever she could to keep that from happening. She closed her eyes and forced the empty thoughts from her mind. Suddenly, she just felt so weary, so drained. She breathed in the close air. Cicadas buzzed their droning blare. Tyne let her mind drift.

Chilliness woke Tyne and she realized they were still outside. Mosquitoes greeted her and she grimaced as she realized they'd probably both be covered in bites. Rousing herself, she gathered up Daisy and crept inside Mrs. Hutchens's house. No sense sleeping outside when they had the room for one more night.

Mrs. Hutchens met her in the darkened parlor.

"Well," she began stiffly, "Your room is paid up until tomorrow after breakfast in the morning so I trust you'll have removed your belongings and have your room tidied by ten o'clock sharp."

Tyne gave a mute nod and feeling a wave of those unwanted tears rise, she mumbled an excuse, stepped heavily to the stairs, and fled to her room. Unknown to Tyne, Mrs. Hutchens stood in the darkened room for a long while before finally giving a sniff and returning to finish tidying the kitchen.

Tyne tossed and fretted the night through. A myriad of emotions from self-pity to anger to bitterness tore through her.

"Why, God? If you really cared, why?" she whispered hoarsely as Daisy slept on. "My life is nothing but a mess. I'm all alone trying to raise Daisy. I have no money, no home, not even a job."

She covered her eyes. If only, if only—Mr. Henricks had been who she thought he might be. They'd have a home and she'd have a new future. She glanced at Daisy and gritted her teeth.

"Oh, God, I'm so alone," she moaned. The familiar drawing she'd felt time and time again rose up. It always seemed to come when Roxie spoke of God, of everyone's need for divine salvation. That swelling force grew, filled her, and called to her until she couldn't resist. "Fine, I give up. Do what you want with my life. I've made a mess of it. Roxie said if I asked you to take over and let go of my sins, you would."

A tear wet her cheek and the anger drained away. "So…I'm asking. Just…help us."

Chapter Seven

Roxie sat up in bed from a dead sleep with a horrible dread in her heart. Tyne and Daisy lay heavy on her mind as if they were asleep in this very room. Her small servant's room in the back of the Wiseforths' home was pitch black, but Roxie didn't bother to light the lantern as she slid her plenteous body to the side of the bed, her pudgy knees sinking to the hard plank floor. For the next hour, the woman petitioned God earnestly on behalf of her friend and her child hundreds of miles away, yet near to her anguished heart.

Oh, dear God. She feared for the woman who'd become like a daughter to her.

❦

Tyne could barely choke down the breakfast that Mrs.

Hutchens had prepared, and it was an especially good breakfast of cinnamon bread, ham and scrambled eggs. In her misery, she missed the cool, puzzled look Mrs. Hutchens passed over her from time to time. Daisy was thankfully very interested in her cinnamon bread with a good slab of butter and seemed oblivious to her mother's state of mind.

Upstairs, afterwards, Tyne shoved their few possessions into the carpetbag once more, straightening each item more times than needed. She tidied the room and made the bed while Daisy rocked her doll in the big rocker by the window. Daisy sang "Hush, Little Baby" in perfect pitch, her expression convincingly tender on the corncob face.

Tyne sorted the meager coins in her pouch. It was enough for food for the next several weeks and then…Tyne stopped her thoughts as she sat on the edge of the bed. Her trembling fingers returned the coins to her pouch. There was no Aunt Clementine to flee to. No Roxie to welcome her in and protect her. She turned red-rimmed eyes to Daisy, so tiny, so sweet, so energetic, so oblivious to their dire situation. It was time to go. Was this what God had planned for Daisy and her?

Tyne tried to make the break as quickly as possible, but Mrs. Hutchens seemed quite reluctant to stop questioning her. But, at last, she and Daisy were on their way toward town. She knew Mrs. Hutchens could only assume that they would board the train, so she headed that way knowing the woman would watch from behind the worn lace curtains. Tyne lifted her head a tiny bit and strode out with false confidence. Once they were hidden from

Mrs. Hutchens's house, she detoured and pulled Daisy down a road that left town.

Not wanting to be discovered, she veered off the road once they left town proper. Tyne cut to a path next to a spreading Mexican plum tree and meandered down by a small stream. She and Daisy picked their way through the weeds for some time. Daisy never once asked where they were going. The poor thing was used to wandering.

The child darted into the shallow water and out again. Then she'd find an interesting stick or pretty rock. Tyne didn't have the heart to scold her even when her best dress became spattered with mud. The countryside had a way of draining Daisy's childish energy in a satisfying sort of way. Tyne would not deprive her of a lovely day of exploring. Tyne only wished she could pass the day in carefree diversions. But her mind stayed fixed on their hopeless situation.

"Mama, I hungry."

Tyne glanced at the sun which had dipped past mid-sky. Of course she was. It was way past lunch.

"Then we'll have a picnic."

Daisy clapped her hands as Tyne drew the child's baby quilt from the carpetbag. Beneath a good strong oak with low spreading branches, she stomped the taller grass and spread it out. Daisy collapsed on it with a small sigh.

Tyne drew out the sandwiches Mrs. Hutchens had thrust at her as they'd stepped out the door. For the train ride, the woman had grunted. Tyne hadn't bothered to correct her. They were delicious. The woman may have been cranky, but she'd been a generous and excellent cook. Daisy, always a good eater, chomped the thick ham with relish.

"Um, um, um." Daisy shoved the last of the bread into her already too full mouth.

"Daisy don't—"

The girl stopped mid-chomp, looking much like a chipmunk hoarding seeds for winter. Oh, how she loved this child.

A smile tugged at Tyne's mouth. "Never mind. Keep chewing."

The heat and the full stomach had a drowsing effect on the girl, and she curled up next to her mother and drifted off to sleep. Tyne stroked the child's golden hair and tears pricked her eyes. How long would this go on? What would happen now?

Roxie had never promised that being God's child would eliminate all hardships. As a matter of fact, she'd quoted something about difficult times producing perseverance. And that it was a good time to be joyful about such times.

But there was no joy, except for the sunshine, and the breeze. What she really wished is that she could close her eyes and everything be…perfect. Well, perhaps that was an overreach. Maybe, everything could be just…fixed—a safe home, plenty of food, and money to see them through.

Yes, that would be wonderful. Tyne let her eyes slide closed and, for just a moment, she convinced herself that when she opened them, all her problems would be solved. Sweat trickled down her temple as she scrunched her eyes tighter. Please, God.

When she opened her eyes, it was much the same—the water trickling by, the flies buzzing around, the oppressive heat. Tyne let out a long sigh. She was long past childish delusions. Instead, she'd have to do the hard work to wait and trust. *What time I am afraid, I will trust in you.* Roxie's Bible verse she'd whispered to Daisy night after night suddenly rose up in Tyne's mind.

"What time I am afraid, I will trust in you." Tyne whispered it to the breeze and pressed it deep in her heart. Despite the dire circumstances, the words breathed a puff of hope in her heart.

When Daisy awoke, they meandered until dark. Daisy pitched pebbles into the creek and waded farther and farther out into the water. Soon Tyne was nearly as wet as Daisy, dashing out to pull the child back toward shore. Daisy questioned every plant and animal they passed, or so it seemed, taking in everything with wide curious eyes.

As dusk settled, anxiousness inched up Tyne's spine. Soon they would be unguarded amongst the wandering night animals and the bloodthirsty mosquitoes. There could be bears or cougars. A shiver ran along her skin, bringing up goosebumps. How could she keep Daisy safe from a huge black bear?

Get away from the water. Yes, that made sense. Didn't animals circulate around the life-giving waterways? Perhaps they could find some sort of shelter. Tyne clutched the child's hand and tugged her daughter toward the high grass. Poor Daisy seemed wilted and gave little resistance. Tyne reached down and lifted the girl into her arms.

As she swathed a path through the grass, darkness fell. A

lined shadow slowed her until she realized it was a fence row. She searched the dark shapes surrounding her and licked her dry lips. With no moon, it was as dark as a cave. As she swept the area, she paused to get a fix on her shadowing surroundings. Ahead there appeared something. A large black shadow loomed in the distance.

With a shuddering inhale, she struck out toward the only landmark she could make out in the darkness, hoping to take shelter there, at least for the night. As they grew closer, Tyne realized the dark structure was a big barn. A rush of thankfulness washed over her. At least they wouldn't be sleeping out in the open amongst the wild animals. Tyne squatted and set her sleepy girl on her feet.

"Daisy, listen to me."

"Uh huh?"

"No, whisper only."

"Like at the Big House?"

"Yes, even quieter than that."

"'Kay."

The darkness seemed to help the child grasp the concept of being hushed.

"We're going to stay in this barn, but you can't make loud sounds. And you can't run around. Do you understand, Daisy?"

In the dimness she saw her daughter's exaggerated nod.

"Promise?"

"Uh huh."

"All right," Tyne drew the child back into her arms.

Daisy turned to jelly against her mother's warm body. Tyne crept softly and slowly toward the building, looking all around for any light and listening carefully for any movement. A small cabin stood off some eighty feet in front of the barn. Tyne froze when she saw a dim light in the window. As she watched, a form crossed the beam of light, and she flattened herself against the side of the barn.

Waiting for several minutes, she finally stepped out to the front. Moving sideways, Tyne kept her eye on the square of light at the cabin as she made her way to the door. A simple piece of wood nailed to the side of the doorpost was all that kept the door closed, but Tyne knew that would make it difficult to shut from the inside. Pushing the piece of wood up past the door's edge, the door popped outward and squeaked just a tiny bit. Tyne froze and swung her head back toward the cabin. After several minutes, all seemed secure and she slipped inside.

By now Daisy dozed on her shoulder, and Tyne wondered how much longer she was going to be able to hold her. She pressed her back against the inside of the barn, fearing to move in the inky blackness. But slowly her eyes became accustomed to the darkness and the little bit of light that came in from one lone window, and she could make out several shapes including the bottom rungs of a ladder running up to a loft. Praying for strength, she set the carpetbag down, waddled with slow searching feet, and struggled up to the top of the ladder while balancing a sleeping child on her shoulder.

By the time she reached the top, Tyne trembled from spent

effort. She sucked in a few breaths and swiped a few stray hairs from her sticky face. Once she caught her breath, she eased forward, trying to avoid any creaking noises. Finally, her eyes adjusted, she could barely make out a mound of hay. Inching forward, she laid her precious bundle down. Daisy never even stirred.

Thank the Lord for small favors. Returning to the floor was much easier without her burden and she made short work of stowing the carpetbag in the loft. The next thing was not so easy. The door had to be closed.

Her eyes could now pick up most of the items stored along the walls. It was a well-organized place. Leathers hung along the wall, stalls appeared empty. Given the warm weather, the animals must be outside. Good. That would be one less thing to give them away. Tools hung in another section above a small bench.

Then her eyes caught sight of a couple of fishing poles hanging just above her head to the right. With a nearby wooden crate, she reached up and fetched the lowest one down. She gnawed her lip. Somewhere there was a hook. She kept her hands near the grip to avoid catching her hand against a sharp point. That would be the last thing she needed.

At the yawning opening, she pulled the door closed and inserted the pole in the crack between the doorpost and the edge of the door. Several frustrating minutes went by as she struggled to get the piece of wood started on its way down. But, at last, the latch slid down a smidgeon and she managed to set the rod's end against it and scraped it down.

Snap.

Tyne caught her breath. Oh, no… Thunk. The wooden latch fell into place, but the broken end of the pole went limp on the outside of the barn. Tyne caught her breath and quickly navigated the fragmented section back through the crack. She pressed her head against the crack of the door, eyeing the dark cabin. Had anyone heard the trifle sounds? They seemed deafening to her. But perhaps it was only because she feared being discovered.

No movement indicated they may still be safe. She pulled away from the door and drifted toward the only window in the barn. In the dim light, she examined the broken pole in her hands. Completely snapped, held together by a mere splinter. There was no way to fix it.

What was best? Put back a broken pole or hide it so the owners would never catch sight of it? She flexed what was left of it and realized that this pole was not freshly cut so perhaps it did not get a lot of use. She would put it back and hope that the pole's presence would keep the owner from looking too closely at it.

Tyne, growing wearier with each step, quickly lifted the rod and flipped it over to make it appear whole. She returned the wooden crate and studied the door. They were secure. She and Daisy were virtually locked in. She swallowed, hoping in the light she could figure out a way to enter and exit. At least being locked in kept them safe.

She gathered a few scraps of straw and swept away her footprints. After backing herself up to the ladder, she stepped on the first rung, swept away the evidence, and crept up to the loft.

She let go of a long breath as she lowered herself to the mound of hay next to Daisy. Funny how the smell of hay settled her nerves. They were safe for now. However, she and Daisy had been reduced to living in a barn. Again.

Chapter Eight

Zeph woke up with a start. He'd slept hard and had awakened even harder. He'd dreamed of people dying and wailing, big and little including the little girl that had been in his wagon. What was her name? Oh, yes, Daisy. As usual, Noreen drifted by in her coffin box, yellower than ever. Beside her, in another pine box, lay the woman with cat eyes and instead of her eyes being closed, they were wide open watching his every move.

With a groan, more growl than moan, Zeph lifted his arms, wiped his sleep-deprived face, and ran his finger through his scraggily beard. Would the dreams never end? A snort flew out as he realized when the nightmares ended, reality set in, and there wasn't a great deal of difference. He heaved himself from the sunken-in straw tick and stood like a man twenty years older than his thirty years.

After pulling on his butternut wool britches and flopping the suspenders over his shoulders, he shoved his feet into the filthy boots by the door. He glanced around at the cheerless cabin. Mud trailed a path from the door and dust lay thick across the few surfaces. He shrugged. What did it matter? His stomach protested at having no breakfast before starting the chores. But he set his face in a firm line and stepped from the cabin to head toward the barn.

Tyne turned over in the soft hay and set the straw to crunching beneath her body. The sound brought her from sleep to totally awake in a mere fraction of a second. Daisy. Frantically she glanced around. Nothing but hay lay around her.

"Daisy."

Dust moats swirled at her harsh whisper in the slash of sunlight making its way through the cracks of the barn loft door. Tyne scuttled up on her hands and knees and crawled around, muttering her daughter's name. This was getting nowhere fast. She rose, banged her head on the low ceiling, drawing a gasp of pain. How had she avoided that last night in the absolute dark?

Rubbing off the sting at the back of her head, she tiptoed to the edge of the loft. Below her, Daisy pranced about, lifting her skirt tail in a spin and singing a cheery, childish version of "Skip to my Lou". Another gasp tore from Tyne's throat, only this time in fear. The child would be in plain sight to anyone who cared to burst through the door, or even wander close as she pranced and yodeled.

"Daisy!" she hissed.

The child halted, spun, and gazed up. Then she waved. "Morning, Mama."

"What are you doing, young lady?" Tyne demanded, trying to keep her voice low and even as she scrambled down the ladder.

Daisy shrugged, her blue eyes huge.

"You are not to come down here unless I know," she said in a firm whisper, reaching her daughter and grasping her shoulders. "Do you understand?"

"Uh, huh," she bobbed her head. Daisy always managed to look so sincere.

How could this child always do this? Tyne blew her bangs up and ushered the child toward the loft stairs.

"But Mama, I gotta go!"

Tyne bit her lip and closed her eyes momentarily in frustration, but didn't change her course. She, herself, could feel her daughter's pain.

"I know, darling. Mama, too. But it's daylight and we must hide until its clear."

She deposited her daughter back in the straw cave she'd dug the night before and quickly scurried down the ladder again to wipe her daughter's footprints away. Just as she was backing up to the ladder she heard faint footsteps outside the door. It was too late to dash up the ladder so she quickly stepped into a back stall just as the door creaked open.

Oh, dear, God, don't let Daisy come running out.

A large form darkened the door and Tyne, feeling her heart racing, pressed against the wall and turned her head, beseeching the Lord to hide her. A person shuffled around from here to there, but thankfully, Daisy stayed quiet. Noises of one moving various objects met her ears and made her want to peek from where she hid. But she remained pressed against the worn wood and closed her eyes.

"Now, where in the world are those nails?"

A low, gruff voice met her ears, and her eyes popped open. She recognized that voice. It was that huge, hairy man who'd picked them up. Zephaniah Rowley. The man to whom Daisy had wasted no time whatsoever telling their most private secrets. Heat filled Tyne's cheeks, remembering the humiliation when his blue eyes had searched hers outside old man Hendricks's shack. A loud thump startled her from her thoughts. A growl from that self-same man met her ears.

"Dad-blasted!" Footsteps then stomped from the barn.

Tyne squeezed her eyes shut as she strained to position him, trying to decide if she'd have time to bolt for the ladder. Nothing but silence met her ears. She leaned from her enclosure to be met with an empty barn and an open door.

It was now or never. She tiptoed to the ladder and leaned over to brush the footsteps away. She turned and could barely hold on to the ladder as she trembled in her effort to be quick and quiet. Looking up as she mounted the ladder ,she blanched to see Daisy's head peeking over the side of the loft.

Tyne scrambled up, grabbed Daisy, and made for the hay

cave just before her ears picked up the man's firm steps returning.

"Where are those blasted nails?" His gruff voice rose to near shouting level. The sound of rough pillaging through objects drifted up to their secret place. Tyne swallowed and scratched at the raw place on her thumb.

Daisy leaned toward her ear. "It's Mr. Zeph."

Tyne covered the child's mouth. From the sound of his anger, she had no desire to come face to face with the bearded scoundrel. There was no telling what a furious man the size of Zephaniah Rowley would do if he found them. Although he'd appeared quite docile at their first meeting, if riled, he could tear them both up without much effort at all. She'd crossed a few men with sour tempers and always she'd been the worse for it. Usually, it had left her nursing bruises or a black eye.

Daisy tugged against her mother, reaching toward a little canvas bag. Where had that come from? Tyne leaned over, keeping her arm firmly wrapped around her daughter and snatched the bag. With a tug, nails spilled from the pouch.

Oh, heavens. Daisy had stolen Mr. Rowley's nails. Daisy looked up at her mother with sweet, pleading eyes. Tyne shook her head and wagged her finger in silent admonition. The slamming around grew louder downstairs until one last loud thump and an angry snarl. Then it became silent.

Tyne pressed her lips against Daisy's ear. "You stay here, you understand?"

Daisy nodded and Tyne grabbed the canvas bag of nails and crept to the edge of the loft. What to do, what to do? If she dropped them, they would spatter everywhere which would make it obvious that something or someone had thrown them from the loft.

If she climbed to the bottom floor, she ran the chance of being seen. Knowing there was no other option, she scrambled once more for the floor, crammed the canvas bag beneath the bench and scrambled back to the ladder, brushing dirt as she went.

Footsteps thumped louder and she scurried up, still breathing hard when she gained the top step. Collapsing quickly at the edge of the loft, she covered her nose and mouth with her hands, trying to cover her panting.

Below, more noisy searching until she heard him exclaim a loud sound of puzzlement.

"What the—"

Everything grew quiet. Tyne could not resist stretching her neck out and peeping very carefully over the edge. There the big man stood, down on one knee holding that blasted bag of nails. After flicking through the contents, he held it out and he stared at it for several minutes. Then, he rose.

Tyne shrank from the edge before he cast his eyes up. Did he suspect? Tyne swallowed with dread. Below, a shuffle before footsteps faded away. Then the sounds of the door closing and being locked assured her he'd left the barn. Tyne breathed an audible sigh of relief. Suddenly Daisy was beside her. She sat up quickly and grabbed her little child's shoulders.

"You must never, never, take anything from this barn again."

Tyne's voice seethed very low and hoarse, but even a three-year-old could recognize the seriousness in her tone. "Do you understand me?"

Daisy nodded and Tyne clutched her to herself.

"But Momma," Daisy whispered, "I couldn't wait."

It was at that moment Tyne realized a dampness had seeped into her dress front and she dropped her head. Oh, glory. Somehow she would have to do better with Daisy. Not only had her daughter snuck away without her notice, the poor child had no way of relieving herself. What kind of horrible mother was she? How could she maintain a normal life for a three-year-old in yet another barn?

"No, baby," she whispered with a catch in her throat, "this is Mama's fault." She squeezed her precious child to herself. "We'll have to figure something out. Let's get you cleaned up."

After creeping downstairs, Tyne located a back door with an inside latch. That would come in handy if they had to stay another night. With her carpet bag in one hand and Daisy's tiny palm in the other, she ducked down and headed for the high weeds along the fence line.

The pound of a hammer in the distance marked Mr. Rowley's location, and he was a good distance off. She stayed hunkered down and whispered quietly to Daisy until they had gained the creek. Just in case, she backtracked toward town. It wouldn't do for Mr. Rowley to want a splash of cool water and spy them perched at the creek's edge.

At last they refreshed themselves and Daisy donned clean

clothing. Tyne rinsed Daisy's best frock and laid it across the bushes. Then they tore into the second half of Mrs. Hutchens's sandwiches for breakfast.

Tyne's thoughts spun for what to do next as she took another bite. Should they return to Mr. Rowley's barn for the night? Though he'd seemed harmless the day he'd given them a ride, it was obvious the man sported a temper. Yet, they would be merely moving to the next barn or shelter that came along.

The barn was a dangerous place given they could be discovered at any moment, but she had seen no other places close. Besides, would one barn be safer than the next? Even though Tyne had shamed herself in front of Mr. Rowley, he had, without doubt, been enamored with Daisy, patient and kind. Perhaps for now, this was the best place.

The loft had certainly been comfortable and private with the small cave she had carved. Even if he took it upon himself to use part of the highly stacked hay in the loft, which was unlikely in the summer, he would have to pitch quite a bit to find their secret spot.

She sighed. Well, at least they'd found a safe haven to shelter from the animals and weather. But somehow, Tyne had to locate a better place, and soon. She chewed her lip. She so wished for Roxie right now. That woman had a faith that moved mountains. What a comfort it would be to feel that woman's arms around her right now.

"Mama. I want Roxie."

Tyne blinked. It was as if she'd read her mind. "Honey,

Roxie is far, far away."

Daisy's eyebrows puckered, and she tilted her head to the side.

"Remember? We went on a long, long, train ride. Roxie is still in Kansas City in the Big House. We're in Texas now."

The girl sagged.

"Come here and let me fix your hair."

The girl flopped into her lap, her silence showing her grief over losing her trusted friend. Tyne decided to enjoy the quiet instead of dwelling on the heartache of Roxie's absence from their life.

"What we doing today, Mama?"

Tyne breathed in deeply. Leave it to her sapphire-eyed daughter to cut right to the heart of the matter. "Whatever we want, I suppose."

"I wanna see Roxie."

Daisy's braid snarled and the girl yelped. "How about instead, we go back up the stream and find some plums?"

"Can we get some lemo—nade?"

Just the thought of entering town made Tyne nervous, let alone, gracing Viney's Victuals with her well-known presence. "I think we'll stick with finding plums."

She stood and gathered their things, leaving the wet laundry on the bushes to continue drying. Daisy's brows drew together and her little arms tightened into a knot. Tyne pulled her doll from the carpet bag. "Here, hug Ginger. She's barely seen you the last day and a half."

Daisy swiped the doll from her and set a tripping pace along the creek. With a sigh, Tyne stuffed the blanket into the bag before scurrying off behind her daughter. If only Daisy could understand their desperate circumstances. But she was just a toddler, really. She would have to learn to make do with what they had. They both did.

The long journey didn't seem to improve either one of their moods. Tyne pointed to one of the trees in passing. "Look, Daisy. It's a pawpaw tree."

The girl's mouth dropped open. "Yay, Roxie can make pawpaw pudding."

"I don't think they're ripe." Not to mention that Roxie was a long way from here.

"Humph." Daisy grunted and crossed tight arms across her chest. Tyne couldn't blame her for her bad temper. The hot sticky weather and the buzzing bugs took a great deal of energy to deal with. And after over an hour of walking, the plum tree's fruit were much like the pawpaws. Not quite ripened and still a light orange. But Daisy didn't seem to mind as she picked the few that had fallen to the ground.

"Done, Mama. Lemo—nade now?"

Tyne stared at her girl, dirt smudges on her cheeks, her blue eyes filled with innocent hope. With a tremulous sigh, she stepped forward and swept up the impetuous child and snuggled her close in a hug. How? How was she going to do this? She couldn't very well raise Daisy meandering through fields for the next fifteen years. Oh—God...

Chapter Nine

No more words came to fuel the desperate prayer. Oh, how Tyne hoped the Lord knew her heart. She knelt and set the child down, reached inside her sleeve and drew out a hankie, and dabbed at her daughter's dirty face. "We will go to town for lunch."

"For pawpaw pudding?"

"No. Lunch."

"Can we have lemo—nade at least? Please, please."

Despite being hot, sweaty, and uncomfortable, Tyne let out a small laugh. "We'll see."

Tyne shrugged the nagging discomfort of showing her face in VV's again. And for a moment, it made her waver. Perhaps they would just stop by Olinki's Mercantile and pick up a can or two of beans. Unfortunately, that meant she would have to build a fire. That meant smoke and the fear of spreading it to the local fields surrounding them. 'Twas too dry to chance that. Perhaps some jerky.

Daisy's eager eyes blinked and made Tyne re-double her earlier decision. No. Her child needed healthy food. The least she could do was to provide a decent meal.

"I'll share with you," Daisy said.

Tyne laughed for the first time in days and swiped the fine, flyaway hairs that encircled her daughter's face. "Well, if you promise to share."

Daisy nodded her exaggerated bobs that seemed to take over the whole top of her body. Tyne slid her hand into her daughter's small one. "All right. Let's go then."

"Will they have pawpaw pudding like Roxie makes?"

Tyne sighed. "Not likely."

More than an hour later, however, seated in VV's, Tyne could feel the stares burning her back. She'd stowed the carpet bag near the plum tree at the creek and brought only her money in a small reticule. It was still late morning, thank goodness, and that made the place relatively empty.

Yet, there remained a few patrons that glanced her way, and she turned her head toward the window. It didn't help that they sat in nearly the same seat as the horrible meeting with Mr. Hendricks. But Tyne was thankful for the distraction of the window. Daisy, in true fashion, took up a small tune of "The Pawpaw Patch" which grew louder and louder.

"Daisy, hush."

"But…we saw the pawpaw tree. And Roxie makes that pudding that's sooo yummy."

"Nevertheless, this is not the place."

"Can I sing later?"

Tyne scratched at the raw spot at the base of her thumb. She knew her daughter. The child always started out so softly and graduated to full volume. Wandering the fields near Mr. Rowley's fields and barn while Daisy shouted her favorite song, all ten verses, would definitely not work. Yet, the child had to have the opportunity to do the things she loved. Tyne didn't have the heart to squelch her childish zest.

"Yes."

This seemed to satisfy the girl and she settled into her seat next to Tyne. The waitress brought the one lunch plate, with lemonade, of course, and set it beneath Tyne's nose. The heavenly smell of fried chicken, mashed potatoes, gravy, and turnips enveloped her and her mouth watered.

Daisy bounced and began to clap. "Oh, Momma, it looks so good!"

Instantly, the toddler maneuvered into Tyne's lap. Loving the comfort of her child's warm body, Tyne spooned the creamy potatoes into Daisy's mouth. This was such a luxury, but one they couldn't become used to every day, or soon her reticule would empty out. But the shared meal tasted so good after a long couple of days wandering and making do with half a dried up sandwich.

If she were completely honest, the chicken wasn't as good as Roxie's, but she wasn't about to complain. It was still good, warm, and filling…and generous. She would be able to save a whole piece of chicken for later.

Once Daisy seemed satisfied, she wedged into her seat and rested her head against the window pane. It was time to find a comfy spot to let her daughter nap. Tyne counted out the money to pay the bill and handed it to the waitress. Daisy, full and sleepy, contentedly tripped along without a word or song as they made their way back along the creek.

Having gained the spot where Tyne had hidden the carpet bag, and after having checked it over to be sure it had been untouched, Tyne laid a blanket in the shade for Daisy. The small child never even fussed about napping but plopped down, playing shadows with her fingers before drifting off to sleep.

Tyne fished a crocheted dishrag she'd started under Roxie's tutelage and worked a few awkward rows. Then she pulled out her journal and removed the wadded up letter. She should write to her friend but couldn't quite pen the words. Instead, she poured out her heart, her fears, and her insecurities of the future.

That made her think of money. She stuffed the cotton yarn in the carpet bag and pulled out her reticule. It didn't take long to count it. Eating at VV's was definitely out of the question in the near future.

Feeling restless and more than a tad hopeless, Tyne rose and stretched her arms above her head. The new day's sky shone bright blue with the fluffiest of clouds. And despite their circumstances, she supposed she should be thankful for the beautiful summer day. If a person had to be homeless and destitute, best do it on a perfect summer day.

"Thank you for the beautiful day," she whispered.

Still, the humidity seemed to have tripled with the extra moisture in the air and soil. She blinked at the sky and parked her hands on her hips. No use complaining. She had things to do.

As she gathered their dry things from the bushes, Tyne thought of types of food she could purchase at Olinki's Mercantile that wouldn't have to be cooked. She needed stuff that would last and food that was cheap.

She returned to sit next to her slumbering child and brushed away a fly. Then she picked up her pencil and made a short list of supplies. Dread and panic rose up, and she pinched her eyes closed. These items wouldn't last long at all. But Tyne couldn't dwell on that now.

Instead, she would somehow write to Roxie. She deserved to know what had happened. Yet, should she pour out her heart to Roxie of all the terrible things that had befallen them? Should she tell Roxie that in less than two weeks she would have absolutely no money and they would be destitute without home or food? Tyne sighed, closed her eyes, and took a deep breath.

The birds chirped, the gentle, scented breeze brushed her cheek, and the creek flowed soothingly by. It was such a calming place. What had Roxie always said when she was worked up with anxiety? Something about being still? Yes, there was a lot to be said about being still. She could feel the peacefulness of her little, shaded spot wash over her and she relaxed. Her eyelids lowered and she curled up on the blanket next to Daisy. Yes, she would write to Roxie, but for now, she would…sleep.

But it was only a short respite. Daisy woke Tyne from a deep sleep a short time later. She yawned and stretched. It was just as well. They had things to do before nightfall.

She stowed their belongings and toted the empty carpet bag to carry her grocery items. Daisy pranced and spun, singing "Pat-A-Cake, Pat-A-Cake." The child reveled in rolling her arms and then throwing the imaginary pan into the oven with quite a dramatic flair.

Daisy just seemed to soak up music. Every song her Aunt Clementine and Roxie had ever sung to her was carefully cataloged in the toddler's memory banks. And while most of the time it was charming, right now it just reminded Tyne how far they were from baking or eating any kind of cake.

Durn, if it wasn't her. Why, today of all days, had he chosen to come and grab some tobacco and whiskey? And the child prattled some sing-songy chant about marking something with a B. Zeph broke off from his place in line even though he was the next customer. Somehow, purchasing his "supply list" in front of the child and the green-eyed woman didn't set right. Instead, he veered toward the soap display. Not that he was short of soap, he just needed to get in the complete opposite corner of where they were.

But that didn't stop his eyes from darting to their movements every few seconds. The woman, Mrs. Bowlanders—blast, he'd thought he'd forgotten her name. *Clementyne.* For all that was holy, that was worse. Thinking of her as Clementyne might just double the needs on his supply list.

The woman clamped a hand on the child whose singing voice had grown much louder. She pulled the toddler toward her and whispered in her ear. A smile twitched at the corner of Zeph's lips.

Then the green-eyed woman placed a jar of pickled eggs into her carpet bag. Odd assortment of items. Jerky, a couple cans of beans, jelly, bread, and now pickled eggs? Either she or her little girl must have a hollow leg to stow away so much extra food. If there was one thing he knew, they were eating well at Mrs. Hutchens's house. The woman could cook.

He plunked the lavender soap he'd retrieved back on the shelf to complete his look of browsing. The pair meandered to the counter. Now was his chance. He could slip from the store, waste a few minutes on a brisk jaunt down the boardwalk, return, and purchase what he...needed.

Zeph crept along the back wall and then quickly slid through the door. A sigh puffed his cheeks. He'd made it. He took two strides before something clamped his leg from the back. His instinctive urge to whirl and square up to the attacker dissipated at the childish squeal.

"Mr. Zeph!"

He froze. Great. Small patting hands tapped at his knee.

"Mr. Zeph, Mr. Zeph. I thought I never see you again."

He twisted to scan the sunny child's grinning face.

Her grip left his lower extremity, and she held up her arms.

"Swing me high, Mr. Zeph."

With a pivot, he now faced his tiny assailant. But his eyes flicked up. Where was her mother?

"Please, oh, please, oh, please."

Daisy clenched her hands open and closed and gave a little hop, as if that would help her fly up to his arms.

Why not? He leaned down, gripped the tiny tot by the waist and gave her a toss. She squealed in glee.

"Again, again."

"No. Not again."

Another voice stopped Zeph stock cold. He tucked the child on his forearm to reveal the opposition. Ah, it was her mother. *Clementyne.*

He tipped his hat with his free hand. "Afternoon, Ma'am."

The pretty, petite woman took a deep breath. Something like panic and despair danced around the anger that sparked in her gaze.

"Please put Daisy down, Mr. Rowley."

He nodded and acquiesced, despite the clawing protest of Daisy. Once the toddler's feet balanced on the wooden walk, she lunged at him.

"No, no. My Mr. Zeph."

Zeph straightened, the child now locked around both his legs.

Mrs. Bowlanders's shoulders hunched in defeat. Then, with a shake of her head, she stepped forward to pry the child from his trousers, but the child fought and slapped in a near fit.

"Hear now."

Perhaps it was his low voice, or the tone of the command. But the toddler ceased and turned her tear-streaked eyes up to him.

"Obey your mother."

Daisy's quivering lip would have undone a weaker man, but he crossed his arms and scowled at her. Finally, the toddler nodded and leaned against her mother's skirt.

"Well…" Mrs. Bowlanders breathed.

From the look on her face, it was obvious she didn't know whether to thank him or curse him. She did neither.

"That's…better. Mr. Rowley has more important things to do than toss you about."

Yep. Like putting away some tobacco and whiskey.

Daisy screwed fists into her eyes and blurted. "I sorry, Mr. Zeph."

It came natural, kneeling on one leg to acknowledge the sincere apology. But he oughtn't have done it, for the child flew into his arms.

"Please be my new papa. I love you."

Her tiny arms squeezed around his neck. But she squeezed tighter around his heart. He crooked an arm around her small body. Glory. How to get out of this when he wished with all his heart he didn't have to.

"Daisy."

The warm hug dissipated as the child was jerked from him. He stood quickly, his Adam's apple jumping at the clog in his throat.

"I apologize, Mr. Rowley. Daisy is quite smitten."

The woman now held the child, Daisy's head buried in Mrs. Bowlanders's shoulder. The carpet bag lay abandoned on the boardwalk. Smitten? He couldn't remember the last time anyone had been smitten with him, except Nor—he cleared his throat.

"Nothing to apologize for. Could I carry your carpet bag to Mrs. Hutchens's for you?" At this point, he'd carry all three of them if she gave the go-ahead.

The woman leaned and snatched the bag up. "No, no. I'm fine. If you'll excuse us."

He swallowed, resisting the itch to follow the overburdened woman and ease the heavy carpet bag from her hands. She wouldn't welcome the help at this time. He'd already done enough damage for the day.

With a growl, he spun, scraping a hand through the riotous thick beard. What did he care? The both of them were merely two more thorns in his side. He stomped through the mercantile's door and halted. The counter was empty and so was his heart.

He dropped his head, turned, and exited.

Chapter Ten

T yne selected a different path for the way back to the creek, though it nearly undid her. The last thing she needed was to be noticed traipsing in and out of town like some hobo living by the creek.

Perhaps it wouldn't have been such a great nuisance for that bear of a man to tote her heavy carpet bag to Mrs. Hutchens's gate. Then she could've picked it up, forced Daisy to walk, and made it back to the creek before the pain in her back had begun to pulse.

But, no. She had to be stubborn. Actually, she really didn't have a choice. Daisy would've ended up riding on Mr. Rowley's shoulders or some such nonsense, babbling about staying overnight in his barn. So, it wasn't stubbornness, it was...self-preservation. The farther they could stay from their unknowing host, the better.

The sun slipped lower beneath the horizon, taking the last orange rays of daylight with it. Daisy sat upon a large rock, peering up at the sky, looking to spy the first star of the night. She pinched her tiny hands, singing "Twinkle, Twinkle, Little Star." Thankfully, the closing darkness seemed to lower her daughter's usual high volume.

"Time to go."

Daisy shot off the rock. "To Mr. Zeph's barn?"

Tyne drew in a long breath. Why even bother to correct her child's first name address, or the fact they were going to his barn. "Yes."

"Yippee."

If only Tyne could muster up such excitement. "You'll have to walk. This bag is heavy."

They hadn't even gone thirty yards before Daisy's song had elevated to shushing level. Daisy's lengthy nap had fueled her energy, and, no doubt, the good food had enlivened her as well. At last the child gave up the song, and though grateful for the silence, Tyne's heart smote her. A child should be able to sing joyfully and embrace a childhood full of love and security.

As they approached the huge barn, Tyne clamped her hand across the imp's mouth. Then, she knelt to whisper in her ear. "Remember, no talking or singing at all."

Her daughter nodded. Inside, she delivered Daisy to their secret hay cave with severe admonitions of being completely silent and lying down.

"But what if'n I haft to potty?"

"I'll take care of it."

"I don't wanna wet my drawers, Mama."

"I know, Daisy. Stay here."

"But—"

Tyne covered her mouth again. "Daisy Belle Ciders. If you keep talking, I will…" What? Make her live in a barn? Force her to spend her days traipsing back and forth to town? The poor child was already doing all of those things.

"Spank me?" Daisy mumbled behind Tyne's hand still across her mouth.

Yes. Perhaps that would work better for now. "I'm going to remove my hand, and I don't want you to say a word, understand?"

Daisy nodded again and Tyne pulled her hand away.

"I must go find a bucket, so you will have a necessary for the morning. You must stay quiet while I search," Tyne explained in a whisper.

"But it's really dark, Momma."

"I know," Tyne replied. "Remember what Roxie used to say about the dark?"

"Uh, huh," she said.

"What?"

"That it's God's hands holding us."

"Yes," Tyne smiled, remembering how Roxie could calm the child, "We're in the cleft of the rock of protection."

"And that's why it's so dark?" Daisy questioned.

Tyne took a deep breath. Roxie could explain this so much better.

"No. It's dark because it's night. But it's like we're in God's hands, because He protects us."

Daisy was still for a moment and then she finally laid down. "I'll whisper to God until you get back."

A relief washed over Tyne.

"Well, whisper very softly."

"'Kay."

Tyne crept away, whispering to God as well, wanting His assurance as much as Daisy. After carefully searching the very dark barn over and over, she found an old bucket in a far corner, that by the feel, was filled with spider webs but empty. It would make a fine chamber pot. She swept the floor free of her footsteps, her back complaining of this task. It brought to mind the day's arduous journey carrying both Daisy, despite Tyne's warning she must walk, and the carpet bag from town. She stepped up the rungs, clutching her temporary outhouse.

Settling into the little nest next to her sleeping daughter, Tyne blinked in the darkness. Oh, to have the faith of Roxie. The woman would assure her all would work out. Roxie had often chided her to give thanks in all things. Even when it seemed a small matter.

Fine. She swallowed. "Thank you for the chamber pot."

Sure. A honeypot that she'd found herself. But was God big enough to take care of the huge problem of being homeless and destitute?

Zeph shrugged off the oilcloth jacket and hung it on a nail just inside the barn. The morning had dawned gloomy and rainy much like his mood. But then, when did he not wake feeling cantankerous? He didn't want to mull over that, for he knew.

Instead, he strode across the cavernous room to the two large wagon doors that opened to the outside and flung them open. As thankful as he was for the rain, the dark thunderclouds clapping violently above only fed bitterness.

He'd planned on cutting out several stumps on the far side of his property toward the creek today. Obviously the weather refused to cooperate. Odd to have such a downpour in the hot weather. So on to indoor activities. Zeph would sharpen his axe and saws, and then wax and repair leather. He knew his saddle needed some attention as the buckle on the saddlebag had worn through on his angry search for the nails last week.

He walked to the rough table that shouldered against the inside of the barn. The sound and smell of the wet soil surrounded him as he rummaged through his equipment on the wooden slab.

The corn crib behind the table showed his corn supply was still head high through the wide wooden slats. It would be enough until the new harvest came in and perhaps it would allow him to sell some of the extra for a little money.

He snorted. Most folks would be thrilled for a little extra money. He, well, he just filled the coffee can and returned it to the high rafter beam in the cabin. He had quite a bit saved up, but wasn't sure for what. His head didn't dwell on the future or plan anything anymore. There was no point.

In disgust, Zeph threw the bridle he had retrieved from a nail to the table and stomped to a shelf and brought down a can of beeswax. After snatching an old rag, he seated himself and pulled the dry leather bridle into his lap and began rubbing with vengeance. He blocked any thoughts and numbly went about the task. The bridle shone in the dim light and he rehung it among the shiny leathers on the wall and then strode to the saddlebag to begin his ministrations of repairing the buckle.

After cutting the old strap and slipping the buckle from the rotted leather, he started back to the table to retrieve a fresh leather strip and an awl. His eyes lit on the fishing poles above the table and he sighed. When was the last time he'd kicked back and fished? He stood a moment and pondered.

But his mind froze, and he stepped forward slowly, carefully examining the old poles. It almost looked as if one had…broken. It must be the light or his imagination, but as his hands reached up, it fell apart. His face puckered. Now what had happened here? He gave his head a shake, his long hair brushing his shoulders. While the pole was almost worthless even whole, yet what would have caused it to break where it hung horizontally above the table? He looked up. Then he looked down, hoping to find something that might have fallen.

He brought his hand up to rub his coarse beard. That didn't make sense. If something had dropped, the pole would've surely fallen. He slipped a hand in his pocket and leaned his hip against the table.

He shook his head in puzzlement and then began removing the line and the hook. It was long past needing fresh line anyway. A huge thunderbolt rippled overhead, bringing a burst of light. Still, it was strange.

He snapped the rest of the pole into several pieces intending to add it to his kindling pile and threw it by the small door. The drenching rains flooded the outside soil and a small stream pooled inside the opening.

Zeph took a moment to stare into the rain. The onslaught slowed a moment, bringing his attention to the sound of a steady drip falling from under the loft. He cast his gaze about the roof. Great. Now he'd have to add patching to his to-do list. If it wasn't one thing, it was another.

With two steps and plenty of pausing to locate the whereabouts of the leak, he sighed. Of course it would be in the loft. That would put the repairs high up near the apex. He thought for a moment to shake his hand at the Almighty, but he refused to even give such an acknowledgement.

Fixing it from the inside would have to do for now. And, in the end, it would mark the area to repair it for good on the outside. With a grunt that seemed to turn on an intense bout of rain drumming on the metal roof, Zeph grabbed a hammer and a couple of shingles and strode toward the ladder.

Daisy huddled on Tyne's lap. The child trembled in total fear of the storm. Pressing a finger to her lips, Tyne managed to keep the child shushed but knew there was no way the man below could hear them with all the racket of the storm.

"I gotta go, Mama."

Tyne pressed her eyes closed. How well she knew, for she had a similar need. But Mr. Rowley worked on tasks in the main room of the barn as the storm continued to beat on the roof. Surely with the noise, a little liquid dripping wouldn't cause a stir. With a nod, she set the child on the rusted bucket. Daisy hid her face against her as a rumble shook the building.

The thundering on the roof calmed a bit and a steady dribble fell from the roof. Near the ladder, a pool of water soon spread down to the floor below them. Suddenly, the floor below them gave a quiver. Tyne smashed herself and Daisy against the far wall behind the tallest section of hay.

Then two thumps shimmied the entire loft floor. Mr. Rowley, in his substantial boots, now stood only steps away. Tyne practically held her breath. She had to stifle a cry when the sharp whacks of a hammer rang out. Then, a long pause. Tyne laid a hand against Daisy's mouth. Each step the big man took seemed to make the whole loft shudder.

Tyne pressed her lips to Daisy's ear and very softly said, "Shhhhh…"

The man's shadow passed against the back of the barn and Tyne cringed as if his mere shadow could uncover their presence. After a few more minutes and few more strikes of the hammer, Mr. Rowley climbed down. One by one the doors closed and the barn became silent. Only the dripping of a steady rain could be heard. Tyne uncovered Daisy's mouth and brought her hands up to rub over her own face.

"What's a matter, Momma? Scared of the storm?" Daisy patted her as the thunder had faded away to a soft rumble.

Tyne shook her head and opened her eyes.

"No, Daisy. Mama—" Tyne stopped and took a breath. "Mama is just trying to keep us safe."

"How come we gotta be quiet? Mr. Zeph is nice," she tilted her head in confusion.

Tyne gave a small smile at her complete trust.

"I'm sure he is, but he doesn't know we are in his barn, and he might not like it."

"Can we go to another barn where they like it?" Daisy questioned.

Tyne dropped her head. How could she explain to a little child that most likely no one would appreciate their presence in their barn.

"It's just that most people live in a house and—"

"Sos huh come we don't?"

Daisy's innocent questions made Tyne want to break down and cry. She quickly shook her head. "Let's not talk about it right now, okay? Just remember that we can't tell Mr.…uh, Mr.…."

"Zeph" Daisy supplied.

"Uh, yes, Actually, Mr.Rowley. He can't know we're here. And I'm glad you…like him," Tyne fibbed a bit here, "but you must remember not to talk or take anything from the barn."

It was going to be tricky staying cloistered in the loft on a rainy day. Daisy's energy level didn't fit into a lazy day in the hay cave. Tyne reached for her carpet bag, thankful she had brought it up to keep it dry and pulled out the piece of chicken.

"Oh, goody. Chicken. I love chicken." Daisy rubbed her belly. "Can I have a bread too?"

Tyne tore a piece from the loaf they'd purchased at Olinski's and handed part of it to Daisy. The other piece she stuffed into her mouth.

"We gots to pray first, Mama."

Why was it that Tyne almost felt as if Daisy were more of an adult than she? "Of course," she mumbled around the yeasty wad in her mouth.

Daisy clasped her hands. "Dear Jesus, thank you, thank you, thank you. Amen."

The child got right to the point. If Tyne hadn't felt so desperate and sad, she would have laughed. Instead she tore off a piece of the chicken and pointed at Daisy. "Now, listen. We're stuck inside until the rains stop and things dry off, perhaps for the whole day. Mr. Rowley may come to the barn at any time. So we must be very quiet. Understand?"

Daisy stuffed her mouth with bread. "'Kay. Maybe I draw on paper today?"

Tyne cringed. She had so few precious sheets left. But it was vitally important that Daisy stay quiet.

"Yes, but you have to use the pencil not the ink."

Daisy nodded solemnly as she stuffed more bread in her mouth. "I need a drink."

Oh, that. They had food. No drink. And come to think of it,

she had no knife to spread the jelly should they have that for dinner. Tyne glanced to the wet wood around the loft door. There was water everywhere, but not a drop to drink.

"We'll get some later."

Daisy's face scrunched up.

Tyne began removing the paper and pencil from the carpet bag. They'd no sooner gotten settled with Daisy on her tummy toward what little light filtered around the cracks of the loft door when a creaking sound met her ears. Mr. Rowley was back. Tyne sighed. It was going to be a long day.

The next couple of days followed the same pattern. Tyne found a jar with a lid inside the barn and swiped a long nail for use as a knife. These items were promptly scrubbed at the creek along with their underthings.

But Tyne's anxiety grew as her money pile shrank and, oh, how she felt the absence of Roxie to talk with and cling to in difficult times. As comforting as the creek spot was, it fast became equally lonely. She followed Roxie's admonition to give thanks to God for all things, and found herself thanking God for Daisy's chatter. Without it, it would have been so overwhelmingly and disturbingly quiet.

Chapter Eleven

A nother fresh day dawned, shining and bright, and Tyne paused at the back barn door. She shushed Daisy so her ears could do a careful perusal of where Mr. Zeph might be. A hum sounded in Tyne's throat as she realized she'd adopted Daisy's name of reference.

She scratched at the sore spot at her thumb base and felt a bit of stickiness. Now she'd opened that small wound she'd been clawing at for three days. Tyne yanked a hanky from her bosom and dabbed at the blood. Then she squeezed Daisy's hand, silently warning her to remain quiet.

They exited, and Tyne bent low to hide her height in the fence row weeds. As they drew near the last field before the woods, the sound of chopping pinpointed their host in the distance. Ah, finally. He sounded far enough away to give them safe passage. Still, she veered off to the right where they met up with the creek a few hundred yards to the west.

It would've been nice to have explored a bit to the east today to see what they would encounter. But with the presence of that hairy Mr. Rowley, she gritted her teeth, determined she would not refer to him mentally as Mr. Zeph, had spoiled that idea.

After the chores of rinsing their clothes and freshening up, Daisy gulped down a jelly sandwich, Tyne resolving not to partake. To keep Daisy occupied, they meandered toward town.

Things appeared quiet as they gained Main Street, and Tyne's ears picked up the sound of music drifting through the air. Following the sound, she shushed her daughter and discovered a charming white-framed church on the far side of town. A fine steeple stretched above a quaint bell tower at the entrance. The windows were wide open along the side and the music now became quite clear.

"What's that, Momma?" Daisy asked.

"It's a church," Tyne whispered. "It must be Sunday."

Daisy leaned forward and brought her hands up to whisper quite loudly into her mother's ear.

"Why do we always have to whisper?"

After setting Daisy down, Tyne took her hand. They tiptoed beneath the open windows until they reached the back of the church. Here, several red oaks lent plenty of shade, shielding them from the heat. Near the base of one, a small weathered bench beckoned. With a thankful sigh, Tyne settled on the seat and pulled Daisy up to sit beside her. Her gaze took in the small yard. What a perfect grove for church picnics and get-togethers. Roxie often told of her small church holding such celebrations. Tyne, however, had never felt comfortable going.

"We have to whisper so we can hear the music."

Daisy sat quite still, entranced to hear the pump organ's wheezy sound and the congregation's voices rising and falling with the notes. The second song Tyne recognized as a favorite of Roxie's. And at Daisy's gasp, she recognized it, too.

"raise my Eb—o—neezer..."

Daisy followed the congregation in a raspy voice, trying to sing in a hushed voice. Without a will to shush her, a tear bit the corner of Tyne's eye and a clog filled her throat.

"...safely to—arrive at home..."

With a sniff, Tyne pulled her daughter, lisping every word, onto her lap. She smoothed the hair behind Daisy's ear. The tot continued to stare into her eyes, singing so soulfully that Tyne could barely breathe.

"...Here's my heart, oh, take and seal it, seal it for thy courts above."

Tyne hugged the girl to her heart and pulled a fresh hanky from her bodice. Daisy leaned into her and became still. A blessed quietness fell upon them. Only the sounds of the birds fluttering and chirping filled the air. Then the distinct sound of a deep authoritative voice echoed from the open church windows. Daisy left her lap and meandered about picking buttercups and Indian blankets.

Tyne strained to hear the faint words. She rose, and while

keeping her eyes on her small daughter, crept near to the corner of the church. Here, she could make out the speaker's words.

"Verse 29 and 30 of Matthew 6 continues, 'And yet I say unto you, That even Solomon in all his glory was not arrayed like one of these. Wherefore, if God so clothe the grass of the field, which to day is, and to morrow is cast into the oven, shall he not much more clothe you, O ye of little faith?'"

The pastor paused here, and Tyne tracked little Daisy plucking the very grass from the ground to add to her bouquet...like an explanation point of the pastor's words.

"We worry for every single thing. Yet God assures us that he can supply our needs. Just think how we fret about nearly everything. Our crops, our homes, our families, why, we can barely greet one another without pouring out our every fear. And Jesus clearly says in this passage that we are to trust him for everything. I want to add the last passage at the end of that chapter. Listen to what our Savior says in verse 34. 'Take therefore no thought for the morrow: for the morrow shall take thought for the things of itself. Sufficient until the day is the evil thereof.'"

A loud thump sounded as if the pastor had fallen over. Tyne strained to hear, but no sounds of disturbance arose. Only the pastor's voice rang out with conviction.

"What does it mean? Don't borrow trouble! Why worry over tomorrow, when there is enough to keep us occupied today?" The pastor laughed softly here. "My goodness, half of what we fear never comes about. So, friends, why do we waste our time? What will be your choice? Will it be faith or fear?"

At that, the organ's deep music began again and Tyne, suddenly refreshed, felt Daisy's hand slide into hers. Faith or fear. She knew what she'd chosen in the last several weeks. But to latch onto a blind faith? Could that be possible?

Tyne ducked and led Daisy beneath the windows as another hymn drifted above them. By the time they'd returned to the road, her daughter had taken up the repetitive chorus. On the trail back to the creek, she allowed Daisy to chatter away noisily like a little jaybird. But Tyne was deep in thought.

It was true what the pastor said. It was a matter of worrying or trusting. She sighed. Or was it? All it took was for one person to recognize her, or the sheriff to peruse through his wanted posters and she'd be done. And what would happen to Daisy? Oh, glory, it was so easy to fall into the fear choice. Quickly, before anxiety took over, she shut down her train of thought. This faith thing would take some practice.

Roxie had put her trust in action, always putting herself out there to help. It seemed the woman feared nothing, always full of assurances and confidence that the best would turn out. But then, she didn't have a sordid past.

Tyne found herself praying, as she settled a chattering Daisy on the small patched blanket. The child's voice grew quieter and more spaced between words. The space beneath the live oak grew still as the girl drifted off to sleep. Tyne pressed a kiss to Daisy's forehead.

As was her habit, she was tempted to pull out her reticule

and count out her money, knowing that dread and fear would mount as she contemplated funding the next week. Rather than give in to the temptation, she chose faith and rose to gather sticks for a small fire. When Daisy awoke, she would heat some bread and warm up some beans for a nice dinner and give thanks for what they had.

At dusk after a can of semi-warm beans, Tyne and Daisy made their way back to their familiar barn. So accustomed to making this journey, Daisy hummed her new hymn along the way before Tyne hushed her.

Armed with her door-locking stick, she and Daisy sealed themselves in the only home they'd known for the last three weeks. Tyne swept the floor clear and climbed the ladder to the loft. Afterwards, snuggled in the sweet hay, Tyne made up a story of a fine horse while Daisy yawned and her eyes fluttered closed. Smiling at her beautiful daughter, Tyne sat against the wall and prayed for the faith to believe in God's deliverance. Her petitions grew slower and her eyes became heavy.

Loud pounding and heavy footsteps woke Tyne from a dead sleep. With a gasp, she sat up and cringed. Daisy whimpered and threw herself into her mother's arms.

"Shhh..." she whispered in the child's ear after her own heart had slowed a bit, "It's just Mr. Zeph fixing the roof."

"Up there?" Daisy pointed to the roof above their heads.

"Yes."

"Can I go, too?" Daisy's eyes rounded into two huge mirrors full of hope.

Tyne shivered. "Oh, dear, no. It's much too high."

"We're up high now, Momma."

"True, but we have no danger of falling off—"

The door below opened. Daisy's mouth opened, and Tyne laid her hand over the tot's lips and shook her head. Rummaging echoed below them, and then, retreating footsteps. Only then did Tyne continue.

"It's too dangerous for you. It's very easy to fall off of a roof."

Daisy's eyes grew wider. "What about Mr. Zeph?"

"He'll be fine."

"What if he falls off?" Daisy's voice grew louder and Tyne shushed her. "Momma!"

"All right. How about we...pray for him?" Tyne suggested. "Would you like that?"

Daisy's head bobbed and she pressed her little hands together. "Dear God..."

Tyne shushed and covered the girl's mouth. The child's understanding of whispering was really come and go.

"How about I pray?"

Daisy nodded solemnly.

Tyne bowed her head and quickly murmured, "Please don't let Mr. Zeph fall from the roof. Amen."

"You forgot to say, 'Please, God.'"

Tyne gave a huff. "Okay. Please, God, don't let Mr. Zeph fall from the roof. A—"

"And the ladder," Daisy prompted.

Tyne sucked in a breath and whispered, "Or from the ladder."

"And don't let the hammer bang his thumb."

Daisy spoke so loudly, the hammering above them paused. Tyne moved to cover her mouth, but Daisy sealed her own mouth with her little hands. The child's eyes spoke volumes. Tyne could only sit there and shake her head, a small smile crossing her face.

"If you don't want Momma to cover your mouth, you must remember to be very quiet."

Daisy merely nodded and settled against her as the loud thumps and bumps continued. She could make out him pausing and sliding the wooden shingles to their place and positioning himself above them to drive the nails home. She surveyed the roof line, shuddering, as he hammered and moved about. Not only did he risk tumbling from the pitch of the roof, his mere size threatened to crash through to the loft.

Tyne hoped Mr. Zeph's task was not an all-day project. Daisy would expect to leave the barn soon. Tyne found her mind on the man she'd prayed for earlier. How strange to pray, especially for someone she barely knew. But she was glad she'd covered him in prayer. Her mind once again brought up an image of him high on the barn's rooftop and she shivered. Dear Lord, do let him please be safe.

Daisy pointed to where she thought he might be on the roof. A scuffling noise ensued and the child stood and meandered across the loft poking her finger to where he moved. *Please let him be efficient so he can move from the barn to another project that would allow us to get to the creek.*

God granted Tyne's prayer just before lunch. Mr. Zeph climbed down and ambled into the barn to put away his tools. Then he disappeared. Perhaps in for lunch?

Glad to be out of the hot, stuffy loft, Tyne let Daisy take off her shoes and wade in the creek to cool off. Daisy squealed in delight as she splashed the water, holding up her dress to chase the minnows amongst the shadows of the smooth rocks.

Tyne pulled the last of the bread from the carpet bag and laid out the strawberry jam. "Hush now. You'll have Mr. Zeph down here."

"Looky, Mamma. A frog."

Another squeal pealed from Daisy. Tyne laughed and scurried forward to snatch up her noisy daughter. Daisy giggled and patted her wet hands on Tyne's cheeks. Ahhh, the coolness of the water felt good.

Daisy wiggled out of her mother's arms and splashed away after the leaping creature, swamping Tyne's hem in the process. With a deep breath, Tyne breathed in. If only they could be so carefree without all the worry of her past and their present situation.

"Remember not to be so loud."

Who knew how far her daughter's high pitched squeal would travel over open fields. Tyne gathered their socks and shoes and collapsed on the quilt. She pulled her lumpy crocheting from the bag and let Daisy play to her heart's content. Today they would explore the land to the west of the road. Perhaps they would come across a fruit tree or a wild raspberry bush. It'd serve to keep Daisy occupied, give them a chance to escape the confines of Mr. Zeph's property, and possibly provide some extra food.

A sigh whooshed from her as she pulled out another uneven stitch. She'd try to be content. Try to put her best hope in the Lord's deliverance. But, it sure was difficult to ignore the small amount of money in her reticule.

Chapter Twelve

Z eph stood stock still. There is was again. An odd high-pitched…coo? Was it some new bird species? Yet, never did he hear it repeat like a normal bird call. Just a random squeal. He studied the trees. But the sound had once again disappeared. He spun, thinking he'd heard it again. Nope.

Well, he must be officially losing his mind. The peculiar noises he'd been conscious of the last several weeks were proof. So was the worn trail alongside the fence row from the barn. And what about the smashed grass under the old live oak down at the creek?

Animals? He couldn't find any tracks. No deer or bear prints. And there was still the mystery of the broken fishing rod. No stray animal had managed that. He shook his head to clear it.

Maybe he'd just needed a break. Sleep had been very elusive lately.

He snatched up the tools he'd been using to mend the fence and meandered toward the barn. Perhaps his time would be better spent locating a new willow branch for a new rod even though buying a bamboo cane from Olinksi's would probably be the better choice.

Zeph ducked into the barn, cubbyholed his tools and extra wire, and reached up for the pole that was still intact. He grabbed up the extra line he'd removed from the broken rod, a shovel, and bucket. The worms were bound to be scarce in the hot sun, so he set off for the creek, planning to dig for some under the shade trees.

Besides, who was he kidding? Wetting a line was a great excuse to kick back, pull down his hat, and nap the hot afternoon away. He dug and dug and only came up with a handful of scraggy worms. But he baited the one good pole, and plopped it into the water.

The next two hours were filled with relaxation and fish. He pulled four plump bass from the waters. Though Zeph never whittled on that new pole, he'd landed enough fish for dinner. And somehow that chased away the nagging bitterness that tried to eat his soul. Especially after he jaunted into town and left two of his catch on Annabelle's porch. Not that he'd stayed around to see her face. He'd only rapped hard and jogged off. She might welcome his fish or whatever else he left on her porch, but she wouldn't welcome him.

❧

It was terribly difficult to let go of the last of her money as the clerk reached out. It had taken Tyne a long time to choose the food to buy. Peach preserves, bread, and pickled eggs. The eggs had been a bargain buy too good to resist. Then they would eat and die.

"Okay, Lord," Tyne whispered as they swung out the door and down the wooden boardwalk. Daisy pranced beside her singing a smattering of her new hymn. "This is it. There's no more. You promised you'd provide. Oh, dear God, you promised."

Daisy stopped.

"What'd you say, Momma?"

Tyne pulled an artificial smile. "Nothing, baby. Nothing."

The smell of frying fish as they approached the barn that evening did nothing to reassure her of the uncertain future. It only made her stomach growl.

"Ummm. That smells good."

Leave it to Daisy to state the obvious.

"Mr. Zeph is a cooker man."

A smile teased at Tyne's mouth as she waved away a spider web. "I guess he is."

"Mr. Zeph's a cooker man, a cooker man, a cooker man..."

Daisy set her made up song to the tune of "The Muffin Man," which made Tyne's salivary glands kick in with the thought of a tasty muffin, with a side of fresh fried fish of course. Ugh, she was hungry.

"Hush now, Daisy. We're close to the barn."

Her daughter yanked at her arm. "How 'bout we visit Mr. Zeph? He might have leftovers."

Tyne licked her lips, very much tempted. "No. We have the preserves. We'll be fine."

The sigh that came from her daughter in the dark deflated Tyne's best intentions too. They slipped into the barn and made their way to the only home they'd known for the last several weeks. Sleep would take away Tyne's hunger pains, at least for the night.

The next several days were agony. The peach preserves disappeared from the jar and the bread dwindled down to nothing. Tyne denied herself food to make it last for Daisy and tried to drink water at every turn to fill her empty stomach. She found herself eyeing Zeph's growing garden as they walked to and from the creek and wondered how long it would be before the vegetables would develop and how she could possibly take them uninvited. And, at long last, it came down to one last pickled egg at the bottom of the jar. The last 'yucky' egg that Tyne had been unable to eat. It was down to that or starve.

She laid Daisy on the straw pallet with a soft song and rubbed the hair behind her ears before she allowed the tears to flow quietly down her cheeks. She prayed like she had never prayed before in soft desperate whispers, rocking to and fro. Finally, she fell asleep, exhausted and ravenous next to her small daughter.

Roxie sat up like a corpse with a muscle spasm. Pray. She must pray for Tyne and Daisy. They had been heavy upon her mind and tonight while getting ready for bed, she had spent a great deal of time on her knees petitioning the Lord on their behalf. There had been no letter and they had been gone for a month and a half. Surely they were settled. They were either settled or…Roxie couldn't think of the consequences. She refused to let her mind go there. Instead she lowered herself to the floor once more. It was going to be a long night and an even earlier morning.

༺꧂

Zeph woke before the light. He slung back the quilt and stood and paced the room running his hands through the mass of hair. Those crazy dreams haunted him. He'd been fishing on the bank and just as he threw out the pole, it snapped in half. And as he looked up, a coffin floated by with Noreen's yellow body in it. The lid snapped shut just as another coffin came floating behind it with that woman in it, Tyne, with those green eyes and shining golden hair.

Daisy was with her and they sat up in the coffin as if it were a canoe. They both held paddles and smiled and waved as they paddled by. Then the coffin suddenly capsized. Zeph stretched out his hand but realized he stood on top of the barn roof with no ladder to climb down. The coffin drifted down the river. There was no sign of life. As he raced toward the edge of the roof, he came awake with a strangled cry.

He groaned and planted himself firmly on the side of the bed

130

and buried his head in his hands. Why? Why did he constantly dream of coffins filled with Noreen's body? And that woman and her child? Why were they always there? Was it because he wouldn't allow himself to think of them when he was awake? He growled at the lack of answers and impatience with himself and quickly threw on his clothing and strode angrily to the barn.

As he drew close, however, he noticed the barn door cracked open. Slowing his pace he crept closer, glancing about to try to decipher if there was anyone about. He stepped through the door and instantly went to the right in the shadowed part of the barn and pressed his back against the large double doors as he slid toward the far wall where he kept an extra shotgun high up on a couple of nails. It wasn't loaded, so he reached even higher to a shelf where the cartridges were. Quietly he opened the box and slipped them into his pocket and kept one in his hand. He wouldn't load it until he stood and listened for a few moments. And what he heard brought a pucker to his face.

༺∾༻

Tyne rolled a bit in her cocoon of hay wakened by Daisy's humming. It was very early, not even light yet. She inhaled deeply and searched for Daisy with her hand. Realizing she was out of her reach woke her instantly.

"Daisy!" she whispered. What if she was too close to the loft edge? Fear raced through Tyne.

"Yes, Mama?.

"Come here," she commanded.

Suddenly a deep voice seemed very close.

"Well, hello, Miss Daisy," Mr. Zeph's voice floated to her from very nearby. "What are you doing here in my loft?"

Fear of gargantuan proportions froze Tyne.

"Hi, Mr. Zeph! We gotta be quiet 'cause…Mama's still laying down."

Tyne heard him clear his throat and felt the tremble in the loft as he gained the top step. "Is that so? Well, I'm afraid we're gonna need to get her up. You think she's decent?"

"Of course. Mama says that only I get to sleep in my under things. She always stays in her dress 'cause we're in a barn."

At Daisy's happy chatter, Tyne cringed. Just when she thought things couldn't get worse, her daughter was talking to a man about her under things.

"Mama, Mama, Mr. Zeph's here," she traitorously chanted as she climbed back into their little cove.

Feeling tears nearing the surface, Tyne scrambled from behind the mound of hay and stood facing him, trembling, while his head nearly brushed the rafters. He shoved his hands in his pockets as he stared at her.

"I…I…," Tyne stopped, her mouth open. No other words crossed her mind.

Just then Daisy jumped up and pulled on his shirt tail.

"Can we have breakfast Mr. Zeph? I'm so, so, so very hungry and Mama only has one yucky egg left, and I don't wanna eat it.

He pulled his gaze from Tyne, gave Daisy a little grin, and ruffled her hair.

"Most certainly," he replied in that deep baritone. He raised his eyes to Tyne before he spoke again. "I think it's only right that we all head up to the cabin and have a little breakfast."

Tyne's stomach jolted. She feared the only thing she'd manage to do was vomit.

Mr. Zeph mounted the ladder first, swung Daisy up in his arms, and easily navigated the steep apparatus. He thoughtfully treaded to the door and waited. Tyne made her way down the rungs. Keeping her gaze lowered, she crossed the barn, and the brawny man, outlined by morning sunlight, held the door.

Daisy chirped like a magpie finding her long lost friend, patting him on the cheek and telling him how she loved taking baths in the creek and eating at VV's, but liked it better when Mama fixed beans on a fire at the creek. Tyne felt herself shrinking with shame as the child spilled her guts about the last several weeks. He grunted and nodded with great interest. Again, he held the door while she moved her leaden feet into the well-built cabin. She stood forlornly by the door as he perched Daisy on one of the wooden benches at the table and grabbed a plate of already cooked bacon and set it before her.

"Oh, goody, bacon. I love bacon! I love it, I love it, ummm..." she raised a thick slice to her mouth and began crunching.

Tyne closed her eyes and wanted to sink through the floor. When she opened them, Mr. Zeph stood before her, close enough to have a conversation away from the child but far enough that she didn't feel completely threatened. He crossed his arms over his wide chest and narrowed his eyes.

"Suppose we start with how long you've been in my barn," he said lowly.

Tears rushed to her eyes, and she clamped her hands together in front of her to keep from trembling. Her voice came out in a strangled whisper.

"About four weeks."

✐

Zeph nodded slowly. Interesting. Perhaps he hadn't been losing his mind all along as he'd feared.

"So you're the one that broke my fishing pole," he stated.

The woman didn't answer. She didn't need to. The redness that rose up her neck and suffused her cheeks bore witness. That and the wretchedness written on her face. Her head dropped and then she nodded.

"I take it you didn't like Mrs. Hutchens's place?"

"It's not that," her voice came out all whispery, "I...I... ran out of money."

One brow rose. Clementyne—Mrs. Bowlanders chanced a glance up. Curious.

"Now, why would a lone widow come half way across the United States towing a young child without the funds to house and feed herself or this little lady?" He gestured toward Daisy.

An odd choking sound came from her. "I thought I'd marry."

He nodded. Her bright red face now seemed as pale as the whitewash he used on the house.

"Oh, yes, Ollie Hendricks." He narrowed his eyes and

perused her. "You corresponded with old man Hendricks?"

"I...," she fidgeted and her eyes slid closed, "....yyyes."

"So, you are Clementye Bowlanders?" For some reason, he felt led to state that, though why he couldn't discern, other that her twitchy countenance.

The woman nodded with one hesitant jerk but didn't dare meet his eyes. Instead, her gaze rested on Daisy at the table, gobbling down bacon. Something seemed rotten in Denmark, and he couldn't put his finger on it. Nevertheless, they were here, homeless, and obviously hungry. Dadburn it.

"So let me get this straight. You need a home for you and the child, so you've been staying in my barn. Now, you've run out of money. I'm supposing you've tried to get a job, but because you have the girl, you've failed to secure one. Therefore, you have no other way to support yourself since the whole thing with old man Hendricks turned out to be a hoax."

She gave an abrupt nod. The strain on the woman's face hurt him somewhere south of his chin, which was probably why he kept talking.

"All right." He scratched the mound of hair on his chin. "Here's a thought. I need someone to clean and cook around the house."

Her mouth parted and her eyes came up to meet his.

"So, here's what I entertain we do," he paused as he grabbed a muffin from the stove and popped it open to slather it with butter and pushed it onto Daisy's plate. Daisy rewarded him with a greasy smile.

"You can work for me keeping house and cooking. I need the laundry done too and you can help tend the garden. The food will need to be put up in the fall and garden planted in the spring." Ye gads. Was he babbling?

"I've got my hands full clearing a new field. I'll not be afoot a whole lot." He scrubbed at his beard as he paced. Grabbing a pitcher of water, he poured a glass for Daisy and delivered it to the table.

"Of course, folks won't understand such an arrangement, so we'll have to get married, in name only, of course, to keep it proper looking."

Chapter Thirteen

He continued to pace, while on the inside, his mind throbbed in shock. He'd just proposed marriage to a woman who was nearly a stranger. "And, if we hurry, we can get into town this morning and have the pastor marry us in time to get back for dinner."

Suddenly, he stood stock still and stared at her.

"Wha...what?" Clement—Mrs. Bowlanders's mouth hung open. "Marry? Why, I hardly know you!"

He halted, pursed his mouth, and narrowed his eyes. "Perhaps you should check with someone you know well, then. Perhaps old man Hendricks?"

Mrs. Bowlanders's mouth snapped shut. The woman glanced at Daisy, delighted at her full meal. Resignation dulled her eyes and for some reason, that stabbed at Zeph. She took a deep breath, and with eyes averted, she answered.

"Fine. I accept your job offer."

Job offer? Blame, he'd made a mess of it. Or had he? It was best to keep her at arm's length, for sure. He didn't need any more grief. So...perfect. He'd just hired a live-in housekeeper. He glanced around at the junk discarded in the corners and the crumbles of dirt clods covering the once fine wooden floor. The woman was certainly getting the short end of the stick.

But, she'd have shelter, food, and necessities for her and the girl. That had to be worth something, obviously. She'd agreed after all.

The thought of what he'd done sent his mind spinning. "I'll get the wagon. You eat."

He didn't mean to give her the once over, but she was as thin as a rail. And he supposed with his brain in a tither, it'd made his words come out a bit rough and commanding, but it couldn't be helped. She only blinked, and he strode to the door. Perhaps she, too, was a little overwhelmed by their agreement.

Before the woman could back out of the deal, he had her and Daisy loaded in the wagon heading into town. Daisy sang and leaned into his shoulder. The tot seemed up for the impromptu trip into town, but her mother had frozen into a statue, her head turned away. Perhaps she was taking in the wildflowers along the road, but he doubted it. More than likely, she was scheming an escape. That's what he'd do if he were set to marry a hairy ogre.

Zeph scratched his head and tried to figure out for the life of him how he had managed to purpose marriage to a woman when he had no such inclinations to do so. It was like the rational 'him,' had stepped out to take a walk, and some insane 'him,' had taken over. He shook his head to try to clear it. It was too late now. The woman and child needed somewhere to go. He couldn't just resign them to live in his barn for the rest of their lives.

But why him, he fought with himself. Why did he have to be the one to rescue the damsel? Why hadn't she stayed where she came from? He wanted to groan and wipe his eyes and wake up from one of his strange dreams. But this was no dream. This woman, who sat so stiffly next to him, had agreed to marry him. And this child, who had just wrapped her little arm around his neck, would soon be bouncing about his cabin.

And...he wouldn't go back on his word. He pulled the wagon to a stop in front of the small cottage next to the white steeple building he'd once known so well. With one bound, he landed on his feet and strode to the pastor's house and gave a firm knock.

Howerlitz Musgrove appeared at the screen door, wiping his round glasses on his shirt tail. He grinned and nodded as he pushed open the door.

"Well, howdy, boy. Long time no see. Shore am glad to lay sore eyes on you." The pastor chuckled, pounding him on the shoulder and remorse pooled deep in Zeph. "Come on in here, you old rascal. I'm sure the wife can scare up some refreshment."

The older man's arthritic hand tried to pull him within, but Zeph stood solid. "I need a favor, Pastor Howe."

That brought the old man's white wiry brows down in a

quick hurry. "What's that you say?"

Pastor stepped to the porch, eyeing the wagon with a keen eye.

"I need to get hitched." No use wasting anyone's time mashing the what-fors.

All the wrinkles in the tall man's face ironed out. "You don't say?" He spun. "Ovaletta."

Zeph scrubbed his beard when the old man hailed his wife even louder. When the woman didn't make an appearance, Pastor Howe snatched at the screen door and scurried in, hollering all the way. Zeph paced to the end of the porch. Didn't the old man know Ovaletta was nearly deaf? This was not going well. Soon, the caterwauling would call up an audience.

"Glory be, Zephaniah Tildee Rowley."

Durn, that woman came on like his long-past mama, middle name and all. And he despised the name. He glanced toward the petite woman in the wagon, hoping she hadn't overheard. But she looked right attentive.

Then the small, aged woman was there, hugging him. He patted her shoulder.

"I thought we'd never lay eyes on you again on this front porch. Why, 'tis the work of the Lord Almighty and that's for sure. Look here, Howie, it's Zephaniah—"

"Hate to interrupt, Mrs. Musgrove, but—"

A pinch to his cheek paused all words. "Now, you know I'm not Mrs. Musgrove. How formal, you darling man. Ovie to one and all. Oh! And who do you have here?"

Zeph's heart sank as Ovie literally leaped from the porch and scooted to the wagon. Pastor Howe's pats on the shoulders were meant to convey friendship and welcome, but they only thumped in more apprehension.

"A wedding!"

Ovie spun and clapped her hands. Well, that hadn't taken long.

"A wedding?"

Another proclamation caught his attention. Up the sidewalk stood Annabelle Hutchens complete in her feathered straw hat and wrap. Glory be. Could the day get any worse?

"Annabelle, dear. Have you heard?" Ovie scrambled toward the frozen woman. "Zephaniah Tildee Rowley's getting married."

Setting his hand up high on the porch pole, Zeph dropped his head. Yes, it could get worse.

He could vaguely decipher the chitter of information, mostly from Ovie, as the two approached the porch.

"Right lucky you came along, Annabelle," Pastor Howe said. "We won't have to scare up another witness."

And Annabelle attending his wedding was even worse. Zeph took a few deep breaths. Would anything be worse than his former mother-in-law, who blamed him for her daughter's death, to stand as witness to his second marriage? He should've never gotten out of bed this morning.

A sick feeling washed over him as the good pastor sandwiched Annabelle between himself and his wife, chatting away, totally ignoring the blanched look on the older woman's face. Here were the same people. The same exact people had been there when he'd pledged himself to Noreen nine years ago. Visions of that day and what became of his marriage almost made him turn and disappear down the street leaving that woman and child in the wagon. But he found himself lifting down the petite woman from the seat, trying to ignore the tremble in the body and the thinness of her waist.

"You mean, you're gonna be my new papa? Hooray." Daisy dove over Tyne's legs and launched herself into the air.

Tyne had only a moment to gasp before Mr. Zeph caught Daisy. The excited tot threw her arms around the big man's neck and slapped a kiss high on his cheek, just above the wooly beard. He set her down gently and she twirled and danced.

"Goody, goody, goody."

Goody. A forced marriage right here in front of God and Mrs. Hutchens. Tyne turned her face away and let her eyelids squeeze closed. Well, at least it wasn't the Fleabag Saloon. And Mr. Zeph wasn't…ancient. Exceedingly unkempt and unshorn, but he wasn't ancient. With an inhale and a long exhale, she condemned herself to her fate. She'd come to marry, and she would. Just not to the person she'd thought. Still, there was something…unsettling in it all…the way her future husband's sky blue eyes searched her face…and her form, and the way his big thick hands sent a flutter through her belly when he lifted her from the wagon.

She sensed some sort of danger here, though she failed to

sort it out by the time he'd reached up, waiting, eyeing her. There was nothing to be done but rise and allow him to once again transport her to the ground with his steady grip.

The next half an hour passed in a haze. There were no rings to exchange, no kiss of true love. Only a couple of I-do's, and a few signatures on the certificate of marriage before the pastor was shaking hands with Mr. Zeph. Daisy tumbled about in her exuberance and then clung to her new papa's hand. Annabelle Hutchens's lost no time nodding to her, slanting a glance to Daisy and Mr. Zeph, and vacating the premises. Ovie plied Tyne with tea cakes wrapped in brown paper, a few recipe cards, and few cotton dishrags and towels the woman had crocheted herself. All in all, it felt like Tyne'd spent the last half an hour spinning in a whirlwind.

"Now you be sure and join us for worship. We won't take no for an answer." The pastor, wreathed in smiles, thumped Zeph on the shoulder for the fortieth time. If anyone seemed pleased by the morning impromptu nuptial, it was the pastor and his wife.

Tyne only wished she could be so contented. Ovie presented Daisy with a peppermint stick, and the girl serenaded the older woman with the new hymn she'd learned.

"This girl has a gift. She must sing at the next service. She simply must."

Daisy gazed adoringly at the older woman who bent to hug the child. Oh, dear. They were knee deep without a paddle.

Annabelle scurried from the church, sweat live across her

top lip. Escaping Ovie Musgrove's gushing had been her only purpose. That and the whole repugnant hitching she'd just legally witnessed and signed off on.

She fumbled with the hanky at her wrist. The bit of white fluttered to the scorched grass along her path. Glory. Rarely did she drop anything. Glancing around as heat surged her cheeks, she stepped back and retrieved the wayward cloth.

Everything seemed bent against her today. This morning, she'd broken the yellow of her sunny-side up egg, snagged her treasured wrap on a knob of her Louis XV dining hutch, and now…this.

Ye gads. The man she despised most marrying what could only be described as an opportunistic wench. The tiniest bit of guilt nudged at her as the memory delved up a vision of the petite woman lugging both her precocious toddler and carpet bag toward her doorway.

With a sniff, she patted the moisture both on her lip and forehead. Perhaps the marriage was merely an act of desperation for the girl. For who could cotton to the slouchy, hairy beast of Zephaniah Rowley?

Again, an unwanted flashback shoved its way to the front of her thoughts. The beast had then been a well-groomed, tall, and sturdy youth with eyes full of a hopeful future. No one could deny Zephaniah's intense fascination for her daughter, Noreen.

Annabelle let out a small squeak. Still, it pained her, the memory of her beautiful daughter, Noreen, in her best pink taffeta, eyes similarly jeweled with youthful hope. How had she allowed the girl to marry for love? The suitor she'd lined up in Chicago would've given her the ease of luxury, not a future of overwhelming farm life sucking the very marrow of vigor from her only daughter's life.

This time Annabelle pressed the shaking handkerchief just under her eye. She stuck out her chin and veered to the right, cutting straight toward her house. Today, she would not gaze upon Leatha's gone-to-seed garden. The comfort of her front porch beckoned now, but she wouldn't rush.

The empty bucket that had contained fish still rested there. Confounded man. He'd not picked up his smelly container yet. Annabelle supposed there would be no more penance offerings appearing on her porch anytime soon. As much as she hated to admit it, the fresh fish had fried up especially good. The woman and the child most likely would be gobbling up any extra portions, portions that should have been for Noreen and...the children. *Her grandbabies.*

She tugged the screen door open and stepped inside the darkened interior. Her inhale came in spasmodic huffs. Why, oh, why today? She had no time for this. Lifting her skirt, she hiked to the top of the stairs, pulled the key from a chain around her neck and opened the first door to the left. A tear dampened her cheek, and then another, and another.

Weeping time had arrived once more.

ജ

"Let's go."

Mr. Zeph was done. From the look on his tense face, he'd

felt the water rising, too, and much too quickly. His gruff reply had both Tyne and Daisy scurrying toward the door, and not for the first time, Tyne was glad for his assertive presence and stern mandates. Daisy never ignored him. That in itself was a wonder.

Daisy chattered in high glee on the ride back to the cabin. The sticky candy, at least, kept her from yodeling the whole way, and Tyne couldn't help but feel grateful for small favors.

Mr. Zeph stopped the wagon outside of the cabin and circled to assist her down. No, she just couldn't let him wrap those big hands around her again. It seemed to fracture her composure. She booted the wagon wheel and jumped free. Dusting her skirt, she rose. But he was there. Terribly too close, a bit of an affronted expression on his face.

She shrugged and lifted her chin. "You don't need to see to me. I'm quite capable of disembarking by myself."

"Get me, Papa. I wanna go high."

The twitch in the corner of his cheek and the tender gleam that lit his eyes when he held up his hands for Daisy brought a strange sort of...pining in Tyne's chest. Silly, she should be glad he tolerated her animated daughter. There simply was no need in her own life for a hairy beast with big...gentle hands. None at all.

For she had to remember, Zephaniah Tildee Rowley might be willing to grudgingly share his name, abode, and possessions with a needy widow and child. But what would he do if he found out he shared all of those precious things with a murdering prostitute toting an illegitimate child? Tyne wasn't about to find out.

Chapter Fourteen

"That door," the big man, who was now her husband, motioned to the one to the right, "is yours and Daisy's room, and that door," he motioned to the left, "is mine.

Tyne stood, a lump in her throat. This is where what she'd done became real.

"I got chores."

Mr. Zeph wasted no time bolting for the cabin door. Tyne glanced around and took a shuddering breath. Dried mud littered the floor. Dirty clothes made an impressive mound in the corner. Dishes covered the wooden table on the far end and cobwebs strung from nearly every rafter.

Mama? Are you sick?"

Tyne uncovered her face, wiping the tears as she did. "You

know what?" she said, managing a trembling smile, "I think I might be a little sick. Let's explore our...room"

"All right, Mama," Whether from sympathy or uncertainty of her surroundings, Daisy slipped her hand into Tyne's. "I'll take care of you, Mama, just like Roxie did that one time you throwed up."

She didn't bother to tell her daughter it wasn't that kind of sickness. Merely, she swung the door open, glad the child was settled for the moment. The room contained a small bed with a trundle tucked beneath. Strangely enough, near the window on the far side of the wall stood a crib with a wooden rocker waiting in the corner.

A dresser, a small table, and pegs on the wall finished out the compact space. This was meant as a child's room. A catch snagged in Tyne's heart. Why would a gruff, hairy man need a child's room?

The answer to that hung in the silent, stagnant air. Something had happened to change such plans. A wisp of sympathy threaded through Tyne's wobbly thoughts. Mr. Zeph had seen loss of some sort.

"Pretty Mama."

Daisy toddled to the bed and clambered up. The bed was neatly made with a pink coverlet and a pillow in the shape of a daisy. Her daughter giggled and embraced it.

"This pillow's for me."

Every surface was clean, though layered with dust. It appeared so very unlike the room they'd come from, as if no one came into this place. Tyne took a deep breath. She couldn't stay mired in the history of the room. Mr. Zeph had bequeathed the space to the both of them. The only thing she needed to think of was practicality. Already she felt a sheen of sweat on her forehead from the unventilated heat.

"We need to freshen the air."

For the next half hour, Tyne aired the room, wiped it free of dust, and shook out the bedding that still smelled a little musty. But there would be plenty of time to deep clean the linens in the days to come.

Daisy's vigor slowed little by little as Tyne set her to work and soon, the girl crawled upon the bed and grew still. Well, Tyne set her hands upon her hips. At least one of them appeared comfortable in their new surroundings. She, on the other hand, had the task of rounding up some lunch. After all, that was what she was here for.

Her job had just begun.

꠸

Zeph unhitched May and Tay in record time, brushed them down, and turned them out into the corral. He returned the harness to the barn and then climbed the loft ladder to collect any belongings that may have been left there. His eyes swept the small cave they had formed in the back of the haystack. How had they done it? Little chatty Daisy had spilled the beans about their barn accommodations in the past. And here, they'd done it again.

He took in the glass jar and a suspiciously clean nail resting on a flowered hanky. Those had come from below he was sure.

Suddenly the day of the missing nails hit him. He chuckled a bit to himself as he imagined little Daisy getting her hands on that canvas sack.

A full-size dress and apron lay stretched out on the straw. Not much to lie on, but then the woman and the girl wouldn't need much space. Which was why the baby's—extra room would work perfectly for them. To cut his thoughts at the root, he snatched up the garments and stuffed them into the carpet bag. He stuffed the nail into the jar and pulled the delicate hanky from the make-shift shelf. Small tatted daisies surrounded the edges with loving detail.

A twitch set up on his lips. That youngster, she was a handful for sure. Having her around would definitely lighten up the place. 'Course, any sparkle the girl would bring would be offset by her green-eyed mother. He'd already thought this through, and he'd come to a firm conclusion. Mrs. Bow—rather Mrs. Rowley—was keeper of the house. Nothing more.

He snatched up the bucket. Though clean, not much brain work was required to figure out the purpose this container fulfilled in the loft. He spun and clambered to the ladder.

The sunshine greeted him at the barn door and he halted. Staring hard and long at the cabin, he again wondered at his sanity. Firm conclusion or not, what would it be like to constantly share the cabin after all this time alone? He'd built the home strong and had put on an extra bedroom when he and Noreen started making plans to marry. Now the bedroom that was to house Noreen and his children was now filled with a strange woman and her child. He bowed his head. It was too late to think on such things. 'Twas done.

He strode to the cabin and opened the door of his house gingerly as if expecting goblins to jump from the shadows. But the main room was empty, floor swept, dishes organized, and a meat sandwich on the table. Zeph could only surmise they were cloistered in…that room.

Clamping a hand to the sandwich, he shuffled to the door of the intruders' room and set the carpet bag down. No use to dirtying up what the new woman had cleaned. So he headed back outdoors, enjoying the hearty sandwich in his hand. Well, one thing for certain. He wouldn't come up hungry.

Settling on the wood-chopping stump, he polished off the last of his meal and then stood to refresh himself at the pump. See, this was right handy. A lunch ready to go. Zeph grabbed up the ax. This would work out fine. Work, show up, eat. Repeat. Sounded like the perfect plan. He palmed a chunk of wood. Nothing like chopping wood to clear a man's head. Perhaps, after all, he wasn't addled in the brain for springing on the marriage proposal.

If everything stayed this smooth, what could go wrong?

Tyne stared at the black lump in the pan. The smoke still hung heavily in the room. Excellent. Her new job was working out just perfect. The only saving grace? She and Daisy wouldn't be in the room when Mr. Zeph came in. She would make sure of it.

"What's that?" Daisy tiptoed, set her chin on the table, and wrinkled her nose.

"Dinner."

A scowl marred her daughter's face. "You burned it again, Mama."

A disgusted sigh whooshed from her. Leave it to Daisy to point out the obvious. She plopped the pan on the stove and took up a towel to wave the smoke toward the open windows. Best to change the subject. "Hush now. Did you pick up your writing mess?"

In answer, the tot sped from the room. Just as she'd thought. She parked her hands on her hips and glared at the lump of burned flesh. Daisy was right. Her cooking skills left a lot to be desired. But she would get it…eventually.

She set the three plates on the table and commenced to sawing on the tough hunk of meat. Tyne groaned. It was nearly inedible. Nonetheless, she plopped on the sliced apples and fresh radishes from the garden, next to the burnt offering. Then she poured the water in the glasses. Small pounding feet echoed Daisy's arrival.

Retrieving an extra plate, she covered one with the most food and laid it back near the stove. "Come along. We'll eat outside."

"Again? I want to see Mr. Zeph."

And that's exactly why they'd eat outside. Tyne had no desire to face his condemnation about overcooked food. Besides, this had become their routine. He disappeared. She cleaned, cooked, and left a meal. They disappeared. A mere nod from time to time when they crossed paths was all that was ever required.

"You can see him later." Tyne wound their way through the yard and into the surrounding scrub woods. There, she set up a couple of busted chairs near a stump. It had become their dining area. Actually, if she were totally honest, it was their hideaway spot.

Surrounded by scrubby cedars and mesquite, it wasn't the best of all hiding spots. But still, it blocked the view from the house, which was essential. If anything, it made Tyne miss their spot by the creek under the imposing live oak. At least she had food for the both of them, such as it was, and a lovely place to sleep. Even if it also housed the huge hairy stranger whom she tried to avoid as diligently as possible.

Daisy wrinkled up her nose at the burned meat Tyne flipped into her plate.

"Can't we have jelly sandwiches?"

A sigh worked its way up Tyne's throat as she seated herself. "No."

"We could go to VV's."

"No."

"What about Misserus Hutchens? She gots sandwiches and soup."

Tyne scratched the sore spot by her thumb. "Daisy. We live here now."

"With Mr. Zeph?"

"Yes."

The tot blinked her large sapphire eyes. "But I don't ever ever see him."

The bite of beef scraped down Tyne's throat. "Eat."

The girl moaned but picked up the hunk of meat with her fingers. Tyne didn't bother correcting her habit of avoiding utensils, only glad she'd chosen to forgo her arguments.

"I miss Roxie," Daisy whispered before cramming the tough meat into her mouth.

Tyne allowed her eyelids to shut for just a moment. She didn't dare let Daisy see how much she, too, missed her friend.

"There you are."

The deep, startling tones jerked Tyne from her wobbly seat and sent her tumbling backward to the dirt.

"Mr. Zeph!"

Tyne scrambled to stand, only to find him there lifting her from the dust. His mammoth hands nearly encircled her waist. Thankfully, he released her and stepped back with an assessing look. Tyne blinked and her gaze dropped to where Daisy had her arms wrapped around one of his tree-trunk legs. Before she could hiss a word, he scooped Daisy up into his arms.

"Hey, Shortcake."

Daisy giggled. "I'm not shortcake. I'm a flower. And I'mma gonna call you Papa."

He chuckled and chucked her chin gently. Then he turned his penetrating blue eyes on Tyne, who'd nearly gone catatonic at Daisy's choice word for Mr. Zeph.

"We got visitors."

"V…visitors?"

His eyes narrowed. "Yup. Pastor and his wife. You best come."

He spun then, Daisy chattering while she ran her hands through his untamed mane.

Tyne had no choice but to trail after the pair, her belly clenching at Daisy's obvious delight to be perched on his arm.

Inside the house wasn't much better. There sat Reverend and Mrs. Musgrove at her well-scrubbed table, faces alight with puppy grins. Her husband set Daisy down and, lo and behold, the child raced to the woman and nearly knocked her from her seat on the wooden bench.

"My, oh my, what a greeting," Mrs. Musgrove chuckled, enfolding Daisy into a hug.

That sore spot on her thumb made its presence known, and Tyne clenched her hands behind her. It took some effort to tug her stiff cheeks into a smile. "I wasn't expecting…" Tyne cleared her throat. "We weren't expecting company."

The woman's raised brows rushed Tyne to add, "but what a pleasure."

The pastor's wife smiled as Daisy wiggled into her lap. "We have missed you all so much. Why, it's been what, three weeks since the wedding? Time does fly."

"Yes, well…" Tyne ran her hands down her apron front, mind scrambling to know what to do next. "Would you care for a drink?"

"Heavens, no." Mrs. Musgrove waved her hand. "We just

wanted to pop in and bring you a little treat."

She lifted the dishcloth from the small basket on the table. A sugary-cinnamon aroma wafted over. Daisy clapped her hands.

"It's Ovie's special. Gooey cinnamon bread."

Lands, the woman knew how to bribe her way into the church slackers' house perfumed with Tyne's last burnt offering. Even Mr. Zeph shuffled on his feet.

"Well, I did come to ask a favor. Come, sit down."

Indeed, the woman seemed to be the hostess of the house that Tyne now called her own. With a sinking heart, Tyne settled on the wooden bench beside the pastor's wife. Across from her, Tyne's new husband did the same. So, they were effectively trapped.

"Mrs. Musgrove—"

A warm hand froze Tyne's sentence.

"Now, now. I'm Ovie to everyone. And my husband goes by Pastor Howe even though that's his first name." She bounced Daisy on her knee who happily played with her long pearl necklace. "What I mostly have in mind is for Daisy to sing. Next Sunday."

Tyne's throat closed up. So, they were not only trapped at the house, they were being baited for Sunday attendance.

"Well, um...I..."

"Yes."

Mr. Zeph's low firm answer swept the breath from her. Did the man know what he was agreeing to? And how dare he commit Daisy's participation without consulting her? His eyes shifted to hers. Resignation seemed to lie there. Tyne was sure that anger simmered in her own.

"Praise Jesus."

Mrs. Musgr—Ovie's burst of praise sent Tyne blinking.

"If you don't mind, we'll start right now. I picked a passel of hymns out, and I just know one of them will shine forth as the one for sweet Daisy."

"Yes, yes." Daisy grinned and clapped. "Let's go, Miss Ovie."

Daisy leaped from Miss Ovie's lap and tugged her to the door. Life had spun fully out of Tyne's control.

Ovie tinkled a laugh. "Oh, this child's sure to completely steal my heart. We'll be about yonder. We want to surprise you. And Zephaniah Tildee?"

The man raised his head. "Ma'am?"

"Trim yourself up nice by Sunday." With a wink, Ovie disappeared through the door.

Things had gone south right fast.

Chapter Fifteen

Had he ever been hoodwinked so effectively? Nope. Never. Ovie and her bright ideas.

Zeph lifted his head once more to eye the monster in the cracked mirror he'd unearthed in the barn loft, Noreen's castoff. As her name whisked by, it turned a knife in his gut. He couldn't think of her now. He had a new wife, Clementyne, green-eyed Clementyne, full of secrecy and vanishing abilities. And he had a child, though not really his, his to care for—little Daisy.

The corner of his mouth quirked. Despite everything, he was sure fond of that little angel. And she seemed right determined to claim him as hers as well. Why, she already called him papa. That sent a thrill of pleasure through his soul. He'd never thought he'd manage to be a father. Even if it did mean Noreen would never know what it meant to be a mother.

He dipped the straight razor in the water bowl in front of him. Best to focus and just do what Ovie had commanded. Trim and not think. He raised the blade and froze. He really had let himself go. His reflection looked twice his age, like an old gold prospector lost in the wilderness. No wonder folks had taken to avoiding him.

With an exhale, he lined up the blade. Who was he kidding? No way this puny razor could tackle all that. With a snort he twisted away in search of the shears he'd used to lop off the long tough strings from the shredded bottom cuffs of his work pants.

He cocked his head, assessing his long hair. For lack of professional skill, he merely lopped off the long scraggily strands to neck length. Snip. Snap. Hunks of hair came free in his hand. He slung it into an old shirt he'd stretched out on the floor and went back to work. Then he attacked the beastly beard and added the mess to the floor.

Shaving was a painful penance for letting it go for so long and his cheeks glowed red from the effort. He ran a hand over his jaw and rasped the surviving whiskers. The cool water balmed his irritated skin. Once he'd run a towel over his face, he stared at his reflection. Not sure it was an improvement, but at least he'd be presentable.

He shrugged on a gray shirt, the best one of the lot. And still, it looked frayed and worn through. It had crossed his mind to set the new wife on the task of purchasing him some new clothes, but the look she'd seared him with when he'd volunteered Daisy to sing stopped him. He'd overstepped, that much was obvious. But, to give his new wife credit—Clementyne, she hadn't mentioned it. My, it was hard to get used to using the woman's given name.

Not that he saw much of her. She and the girl were like two imaginary sprites hiding amongst the woods. Usually, the only sign of their presence was the fresh clean house and a meal of some sort left out. Most often than not, it was slightly burnt.

He glanced around his room. Obviously, she hadn't set foot in here. And he liked it that way. No sense messing up his workable system. Zeph wrapped up the hair and took it outside to sprinkle around the garden to keep the wild animals at bay. Then he dropped the shirt in the corner of the living area where it might be found for washing. Time to hitch up the horses. He assumed the other two were up and about because he could hear the murmurs from the next room.

By the time he'd steered the team to the front door and dismounted, the girl and her mother stepped out on the porch. The woman had donned a serviceable green dress that matched her eyes, her hair tightly pulled to her nape. He hated to admit it, but she looked more than pretty. Her dainty form complemented the plain dress. The simple bonnet made her downright charming. Daisy pranced at her side with a white fluff of a dress. The girl grinned at him. He couldn't help but grin back.

Tyne glanced up and skidded to a stop. "Daisy, wait."

Suspicious eyes raked him over and back up with growing understanding. Realization dawned like a splash of cold water. She hadn't recognized him.

Daisy blurted the thought her mother couldn't express. "Papa, you lost your hair."

He chuckled as he lifted her into the wagon. "I reckon I did."

Turning back to do the same to her mother, he found her gone. She'd scrambled to the other side of the wagon and clambered up to the seat. He shrugged and boarded.

"Morning…Clementyne."

She bobbed her head.

"Sorry to give you a start. I hadn't thought you might not recognize me without all the…" He waved a hand past his face.

"Oh."

The one word she breathed came out soft and stretched long into a deep groan. That could be good, or that could be bad. "Ovie said to trim."

Daisy squeezed through the middle and plopped in Zeph's lap. Her little hands came up and rubbed his slick face.

"You're pretty, Papa."

He chuckled and pried the girl from his face and set her between the two of them. He glanced up, a grin still firmly fixed on his face, and met with Tyne's stony stare, brows like thunderclouds. "Something wrong?"

"No." She turned a stiff profile to him.

"Don't worry, Papa," Daisy filled the awkward silence. "You still gots plenty of hair."

The girl patted his fuzzy forearm.

Zeph set the team in motion, enjoying the prattle of the girl who'd become his daughter. But, for the life of him, he couldn't figure out the strained silence of the woman, thick as lake fog in fall, on the far side of the wagon seat.

Tyne fumed. Why hadn't she recognized the man she'd come face to face with as the same hairy beast she'd married? And, why did that make her so angry? Just because he'd flustered her with his unfamiliar…face? She'd seen decent-looking men before. Well, occasionally. After all, the Fleabag Saloon catered more to the less-than-average Joes, usually scruffy, ripe in their own body odor, and oozing with alcohol. But every so often one would come through the doors, all slicked clean and greased for action. Nevertheless, there she'd been prepared to meet her doom.

But this one—she cut her gaze back to him, Daisy still toying with his arm hair, chattering nonstop—with his features full of gentleness and affection had stunned her. Not that he'd turned that tender gaze on her. That had been reserved for Daisy.

It was just…hmmm. Well, the problem was… It was… All right, the straight truth. He was…*handsome*. Without all that beastly hair, rag bin clothes, and grim silence, he was quite…attractive. Maybe a little rugged around the edges, not the uptown dandy-sort of crisp good looks. But the strong jaw, the slightly dominant nose had all been quite effectively disguised by the unruly beard and overgrown hair. And she'd been so very unprepared for this unveiling.

She licked her dry lips, scrubbed at that spot near her thumb, and cast another sidelong peek at the good-looking stranger who was her…husband. He chuckled as Daisy gasped and giggled at the butterfly that landed on the horse's head. His laugh was low, a deep pleasant rumbling. It brought all kinds of strange tinglings in her belly. These unfamiliar sensations made it harder to breathe. Tyne forced herself to swallow and snapped her chin forward.

All kinds of instinctual protection hackles rose. *Remember, a laughing, handsome man always wants something...* Tyne's eyes slid closed as she remembered Rose Yates's—better known as Miss Emerald to the general population—constant caustic prediction. One of many omens she'd whispered to an innocent fourteen-year-old Tyne cowering in the corner, a new recruit to the Fleabag Saloon. An oft repeated phrase that Tyne discovered later, was more than not, true. After all, Miss Emerald knew, having spent close to thirty years in her trade.

She tugged her thoughts away from those dark days as the wagon came to a halt. The same church she and Daisy had snuck around, the same one in which Tyne had married a stranger, loomed in front of her surrounded by buggies. That sore spot by her thumb grew itchy again and she scraped at it. Mr. Zeph appeared below her. Those sky blue eyes assessed her. Perhaps he wondered if she'd lurch from the wagon without his help.

With shoulders pulled back she stood and allowed him to assist her. Then Daisy, who'd waited as patiently as a crouching cougar, launched into the air. Without fail, her new husband's sure hands snatched the child safely from flight and then tucked her on his arm. Daisy grinned from ear to ear and planted a kiss on his now bare cheek.

Tyne bit back the desire to scold her daughter. What good

would it do anyway? The child was smitten with the big lug. And getting Daisy to mind was like skipping rope on a fence post.

Thankfully, they ran late for the service. They entered the white building and slipped into the last empty pew. Heads turned and many patrons stared and whispered. Tyne cast her eyes down. Surely, she didn't belong here.

But soon they stood for the congregational hymns, the familiar pump organ's sound blowing out the breathy notes to follow. Tyne puckered her lips at the unfamiliar lyrics. No doubt folks stared at her lack of knowledge. But to her shock, Mr. Zeph joined in, albeit a bit less enthusiastically than her daughter who seemed to pick up the words quicker than a starving cat lapped a platter full of milk.

Once the singing ended, Miss Ovie stood and called Daisy forth. The child scooted out of the pew before Tyne had a chance to whisper any behavior warnings in her ear. But Daisy appeared a vision of a perfect angel on the podium, staring lovingly up at Miss Ovie. Tyne swallowed, a sense of pride swelling her chest.

The pump organ wheezed again and Daisy, in a high clear voice, perfect in pitch, lifted the words of a new song that Tyne had never heard. *All things bright and beautiful…*

That pride that latched onto Tyne's chest slowly changed to awe. Daisy had only practiced with Miss Ovie a couple of times, yet she never stumbled, never wavered. Tyne shifted her gaze around the congregation. Every eye stayed glued to her daughter and her sweet rendition. Clearly, a higher power had blessed Daisy.

Daisy finished, curtsied, and walked with her head held high to their pew. Was this really her child? Daisy plopped next to her as if she performed every day exactly the same. Tyne's eyes snagged on Mrs. Hutchens across the way near the front. Did tears really glint in the hard woman's eyes?

Pastor Howe stepped to the podium. "Now, wasn't that a stuffed-turkey blessing, overflowing with pure goodness and spiritual meat for our starving teeth! The Lord's done filled that baby child with talent to sing high praises. Give her a hand, folks."

A smattering of claps circulated the group and the preaching commenced. No matter how hard she tried, Tyne could not relax, even with Daisy plopped in her lap, nearly asleep. These people would throw her and her ill-begotten daughter out if they knew who she was and what she'd been. These thoughts rotated inside her brain. Then they cycled back and began again, shaming her even further, bringing her so far from the present action that when everyone rose to sing, she had to jump up to join, drawing several sets of eyes.

They sang the same hymn from the day they'd spied outside and Daisy sang along with careless joy. Fine. For her daughter, Tyne would endure the service. She didn't belong here, but clearly Daisy did.

Tyne threw a glance to her husband who followed along, somewhat reluctantly from the volume, but still, he sang. How keen was he to continue attending? Tyne hoped not too much. Perhaps, like her, he felt out of place.

The music ended and the people began to stir. She couldn't wait to hit the door.

"Howdy, folks. Glad you were able to attend. My, your daughter's talented."

The dark-haired man behind them nodded to her and shook Zeph's hand. "Congratulations on your wedding. It's been the highlight of talk as folks have moved through my office this week."

Tyne blinked, noting the suntanned face of the man standing behind their pew. Drats. She was trapped again.

"The gossips love to stop by and chat over a game of checkers. Ain't that something?"

Zeph bobbed his head. "Sheriff."

That word drew Tyne up tight. She cut her eyes toward the door instead of looking at the gap-toothed woman leaning forward. Tyne could only guess this was the sheriff's wife.

"Now, I believe word about town is that you came in on the train 'bout two months back. And, of course, by newspaper account, from Kansas City?" Her southern twang lay a bit heavy. "Gracious, you look right familiar."

Tyne attempted a smile as bile rose up to choke her. But the woman's eyes only brightened.

"Ya'all must come to dinner at our house today. We insist."

No, no. *NO.* How could she stop this? But Zeph nodded his head.

"That'd be kind of you, Mrs. Elwood."

The tall woman giggled. "Stop, Zephaniah. We've been

good acquaintances since grammar school. It's Helen, as you well know, and your wife is…"

"Tyne."

"Clementyne."

Both she and Zeph had blurted out together. She cringed. Insisting on Clementyne would muddy the waters and her new husband would expect an explanation. Already, his eyes rested on her, brows drawn.

"Uh, my nickname is…Tyne. Like the fork tine. Short for Clementyne."

Drats. Tyne was also most likely the name smeared across her wanted poster if anyone were interested in that snippet of information. *Tyne Ciders, also known as Miss Sapphire, former strumpet at the Fleabag Saloon, wanted for murder of one Ervy Gumpers.* The big-shouldered lawman swelled up with a long inhale.

"Tyne? That's unusual. Quite unusual."

Horrendously unusual. Why hadn't she just given her full name? Tyne gripped Daisy to her. How long before the man connected that unusual name to one of much more interest? One linked to murder?

167

Chapter Sixteen

In Zeph's way of thinking, his new wife looked more nervous than a treed boy facing a hornet's nest. She'd been seated directly in front of him at Helen Elwood's gleaming oak table, face pale, picking at her food. Daisy, at the end of the table between them hummed a quiet tune in between bites of cold fried chicken.

"So, are you enjoying our summer heat, Mrs. Rowley?"

At the sheriff's questions, Tyne jerked to attention, her eyes wary. She cleared her throat.

"I suppose."

Helen giggled. "It's the evenings I dread the most. That hot wind."

Zeph nodded, polishing off the rest of his chicken. He pushed the plate back. "That was right filling, Mrs. Elwood."

"Stop," the woman's flaxen curls bounced as she flipped her hand at him. "It's Helen. But enough about the weather and my name. Let's have some of my yummy lemon jelly cake."

"Let me help," Tyne jumped up.

But Helen flopped over a hand. "Nonsense. Ya'all are our guests."

The skin around Tyne's mouth tightened, and she sank back into her seat to scrub at the wound near her thumb. Daisy, however, couldn't resist an opportunity to blurt out a song.

"Lemon cake, lemon cake, baker woman. The lady baked a cake as fast as she can. Roll it up, roll it up—

♥~♥

Zeph's mouth quirked as his wife stifled Daisy's song. When the child struggled against her, Tyne gathered her into her arms and whispered into her ear.

"That girl can sure turn a tune," the sheriff grinned at Zeph.

Daisy, now in her mother's lap, merely blinked. Zeph had a feeling the child would sing nonstop if she had an opportunity. He couldn't help but wink at her and the Daisy grinned. When he met her mother's eyes, however, she glared at him.

Helen placed small plates around with generous pieces of cake oozing yellow goo between the layers. Zeph's mouth watered. Helen sure could cook. A smile bloomed on his face. He hadn't had a dessert of this quality for a coon's age.

He couldn't help but dart a glance at his wife. She lifted her gaze from the perfect triangle of cake decorating her plate. Did her glare contain a bit of sorrow?

"Ummm, yum." Daisy clapped her hands. "Bee-you-tee-ful cake Mrs. Lady!"

Their hostess gave a curtsey bob. "Well, thank you little Daisy. It's my specialty."

"Mrs. Elwood."

Tyne's whisper was not lost on Zeph. Hardly did the toddler even hear before she'd snatched up a fork to jab the perfection. Tyne's surprised inhale made his eyes lift from enjoying his own bit of heaven.

"Dais—

The name clipped in half as his wife pried the fork from her daughter's hand. Again, a round of whispering in Daisy's ear.

"Here, Daisy. I've got a slice just for you."

Helen laid a plate on the table and the child scrambled off her mother's lap to clamber into her own chair. The frustrated sigh from Tyne was hardly noticeable when a knock sounded at the door.

"Huh. Wonder who that could be on a Sunday?" The sheriff rose and ambled toward the door.

"Oh, I hope there's no trouble." Helen rose and joined her husband.

Zeph ignored the voices of the visitors and took another opportunity to fork a generous-sized bite into his mouth. His wife, however, turned deathly white and clutched at the neckline of her dress. He set the fork down. Had she choked?

"Tyne?" He pulled the napkin from his lap and rose.

But his wife jumped up, her head swiveling from left to right as if she were searching for a way to escape.

"What's wrong?"

Tyne gave no answer. She only swiped Daisy from her dessert-gobbling coma. Before she could take even a step, the sheriff and Helen brought in the visitors and they strode to the table. A man and a woman were trailed by a long line of stairstep children.

"I hope you two don't mind, but I've been waiting for Jenks clan to light into town. This here is Wylen and Pansy Jo Jenks."

The swarthy-skinned man nodded and the red-headed woman grinned, wasting no time to speak up.

"Again, we apologize. Our train schedule got turned around and wouldn't you know—" The woman's mouth fell open. " Miss Saph—Tyne? Tyne Ciders? Oh, my gracious."

The woman scurried around the table and all but pounced on Tyne. The strained, frightened look on Zeph's new wife's face spoke volumes.

"Well, I reckon she's already acquainted with your wife, Zeph." The sheriff swelled with a long inhale and crossed his arms over his barrel chest.

Yep, it surely did appear that the women were acquainted. But from the looks on his wife's face, it wasn't a welcome reunion.

◦◦◦

Tyne tried to school her features, but she was fighting a lost cause. If Pansy Jo hadn't wedged her in a vice-grip hug, she might have slumped to the floor. Pansy Jo, better known at the

Fleabag Saloon as Miss Ruby, seemed right glad to see her. However, this was Tyne's worst nightmare. All she'd done for the last four years to escape the past had been for nothing. This woman, who now grinned at her, first caressing her face and then Daisy's, knew everything. *Everything.*

"So you know Mrs. Rowley?"

"Know her? Land sakes, yes. Only, I don't know this little one."

"I'm Daisy."

Pansy Jo's laugh tinkled across the ceiling. "Aren't you a bundle of character, you sweet thing."

Mrs. Elwood scurried forward, excitement dancing across her thin face. "Why don't we all have a seat? Lester, grab a couple more seats."

The woman she'd known as Miss Ruby spun. "Oh, children. Why don't you settle out on the porch and enjoy a little shade?"

A few yes, mama's were murmured from the group of five— no—six children as they filed out the door. Pansy Jo pulled the toddler from the man next to her.

"This is Wylen Harker, Wy Harker for short. He's three." Pansy Jo grinned, stroking the child's auburn hair with gentle love gleaming in her eyes. "I just bet he'd like to play with your Daisy. Here, I brought some blocks."

She parked the little tyke on the floor and spilled a jumble of blocks out for the two of them.

"Glory be, what a wonderful get-together we're having. And you know what? The Lord impressed on me to make two of those lemon jelly cakes and now I know why. We'll have enough for everyone." Helen buzzed away to ready the dessert.

The sheriff gestured toward Zeph. "This is Zeph Rowley and I guess you know his new wife, Tyne."

Again the redhead giggled. "Well, I do. But Wylen's never set eyes on her, have you darling?"

Tyne sank into her chair which could have been a pile of hot coals, she was that anxious to bolt. But everyone bellied up to the table, and she had no choice but to stay. Mrs. Elwood set out new plates of dessert and sent out cookies for the children.

"Now, tell us all how you are acquainted with Glennis Bluff's newest citizen." Mrs. Elwood picked up her fork, the glint of grapevine eagerness in her gaze.

With an unsteady breath, Tyne glanced at Pansy Jo. Dear heavens, the woman had been known as a bold, devil-may-care, forthright woman even at the Fleabag Saloon. She'd faced down many a meeker man and woman. Many a time Tyne had hidden in her room while Pansy Jo, or rather Miss Ruby, castigated an unwanted interloper. Except the very night Pansy Jo had been accosted by Ervy Gumpers…

Pressing her lashes closed, Tyne gulped. Her very life rested in Pansy Jo's hands. Her lashes fluttered open in time to see Pansy Jo grin.

"Oh, we lived together for a time."

"Oh, in Kansas City?"

Pansy Jo turned toward Tyne with her brow slightly quirked. "Hmmm. There 'bouts. All water under the bridge."

Then the woman tapped on the table with both hands. "But what we want to focus on is horseflesh. My husband breeds and trains Quarter Horses. I believe they are the best in the country. We've come to deal here with some local ranchers. But, when we come to a particular location, our first thought is to donate one of our horses toward the local law force. And apparently, Sheriff Elwood, that is you."

Amazing how Pansy Jo had turned the tide of conversation to something completely different. Both Sheriff Elwood and his wife leaned forward, their interest obvious. Even Zeph's face puckered in attentiveness. Pansy Jo turned the narrative over to her solemn husband who began to explain the details in his low baritone voice.

Tyne glanced down at the two toddlers, engaged with the blocks, babbling and staring at each other. Thankfully, her contribution to the conversation was unnecessary. She forked a bite of lemon jelly cake. It would seem her secret was safe.

At least, for now.

❦

"Those children are mine, but I didn't give birth to them. Only Wy Harker. We had what you might call, a marriage of convenience."

The conversation had swung from horses to kids right quick. Pansy Jo leaned into her solemn husband and patted his hand. A ghost of a smile lit the corner of Wylen's cheek.

But that bit of information perked up Zeph's ears as he shoveled in the last bit of Helen's lemon jelly cake. His gaze traveled to Tyne's, but she kept her head down and picked at her dessert. Come to think of it, she hadn't participated much in the conversation around the table.

"Really? I never would have guessed. Do tell." Helen almost purred as she leaned forward.

Pansy Jo let go a bubbly laugh. "Oh, my. But it was the Lord's doing. And I wouldn't change a thing. It was a blessing in disguise."

The woman bobbed the little boy who'd climbed into her lap. Zeph couldn't help but study the boy and the contentment on the woman's face. Marriage of convenience? That struck a little too close to home. He flicked a glance to the woman beside him, but she'd frozen into granite.

Zeph couldn't help thinking about that whole pronouncement as he drove his new family home and over the next week as he did the chores. By Friday, he was in a right cantankerous mood.

He'd just spent another week with the two shadow beings, never once having an actual conversation with either of them. Food was left on the table, his clothes cleaned and folded. And that was the sum of it. Yet, things had seemed quite rosy for Wylen and Pansy Jo Jenks. He would've liked to have questioned them further, rooted to the bottom of how their relationship had gone from forced to...bliss.

He snorted as he turned out the cows into the pasture for the night. Bliss. That was a joke. Zeph hadn't known bliss since he married Noreen, and he wasn't likely to see it anytime soon. He grabbed up the hoe and strutted to the cornfield. Chucking the weeds from the rows seemed to feed his discontent. It might have worked out for that couple he'd met today, but that wasn't likely to be the case for him.

It was bad enough being cursed to be single for the rest of his life, doomed for a life of bitterness and regret. But it was quite another to be married and sustain a family who had no use for him. He'd married to give both Tyne and Daisy a home. Now he'd have to face the consequences of his choice.

Dagblasted, he was a fool to be stuck in a relationship with a woman who hated him. He strode to the barn and threw the hoe in the corner. In a flash he had Tay saddled up, heading to town. No need to inform anyone of his whereabouts. The woman didn't care anyway. As far as she was concerned, the more he stayed away, the better.

Tay didn't like the hustle Zeph put in his ribs with the heel of his boots. But he had little care about the horse's agitation and halted him in front of the only bar in Glennis Bluff, Butch's, known by its respectable name of the Swank Hotel, Saloon, and Boarding House.

Through the batwings to the left in the foyer, Zeph busted through, not bothering to swing his hat from his head. No sense in sticking to manners at this point.

"Whiskey, straight."

The words came out harsh and low. It took a bit of effort to force them from his throat. The barkeep filled the shot glass and scooted it to him with an expert shove. A bit of it sloshed over the side onto his hand. Zeph slapped his coin on the beaten wood and clamped his fingers around the small glass. The amber liquid swayed in the cup, and he watched the light dance on the surface. The boisterous noises around him dulled to a silent vacuum as he contemplated. Once he tipped it down his throat, it would burn. Then a fire would leap in his belly.

Then, he'd drink another and another until a numbness spread through his body. Then, everything would become brighter somehow. No, hazier would be a better word. And his troubles would shuffle to the dark recesses of his mind. Zeph worked his jaw while his hand rotated the glass on the bar counter.

"You going to drink it, or stare at it?"

Zeph raised his head. On the stool next to him sat Dells Tucker, town drunk. The man grinned, his hairy mustache hiding the only two teeth he sported, face like leather chaps. The noises of the barroom seemed to flicker to existence like a flame to oil-soaked cotton. The card game in the corner brought up an uproar, and Tichious Smith threw his cards down and jumped to his feet.

"I'm out, you cotton-picking cheats."

The chair tumbled to the floor, accentuated by the guffaws of the others around the table. Most of them were lazy farmers or just downright drifters. Lenny leaned against the piano and jutted out a lively tune that sounded quite good until he hit the dead keys lined up and down the board.

Realization cut through Zeph like a freshly sharpened Bowie knife. He didn't belong here. He didn't need Noreen or anybody else to tell him that. Zeph felt it deep in his soul. He stood.

"You know what? I ain't going to do either. Here, with my compliments."

He thrust the shot glass to Dells who grinned, delight jumping in his eyes. Zeph spun and encountered another dedicated patron who promptly spilled half a glass down his arm. Zeph cringed at the wetness creeping down his sleeve.

The man swore and mumbled. "Why don't you get outa the way?"

Why didn't he indeed? "That's exactly what I intend to do."

Zeph strode to the exit, stepped out into the night, and slung his arm to rid the rest of the whisky drops from his sleeve. His chin lifted and he studied the dark sky lit with a thousand stars. With clenched fists and gritted teeth he squelched his desire to curse.

For here he was. Cheated both times in marriage. And still he could not drown his sorrows because of conscience. Indeed he was a dang idiot fool.

He climbed aboard Tay and let the animal meander home at a snail's pace, the animal stopping to sniff at the plums.

A thought froze Zeph in the saddle. The nightmares were gone. Odd he hadn't had one since…well, since he'd married that green-eyed woman. He snorted. Luck of the draw. Most likely his brain merely had other things to think over and had completely forgotten to settle back into its punishing groove.

Still, it was strange. And he couldn't help but wonder if something had really…shifted.

Chapter Seventeen

Except for the distant sound of the cherry longcase clock's methodical tick-tocks, the house was completely silent. Daisy gave up her plan to stay up with her mother, climbed in the bedsheets, and drifted off to sleep. Tyne set aside her pitiful crocheting due to the lack of light. And, actually, she wasn't sure why she continued to sit in the rocker while the moon cascaded a stream of light into her lap.

The only explanation was...she hadn't heard him. While Tyne did her best to avoid coming face to face with the man she'd married, there was still a bit of a pattern to their days. In the evening, she'd leave out his food and retire to their room. The early bedtime proved a challenge to keep Daisy settled for so long, and if Tyne were honest, for herself as well. But it seemed a workable plan.

Tyne would often hear him puttering around and then, he'd close the door, shuffle about his room, and all would become quiet. But that was not the case tonight. As a matter of fact, his dinner still lay upon the table.

Perhaps he too, had a week fraught with worry. After all, she half expected Pansy Jo to show up, leading Sheriff Elwood and the Cairo lawman right to her door. She sighed. Pansy Jo had been a friend. That was silly to think such a thing. But still, couldn't the lawmen have trailed her and her husband?

And that was a whole other thing. Pansy Jo, former Miss Ruby, appeared happily married. The woman fairly mooned over the rawboned man at her side. And he too, had seemed quite smitten with her. If Tyne hadn't seen it with her own eyes, she might never have believed it. Did Pansy Jo's husband know of her shady past? Knowing the woman's outspoken nature, it did seem unlikely that he'd still be in the dark about it all.

With a disgusted sigh Tyne pushed herself to her feet. Goodness, it'd been all she'd thought of the entire week. She was as worn as Grandma's shabby carpet with the whole thought. With crossed arms, she paced. She shoved away thoughts of her former friend in crime and focused on the more immediate question.

Where was her…husband?

She tiptoed to the door and cracked it open. Soft tinkling chimes indicated the top of the hour. Tyne stepped through and pulled the door closed. The oppressive heat still permeated the room even hours after cooking. She bellied up to the expensive clock that stuck out like an albino deer in a forest so out of place in the simple cabin. Her eyes squinted at the hands.

The hands pointed at eleven o'clock, nearly two hours past her husband's usual time of retirement for the night.

She trod to the table. Yep. The ham slice, well-cooked if she said so herself, and potatoes were doing nothing but drawing flies. He hadn't even bothered to come in and eat.

With a flip of her hand, she recovered the plate with the cloth napkin and stepped to the door, cracking it open in the night air. Night had always struck her as an uneasy time. A hoot owl hooted in the distance, adding to the eeriness of the darkness. Her eyes latched onto the barn. Surely he worked inside, but no light leaked from any crevice.

Trepidation crept up her spine. Had the man hurt himself? Perhaps he lay in the barn, bleeding out with no one to help him. She caught her breath. Wouldn't that be a mess? Not just literally, but figuratively. She and Daisy would be on their own again.

Tyne sniffed and stepped out, impatient with her own selfish thoughts. If the man were injured, she needed to get to him. She sped across the wet grass and pushed the barn door open. Inside the cavernous building was solid darkness. Great. She'd failed to bring a lantern. The only light was the bit of moonbeams streaming in the doorway at her feet.

Her hand went to the wall near the doorway. There she could just make out a kerosene lamp. With a few fumbles on the spidery shelf, she located the matches. Just as her fingers found their way into the box did she hear the shuffle and then another.

Someone was in the barn.

Tyne stepped into the shadow. Was it her husband? Or someone else? Perhaps an interloper lay hidden, much like she and Daisy, only with more sinister intentions. She slunk along the walls, freezing when a hanging tool snagged her dress and made a rattle. Ordinarily, such a low volume noise wouldn't have been noticed. But in the dark, with questionable company, she might as well have perched on the roof and banged a spatula against a frying pan.

She stood, struggling to keep her frightened gasps for oxygen quiet. When no other noise met her ears, she tiptoed forward, avoiding the tool-laden wall behind her. A few stomps alerted her that she approached the horse stalls and caused her to stutter-step to a stop for a moment.

Maybe that was it. Merely, the movement of a couple of animals had caught her attention. Nevertheless, she peeked around the first stall. Through the small window in the back, the light filtered in to outline the first horse, head slumped in slumber. My, she was being silly. Scared of an old—ooof!

A solid body knocked her to the ground, man-sized and smelling of liquor. Then hands gripped her shoulders. Everything in her rebelled. She was no longer in the barn. She was back at the Fleabag Saloon, fending for her life. She clenched her hands together and swung with all her might.

"Let me go!"

Her forearm banged painfully against a skull and, despite the throbbing now in her arm, the man's groan fueled her desire to fight her way free. With a swift kick, earning her yet another cry of pain, she drew free of his arms. Tyne scrambled backwards like a crab once she'd escaped from his clutches. With frantic hands, she lifted her skirt to the small knife she always kept strapped to her thigh. Once it came free, she bounced up, and took to a wide stance. He wouldn't lay another hand on her.

"Touch me again, and I'll stick you."

A match scrape caught her by surprise. There, holding the lit kerosene lamp, stood her husband, hair mussed and rubbing his jaw. "By gum, woman. I was only trying to help you up."

She stood and panted for a moment or two, arms out, knife still drawn. He took a step forward, and she raised the weapon.

"That's far enough right there."

"I'm just getting my hat."

She made a slashing motion. "Oh, no you don't. I know that trick."

With a flip of her boot, she cartwheeled the hat to his feet. He swiped it from the dirt, planted it on his head, and then motioned to her knife.

"Is that necessary?"

"A woman needs to protect herself. Drunks can't be trusted."

"Drun—I'm not drunk."

Tyne narrowed her eyes and gave a snort. "I've little trust in men and you reek of whisky. From experience, that's a lethal combination. I don't fancy being beaten in submission."

That seemed to stun him for he stepped back and slid one hand into his pocket. "I see. Well, you can rest assured that was never my intention. And the whisky is on my shirt, not in my stomach."

ᢟᢟᢟ

Zeph eyed the fierce woman in front of him. She stood braced for an attack. Something cold and dangerous sparked in her eyes. He could take the knife from her, but he'd have battle wounds for sure. Her gaze stayed latched to him, body ready to strike. He'd seen plenty of men poised for self-defense with such furor, but never a woman. It saddened him somehow and made him wonder what lay in her past. He decided to take a different approach.

"You're right. A woman does need to know how to protect herself. It's good to know you're prepared."

Her two blinks told him she hadn't expected that comment.

"Anyway, I'm tired, and I'm going in for the night. I apologize for making more laundry. Some sap spilled his drink all over me."

No sense telling her he'd gone into town with the intention of getting soused. He turned, hoping he wouldn't regret putting his back to her. But it seemed the only way to diffuse the situation.

He paused at the door and hung the light on a peg. "Bring the lantern to the house when you're done, if you don't mind. I need to refill it."

Zeph stepped into the night and let a little whistle lighten the heavy atmosphere. When no blade spliced his back on the journey to the cabin, he cast a glance over his shoulder. Tyne followed at a distance, holding the lantern aloft. Good. Now, he'd turn in and let the woman do the same. But he was afraid his ruminations on the woman's skill with a knife wouldn't let him sleep so easily.

In the morning he sat fully dressed on the corner of the bed. Morning chores had been done a tad early and now, he sat in silence, waiting. When his ears caught the sound of chatter and a door creak, he knew his plan had worked. Tyne had emerged from hiding and now would start the breakfast chores. To her mind, he was still outside tending to chores.

After last night knife fiasco, he'd pondered a right long time. Perhaps it'd be sweet release to be knifed to death on his mattress, with no more than a slight echo of pain. The only problem was, with his luck, she'd miss and he'd bleed out a long painful death. Or worse, he'd lie in agony, destined to spend life a feeble simpleton.

Besides, this wasn't about him fearing the blade. What stoked his curiosity about this mysterious green-eyed beauty was the deadly knowledge that lay in her eyes. Her desperation, her absolute willingness to shed his blood so eagerly. He'd toted that same delicate mail-order-bride to an old man's doorstep where she'd nearly fainted, devastated with lost hope. His wife was an enigma, and he wanted to know more.

Something sizzled in a pan and Daisy, true to her spirit, babbled about everything, including the odd knots of wood in the plank floor. He grinned. That one was no mystery. The child was as she appeared to be, open, innocent, and willing to embrace those around her without a hesitation.

And become as little children…

He swiped that haunting biblical truth away and walked to the door. When he swung it open, the woman at the stove jumped back, spatula in hand, grease dripping to the floor. Well, he supposed, it was better than a deadly blade.

"Papa," Daisy squealed her delight, thudded across the floor, and flung herself against his legs. She turned her face up, looking like a charming, little cherub.

He hefted her up into his arms, and she locked her small arms about his neck. Tremors of contentment traced down his spine. What would it be like to wake up every morning and be embraced by this child's sweetness? He paused a moment to soak in her hug and then glanced up. The guarded expression on Tyne's face was enough to kill the snatch of homey tenderness of Daisy's greeting.

"What are you…" Tyne modulated her commanding tone, "doing here? I mean, you're usually…out."

In other words, had the woman known he was still inside, she would've never had made an appearance. Thus, the reason for his whole plan. Now should he be direct, or indirect? He chose the latter.

Zeph shrugged and parked Daisy on the dining bench. "I finished early. Thought it'd be nice to eat together."

His wife passed a pink tongue over her bottom lip.

"Is that okay?"

Several blinks ensued before she answered. "Of course. It's your house."

"And yours, too."

She stepped back as he approached. "What...are you doing?"

He pointed behind her. "Getting coffee."

With a cry of surprise, she whirled away, as if he carried some deadly disease, leaving more than enough room for him to stride through. Instead of commenting, he grabbed a mug and filled it.

"Sorry, I guess I should've poured it for you."

"Why? I'm capable. You've got enough to deal with." He motioned to the darkening bacon sizzling in the pan.

"Yes, I—my biscuits!"

With a flurry the woman had the pan out of the oven. But she needn't have worried. They were fluffy and golden brown. She let out a sigh and he seated himself. Perhaps the best thing he could do was entertain Daisy who now stood in a chair.

"Papa, Miz Ovie's teaching me a new song, wanna hear it?"

Of course, darlin.'"

Daisy giggled at his endearment, hopped down and tumbled into his lap. Once she got settled, she began to belt, "Hark 'tis the Master's voice I hear..."

"Daisy. Not so loud."

"Yes, Mama."

The child began again in a more normal tone, her clear pitch-perfect voice ringing with each word. She stopped after the first verse and chorus.

"That's all. Miz Ovie didn't teach me the whole thing. But I can do the New Test'ments with the same song. Matthew, Mark, Luke and John…"

When she finished, she sat peering at him. The strangest warmth spread through his gut.

"I'm proud of you. I've never heard any girl be able to sing so sweet.

Daisy giggled and patted his cheeks. "Now, you sing, Papa, so's I can be proud of you."

He cleared his throat, conscious of the woman frozen near the stove, peeking over at him.

The girl patted again. "Please, Papa?"

This child had a way of pinning him down for a reaction. He opened his mouth and sang a well-known hymn. "Amazing Grace, how sweet the sound…"

Not only Daisy but the whole room seemed to quiet. Zeph closed his eyes momentarily, drinking in the words he knew so well. "I once was lost, but now I'm found, was blind but now I see…"

A pan ricocheting across the floor broke the spell, and Zeph jumped to his feet, Daisy firmly in his grasp. The last pan of frying bacon now lay scattered across the wood floor, grease staining the oak. Tyne's face was a sight. With a small strangled cry, the woman scrambled across the room, ran into her bedroom, and slammed the door.

Chapter Eighteen

"Uh-oh."

The exclamation from Daisy explained it all. His whole plan of digging into his wife's past had just splattered across the floor.

"Well, I guess we got a mess to clean." He set the child on the floor.

"We do?"

"Yep."

Zeph grabbed a towel, and picked up the pan. That batch of bacon lay ruined, but the pigs would enjoy it. He swiped at the grease with a towel. A sharp knock sounded at the door.

Daisy squealed and shot across the room. "Miz Ovie!"

Zeph rose, pan in one hand, towel dripping grease in the other. Only, it wasn't Miz Ovie. It was the woman they'd met at the Elwoods' home, Mrs. Jenks. On her hip rested the youngest of her clan. Daisy clapped her hands.

"It's not Miz Ovie. It's Wy-Wy and his mama."

"Oh, my." The woman grinned. "Looks like we interrupted at a bad time."

The woman stepped in, set down the toddler and the bag she carried, and scurried over to pull the pan and towel from Zeph's hands.

"Lands sakes, what a mess. But, I reckon it'll clean up in a jiffy."

"Mrs. Jenks, I—"

She waved away his protest. "Now, now. No fuss. Looks like we need to get breakfast on."

There was nothing to do but sit at the table. Daisy and her little friend climbed up into the same chair. The poor boy, all blue eyes and solemn, nodded to Daisy who chattered her head off.

"We gots bacon. Some off the floor, but some clean. Then we gots eggs. Ooops. Mama forgot the eggs."

The girl scrambled off the chair and ran to the bedroom and flung it open. Zeph had no trouble hearing her conversation.

"Wy-Wy is here, Mama, and we needs eggs."

No sooner had the child spoken the words, than Mrs. Jenks cracked several eggs in a pan and whipped them around, salt and pepper sprinkled liberally. Tyne appeared at the door, her face a stiff mask.

"Oh, Tyne. Please forgive my rudeness at arriving so early." Mrs. Jenks left her eggs sizzling in the pan to hug the woman.

"But I brought apple fritters from the diner downtown. VVs, I think. Oh! The eggs."

Between the two women, eggs, bacon, and apple fritters soon decorated the table. Mrs. Jenks plopped on the bench seat and pulled her little one beside her. Then she reached out her hands. Zeph blinked and Tyne gingerly gripped Mrs. Jenks's hand. He did the same, holding Daisy's tiny one in one hand and Tyne's cold one in the other. The two little ones grinned at each other as they grasped each other's hands.

Mrs. Jenks smiled, approving of their prayer circle. "Shall we all pray? If'n you don't mind, Mr. Rowley, could you do the honors?"

'Twas hard to pray for thinking how small and clammy Tyne's hand felt. "Thank you, Lord, for this bounty and the hands that prepared it. Amen."

"Amen." Mrs. Jenks burst forth. "And hallelujah, I say."

Daisy bumped the bacon plate against his arm. He grinned at the careless toddler yapping at her friend and took the plate before it ended up shattered against the floor.

"I know I'm being as bold as a blizzard in April, Tyne, but I just couldn't leave town without stopping in. I do hope you don't mind."

His wife shook her head, and she bypassed the bacon platter. Probably preserving the meat for the guests given the airborne delivery of the last batch.

"No, no. Of course not. You have perfect timing."

Perfect timing? Maybe for saving breakfast, but certainly not for what Zeph had planned. But, maybe it was more important for Tyne to visit with her old friend than be pinned to the wall about her skill in knifing folks.

Or perhaps, just perhaps, Mrs. Jenks held the key to all his wife's secrets.

ॐ

Pansy Jo dried the last plate and laid a hand to Tyne's arm. The children had scattered to play in the front yard, and Zeph had lumbered off with some excuse to trim some weeds. The woman gently guided Tyne back to the table.

"Let's just stop all this polite chit-chat and be honest."

Tyne dipped her head as she slid into a chair. She'd hoped they could avoid the past. With all her heart, she'd tried. They'd made it through breakfast and clean up, but here the past was about to vomit all over in her kitchen. At least they were alone.

Her friend of old fixed her with an intense gaze. "How in the world did you end up here?"

The exhale Tyne let loose blew up her bangs. In a way, it was cleansing to talk of it. It took such energy to keep the horrid information tucked away. "That…night, I snuck out the window and ran. Headed west. Stayed here and there for a time. Ended up in Kansas City. Had…Daisy."

"Do you know who the father…"

"No," Tyne couldn't say it fast enough.

"Someone from the Fleabag, no doubt?"

Tyne could feel her face burn and simply nodded. "Then I ended up working in Kansas City with my aunt in a big house.

She'd been corresponding with a man in Texas. Poor Aunt Clem. She always wanted to retire from being a maid, and she finally secured herself as a mail-order bride. But, she passed before she could make the trip. So, instead of my aunt going, I became the new…Clementyne Bowlanders."

Pansy Jo's brows crinkled, and she thumbed a hand over her shoulder toward the door. "So your new husband had been corresponding with your elderly aunt?"

A snort shot from Tyne. She covered her mouth. "Sorry. But no. The man she'd linked up with was an old coot who didn't even know he was part of an elaborate, human-interest newspaper story."

"Glory and gone. You've got me all up and confused."

With some explaining, Tyne cleared up the whole mess of her arrival in Glennis Bluff. And Pansy Jo's expression became more and more concerned at every word.

"So, it's public. This affair, forgive my choice of words. It's in print. All of it. The whole kit and caboodle. In the newspaper?"

Tyne swiped her dry lip with her tongue and scraped her fingernails at that bothersome spot at the base of her thumb. Pansy Jo's hands covered her agitated hands.

"Yes," Tyne whispered.

"Oh, dear. Well, that's a mess."

Daisy's squeal made Tyne rise from the table and stride to the open window. Both children giggled and ran, wagging the new kittens from the barn as they played. Pansy Jo stepped up beside her as they watched the carefree children.

"I want my daughter to know love, Pansy Jo. Stability. Safety."

"Things we never had much of," Pansy Jo murmured.

"Yes."

"What will you tell her? You know she'll ask."

Tyne sucked in a shaky breath. "Nothing. Better to not know anything than to know you're an illegitimate child of an unknown man with no morals."

Pansy Jo laid a hand on her arm. "But Tyne, she'll find out somehow. Perhaps it's best if it comes from you."

"I don't want to talk about it. Not any of it. Ever. I just want to forget it."

"We all want that." Pansy Jo sighed. 'But doing what we did…it haunts a person."

Tyne blinked, fixing Pansy Jo in her line of sight. "You, too?"

The woman nodded. "When I'm not prayed up and I let it in. It was a terrible life. Doing what we did. One horrible man after another. Danger at every corner. Beatings, cruelty, scraping by with nothing to call your own. No one ought to live like that."

Tears threatened but Tyne hardened her jaw. "And it won't. Never again." Tyne let the curtain fall into place. "As long as I have breath, Daisy'll never know a life like that."

A few moments lay hovered in silence before Pansy Jo spoke again. "I never did thank you for what you did. You saved my life, Tyne."

An unsteady breath did little to fortify Tyne's heart, that

night coming like a horrific repetitive nightmare. She could still feel the hot gun in her shaky fingers, smell the caustic smell of spent gunpowder, see the man in a pool of his own blood. She shuddered.

"The police questioned Kerth that night."

The bald-headed bulldog of a man popped into her head. He'd been both a defender and a lecherous menace. One never knew which he'd morph into.

"So…they've pinned it on him then?" Tyne could barely hiss out the words, ashamed a dash of relief shivered up her spine.

"No, Tyne." Pansy Jo's eyes held gentle pity, even regret. "The police let Kerth go, and he just disappeared. The person they're really looking for is…you."

With a cry, Tyne stumbled back, pressing a hand to her thudding heart. Pansy Jo steadied her and led her to a nearby rocker. She hadn't escaped. The other girls had sold her down the river. All this running and they still pursued.

Pansy Jo pulled a crumpled paper from her apron pocket and unfolded it. An amateur sketch of Tyne stared back at her. Under the bold letters of WANTED FOR MURDER, it listed: Tyne Ciders, alias: Miss Sapphire, Lady of the Evening of the Fleabag Saloon. $200 dollar reward for information. $500 for capture.

A brief description ran on in smaller letters describing her height and weight, hair and eye color. A black haze brushed across her vision. It was just as she'd feared.

She was a wanted woman.

෴

Zephaniah shook his head as the train pulled out. Mr. and Mrs. Jenks and their passel of children were safely aboard heading back to Missouri. And—he hadn't learned a dang thing about his wife.

Seeing Mrs. Jenks leave the cabin with her tot on her hip had sent him hustling to offer a ride back to town. But the woman had been a sealed trunk, carefully sidestepping his questions with her brand of Scripture wrapped in her own homey slogans. Her avoidance of his questions had been doggone effective.

His, "So, where 'bouts did you meet my wife?" was met with "Mercy, we've traveled through waters and rivers together and the flame consumed us not. We've come a long way. The past is not worth remembering." Even his point-blank, "But you and…Tyne, what did you do?" was answered with "Many things, though we rarely prospered. But God, in his great mercy, saw to give us a new birth. A new beginning. Praise Jesus."

Now there were a lot directions that Zeph's mind could've wandered to. Instead he shut up, and the woman prattled Scripture intermixed with life stories until he'd felt like he'd spent a good long afternoon at the church house. Despite the fact Mrs. Jenks probably carried important information about his wife, he was right glad to see her off.

He rubbed his bristled chin as he boarded the wagon seat. Time to form a new plan. There would be no more beating about the bush. He had a right to know why his new wife could swipe a Bowie knife at a man with the expertise of Daniel Boone gutting a deer, didn't he? Therefore, he'd sit her down at the table, dismiss Daisy to play in the yard with the kittens, and barrage her with questions until he was satisfied.

A grunt flew from him as he pictured that. He, demanding answers, and she, turning red with brows as thunderous as a stormy night. Yeah. That didn't sound like the best plan. He could picture her jumping to her feet, demanding the same from him, or storming completely out of the house and he'd be no better than he started off. Actually, he'd be worse off. He'd have damaged any connection between them. It would be right hard to rebuild from that.

The Lord knew everything about Tyne, as Mrs. Jenks had referenced. Several times. But she was right. *He knows all about all of us. The warts and secret sins. And He forgives them, every one, if we only ask. He loves us that much. Ain't that amazing?* It was, but Zeph had a hard time admitting it. He hadn't been on talking terms with the Almighty in a good while.

No matter how angry we are, no matter how far we run away, God is always waiting to welcome us back. God's always looking for us down the long, long lane, hoping we will come to ourselves and remember how good He is, Hallelujah! Just like the prodigal son. No man can pluck us from His hand. No one! That's God's promise. Woo, don't that just speak to ya?

Durn Mrs. Jenks had him pegged like a new barn beam. Well then, fine. Let the Lord sort it out.

"The truth needs to come out, Lord," he groused. "Do it your way."

Zeph pulled the reins to steer the horse out into the road.

What a fool desperate plea. He had to be truly losing his mind. In his experience, his prayers had never reached past the top of his head, let alone get answered. Didn't he already have three dead babies and a dead wife he'd prayed earnestly for? Didn't that prove God didn't answer? Didn't care one—

"Zephaniah."

He turned his head to catch a glance of Sheriff Lester Elwood gaining on him on his glistening bay. Zeph pulled back on the reins, stopping May and Tay. Lester bobbed his head as he came abreast and pulled his hat from his head.

"Sheriff," Zeph nodded.

"Trouble comes knocking," was the lawman's greeting, his dark eye unreadable.

It was a matter of self-control that Zeph didn't roll his eyes. But he did let his annoyance be known by exhaling a low exasperated growl. He'd about had his fill of worn out adages from Mrs. Jenks.

"Well, I'm sorry I don't have the time to lend an ear, but I need to get back to the farm—

"It's about your wife, Zeph."

He turned to the sheriff, face set in serious lines. "And?"

The sheriff shuffled in his saddle, looking way more somber than he ought. "I'm afraid I'm going to have to…arrest her."

Chapter Nineteen

Prostitution? Murder?!

Zephaniah shut his mouth and leaned back in the chair. Sheriff Elwood finished loading his Colt and slid it into his holster. Then the lawman leaned back in his seat and drummed his fingers on his desk.

"I know this isn't the kind of thing a man wants to hear about his new wife, but I thought it best to let you know the details first, before I bring her in."

That brought Zeph's head up. "You can't be serious."

The sheriff leveled a sober gaze at him and then rose. "It's murder, Zeph. I can't just look the other way."

The sheriff held up a crumpled piece of paper in front of Zeph's nose. A rough sketch of a woman combined with a description too uncomfortably close to his wife was displayed there. *Small of stature, dark hair, green eyes.* Yes. It could be her. Her green eyes had certainly haunted him on many occasions. At the bottom of the sheet in bold letters, *Contact Sheriff, Cairo, Illinois.* But it was the large print words, *for murder*, and the smaller print letters that spelled out *lady of the evening* that hit Zeph mid forehead.

"I knew her name sounded familiar. But it had been a while since I'd been through this pile of wanted posters."

"No. This can't be. It says Tyne Ciders. My wife's name was Bowlanders."Even as he said it, he remembered Mrs. Jenks addressing Tyne with this same last name.

"Name's been changed. I've been in contact with the Kansas City office. They turned up a woman named Clementine Bowlanders who died a year or so back in Kansas City. Your wife has connections both with this dead woman and Cairo, Illinois. Possibly this woman was a relative. It's got to be her."

Zeph rose clenching the offending page. Sheriff appraised him with his sharp, dark eyes. The lawman was a big man. He'd be tough to take down. But then where would Zeph be? As if Lester read his thoughts, he spoke.

"This can be easy or difficult. It's your choice."

"Easy?" Zeph snorted. "I can assure you arresting my wife for murder is anything but easy. But I'm not going to brawl with you. You're the sheriff."

He didn't dare bring up the phrase *lady of the evening.* Layering that description to murder just struck Zeph stone cold silent.

Tyne never flinched. Not once. But her face turned so white Zeph thought she might fall off the porch steps. She asked to gather a few items, clutched Daisy to her chest, and then trailed a reluctant path to Zeph. She swallowed before she spoke.

"Pl...ease. Take care of Daisy."

Then Sheriff Elwood handcuffed her, loaded her into the back of the wagon, and drove off. She never once looked Zeph in the eye. Never once did she deny any of the charges.

As the wagon rumbled away, Daisy clung to his leg, sobbing. He leaned over to hoist her up. The girl buried herself against him.

"Mama, Mama, I want Mama," the child mumbled against his neck.

That deep, dark ache set up house just six inches south of Zeph's chin. Just when he thought he might come up out of a long dark cave, he'd been jerked back into survival mode. Daisy needed comfort and something to fill her belly. Then he had some hard thinking to do.

For as painful it was to bear, the Lord had brought out the truth.

ৡৄৢ

Tyne pressed her head against the cold stone wall. The cot was thin beneath her even with the colorful quilt Mrs. Elwood had sent along with the tray of noodle soup sitting ice cold on the small table near the barred door. The woman hadn't shown up in person, of course. Proper ladies didn't mix with bawdy girls, let alone murderers.

She wanted neither food nor the steely gaze of the sheriff across the room. It was just that she missed...Daisy. How bereft Tyne felt without the girl by her side. Her heart squeezed just thinking of the child sitting in her lap singing some sort of silly song, little hands patting her face, tugging at her skirt. She'd almost begged to bring Daisy with her. But that would've been foolish and selfish.

After all she'd accomplished to get away, stay hidden, change her name, she'd been found. Everything she'd done to protect them had been in vain.

Not only that, but she'd married a man ignorant of her past. He'd been duped into her little escapade in the hope that his name and his location would shield them. And now, he was married to a despicable criminal. But he wouldn't be for long. He'd be free to live his life unburdened by her past. He'd be free of...her.

And she'd be free of him. But no comfort came of that thought. If anything, it left her heart aching, and she pressed her fingers to the middle of her chest. It hurt so fiercely she wondered if she'd die right here in this cell. Perhaps that'd be a kindness, for she wouldn't have to yearn for what could've been—yearn for a man she barely knew.

The scrape of chair legs made her blink and press her head deeper against the grit of the stone. Footsteps indicated Sheriff Elwood approached the cell.

"Listen Mrs. Rowley. It's late. Right now, I don't have a deputy to be on duty through the night. I'm going to have to—

A rap on the door ended his speech, and the man spun to see

to the intrusion. The door opened and the mumbled sound of the voice lifted her head. It almost sounded like…her husband, the very man who occupied her thoughts. But it couldn't be. Surely he was busy separating himself from her in every aspect.

She stood and tiptoed to the bars. Even squinting in the dim light of the lantern, she couldn't make out the face of the figure at the door.

"…highly irregular," the sheriff's voice drifted back.

Only mumbles of a few words met her ears from the late night visitor at the door.

"Fine. Fine," the lawman finally agreed and swung the door open.

The man stepped through the doorway. A small figure clung to him. Daisy. And…him.

"Mama, Mama."

Daisy twisted out of Mr. Zeph's grip and bolted across the floor. Tyne gulped a sob and dropped to the floor. Small arms reached through and patted and hugged. Tyne squeezed her against the bars between them, tears washing her face.

"I missed you so much, Mama. I told Papa we had to come and sleep over. And he said yes."

A strange little giggle popped out of Tyne.

"And Papa brought lots of blankets and pillows and even some biscuits."

Tyne clenched her eyes closed and tried not to squeeze the child too tightly. She'd do most anything not to look directly at the man in the room. Daisy wiggled out of the comforting embrace. She had no choice but to rise and put eyes to—her husband.

Those light blue eyes held reservation and questions. "Thank you for bringing Daisy. I—"

The door burst open behind him. In scuttled Ovie and Reverend Musgrove. Lands, it was becoming a city wide peep show. Surely hawkers would appear outside to bellow, "Step up, step up! See the murdering trollop, five cents!" Tyne drew back from the bars and hovered in the darkened corner.

ᴥᴥᴥ

"Well, here we are."

Miss Ovie had stated the obvious. Here Zeph had just been wondering how quickly he could settle Daisy into slumber on a pile of blankets and interrogate Tyne. His need for the truth burned like a bonfire within. Instead, he nodded to the preacher and his wife, not sure what to say. Daisy held no uncertain reluctance and launched herself at Miss Ovie.

"Now, there's my girl. Sweet as sugar pie." Miss Ovie swung the girl up and settled her on her hip. "I reckon there's no bed for a child here."

"I brought my blankets," Daisy motioned to a pile near the door.

Zeph nodded to the preacher as Miss Ovie turned her eyes to his.

"This is no place for a child. No place at all. How about we take her on over to our house? We have a spare bed." She laid a hand on his arm and shot a glance toward the barred cell. "You're welcome as well."

Zeph cleared his throat. Deciding the child's lodging for the night should fall to her mother, but she'd ducked out of sight. Reckon getting arrested and jailed for murder and exposed for prostitution sort of transferred some of those responsibilities his way. "Take Daisy. My place is here."

Miss Ovie nodded and gathered the child like a hen winging her chick. "You know where to find us. And I can always scrape together some food when you're hungry."

They waved as they made their way through the door.

"Welp, I best be off to the Missus. Zeph, I'm trusting everything to you. A deputy of sorts. Don't let me down. No visitors and lock it up tight."

With a bob of Zeph's head, the sheriff donned his hat and exited. Zeph stepped over to watch both parties meander down the boardwalk and then flipped the lock as he'd promised. He picked up the lantern and scooted a chair over to face the cell in the narrow hallway.

Tyne sat huddled on the cot, leaning into the stone wall, clutching her wrap about her. She didn't move as he situated another chair for a foot rest. Once he sat and elevated his feet, he gave a sigh. "This all we're going to do?"

Her hands tugged the shawl closer.

Zeph stared at her huddled figure for a moment. Then he tossed his feet down from the chair and scooted forward until his knees brushed against the bars. Leaning forward, he pressed his forehead to the iron. He turned the lantern low and set it at his feet.

"You were running, weren't you? When you showed up to find Oliver Hendricks?"

A few moments ticked by and he thought for a minute she wouldn't respond.

"Does it matter?"

Her harsh whisper brought him upright. "Yes, it does. Don't you think we're at the place of complete honesty?"

Her bowed head shook from side to side. "And so we are. I've made arrangements with the sheriff to proceed with the divorce."

"Divorce?"

At last her head lifted and her eyes locked with his. He couldn't make out their startling color in the dim light, but tone and stiff posture indicated an intense earnestness. When she said no more, he leaned over and twisted the lantern knob and the room brightened. He wanted to see her clearly, know what she was thinking. But in the glare of the lantern light, her face looked hollow and lost. A woman totally defeated.

She continued in a monotone. "You need not stay. Once the proceedings conclude, everyone will know you had nothing to do with…it. I told the sheriff as much. Your reputation will be intact."

Reputation? He stood and paced toward the darkened main room, stuffing his hands beneath his armpits. Could she truly just coldly dismiss him as easily as that?

He strode back to the cell. She stood near and stepped back

as he approached. His hands clenched the bars. "Tell me one thing. Did you murder a man?"

Her lips twitched and her chin lifted. Silence stretched.

"You owe me at least that."

With a shuddering breath, she closed her eyes. Then her green eyes flared open. "Fine. I held the gun. I pulled the trigger. But the man murdered himself when he attacked my friend."

So, it was self-defense...with a witness. It was an open and shut case. "What friend?"

Her tongue appeared and licked the corner of her mouth. "Pansy Jo."

Mrs. Jenks? He yanked his hands down and shoved them into his pockets. Surely the woman would be willing to testify? It'd be only a matter of a quick court date and it would be over. Except...

"Where exactly did this happen?"

Tyne spun and melted back to the shadowed rear of the cell.

"Well?"

"You don't want to know. It's not important."

She spoke them so lowly, he could barely make out her words. Suddenly he knew more than ever he needed to know.

She lowered to sit on the cot sticking out from the wall. "Please...don't ask."

"Tyne Rowley, tell me where you shot that man."

She swung her gaze to him then. "You want to know? Really? Okay, then. It happened at the Fleabag Saloon."

"And you were there because..."

Her eyes lowered, her lush lashes brushing her cheeks. "I worked there. Upstairs."

Hearing it from her lips all but took his feet out. He collapsed in the chair. So, the terrible accusations were true. "And Daisy?"

His wife shrugged. "The fruit of my labor."

A groan rolled from his throat. He pushed to his feet and moved to the far corner, of the office. Before the paned window, he paused and stared out onto the darkened street. Well, that explained a lot. How'd she'd come to be so desperate over Ollie Hendricks. Why she had holed up in the barn loft.

Or at least he thought so. He didn't have the heart to press for any more details.

"Don't worry." Her voice floated to him in the dimness. "Once Sheriff Elwood finishes the paperwork, you'll be free."

Zeph took a deep breath, spun, and strode back to the bars. The small woman hadn't moved from her huddled position on the cot. He cleared his throat.

"There will be no divorce. You're my wife. We'll see this through."

Slowly her head lifted, disbelief live in her features. "You...you can't be serious."

"I am." He jerked the chairs around until it suited him, flung the covers about, and reached down to snuff the light. The room fell into darkness. With a sigh that was more a rush of air, he settled against the wooden spindles of the chair, his feet propped in the other.

An impatient sigh that wasn't his own met his ears. "Then Mr. Rowley, you must be some kind of daft fool."

He shifted his backbone between two particularly bumpy spots, but it didn't seem to help much. The woman was right.

He was a daft fool.

Chapter Twenty

Tyne couldn't help but think of her words to her husband from that first night as she hugged Daisy next to the train station. Cairo had sent a man to expedite her back to Illinois, and Zeph Rowley insisted on going along. She might have rightly tagged him as a daft fool for holding onto a marriage with a criminal, but he didn't seem happy about it. The man had slept on those two stiff chairs for four nights past, and now he'd trail her back to the city of her crime. He'd barely spoken two words since that night. Was he indeed supporting her, or making himself available to watch her suffer?

If that wasn't enough, she was leaving Daisy in the hands of Miss Ovie and Reverend Howe. For what good would it do either of them to tote the child on a long train ride to sit through despicable evidence against her own mother. Not to mention that

Mr. Rowley would have to care for her throughout the trial. Still, it was difficult leaving her. With a peck, she untangled her cuffed hands from around the wiggly body.

"I love you, Mama." Daisy pecked her cheek and scrambled over to latch onto Miss Ovie's hand.

Tyne spun and stepped behind Deputy Caffey, though a smallish man, more than large enough to adequately block her from Miss Ovie's gaze. She dared not look back to the swelling crowd of curious onlookers that had gathered. Most wore disdainful expressions. And as if that wasn't enough, Mr. Caffey clamped another handcuff on her left arm, linking them together.

Boarding the train gave no comfort from the cold accusing stares. Tyne fixed her eyes on the plank flooring, following blindly, and then settled into the seat next to Mr. Caffey. Mr. Rowley remained standing.

"Suppose you sit over here?"

Tyne worked her eyes up her tall husband but found he addressed Mr. Caffey.

"I'm sorry?"

"Well, just seems strange. You sitting by her. She's my wife."

Mr. Caffey cleared his throat. "But she's my prisoner. I must see that she stays secured."

"Then secure her to me."

A grunt sounded from the officer. "I cannot do that, sir."

"Then—"

"Stop." Mr. Caffey removed the key from his vest pocket,

clicked the cuff on his arm open, and secured it to the arm of the seat. Then he rose. With a cutting glance, he adjusted his bowler, sat opposite Tyne, and pulled a small book from his pocket.

Her husband nodded and sat next to her. "Thank you."

But Mr. Caffey seemed absorbed in the leather-bound journal. Tyne shifted toward the window. While she hadn't relished sitting next to a complete stranger, he'd been smaller in stature and less...unsettling. Now, Mr. Rowley's—her husband's—brawny leg pressed against her. How silly. She, a publicly exposed bawdy woman charged with murder, disturbed by a little physical contact.

She set her eyes on the scenery as they pulled out of the station. Yet, it was more than that. She'd...deceived him. And she, as much as she'd like to deny it, felt...something. Something she didn't want to nail down. Tyne let out a small sigh which drew the deputy's eyes across from her. She schooled her features. Little good it did to focus on anything she "felt" at this point. Beyond a doubt she was a ruined woman and why he stayed with her, she hadn't a clue.

The train chugged its monotonous journey, stopping every twenty miles or so. Along about mid-afternoon, brown bags arrived, filled with sandwiches hawked by a uniformed dining attendant. Mr. Caffey purchased one while her husband acquired two. Between her soured, tossing stomach and her cuffed hands, the meal left much to be desired.

The train pulled out of Tyler, Texas and resumed its journey northward, on the St. Louis Iron Mountain Railroad. At

Texarkana, the train puffed into yet another station. Tyne thought for sure she couldn't stand another hour without stretching.

"Why if it isn't Mr. Caffey."

A low woman's voice, seductive in tone brought up Tyne's gaze from the hustling folks that occupied the station's platform. That voice was painfully familiar. Tyne sucked in a small gasp. Rose Yates, better known as Miss Emerald, sauntered up the aisle and settled her shapely hip against the side of Mr. Caffey's seat. Older than Tyne by at least twenty years, the woman was an institution at the Fleabag.

Despite the lines of age on her porcelain skin, she still managed to look quite stunning. She was a sizable woman and had taken down many unruly men. But she was also cunning and crafty, and definitely beguiling. Many of the girls had wondered why she hadn't already left the profession. Word had it that she had a full-grown daughter, somewhere. Perhaps she'd become resigned to her life on the edge.

To avoid the passengers scurrying to disembark, Rose twirled her satin dress into the booth and plopped next to the deputy. His narrowed, mustachioed face turned tomato red.

"I haven't seen you in a coon's age, doll."

Tyne licked her lips and scraped at her finger against the base of her thumb. Rose swung her gaze to take them in, her brows lifting at the sight of Tyne. Her keen appraisal didn't miss the cuff latched on her hands.

"Indeed, you've brought quite an entourage, Caffey boy. How do you do?" Rose's husky voice dropped as she reached out a hand to Mr. Rowley.

But he merely bobbed his head.

"Caffey, darling. You've not introduced us." The black feathers sweeping around the base of her wide hat dipped.

"I'm working, if you don't mind." Mr. Caffey shuffled in his seat.

A provocative smile vined across Rose's mouth as she tucked her hand into Mr. Caffey's elbow. "Obviously. But can't we be, hmmm, civilized?"

Tyne shifted her eyes from the voluptuous woman to the uncomfortable deputy. How was it that Mr. Caffey seemed to know Miss Emerald, but didn't connect her to Tyne?

With a grunt, he motioned toward them. "Mr. and Mrs. Rowley.

Her thick mahogany brows rose. "Mr. and Mrs.? How lovely. Emerald...Cluford. Very nice to meet you."

Emerald Cluford? If the situation weren't completely morbid, Tyne would have laughed. Rose used the secret Fleabag code. "Clue" was always used somewhere in the conversation to test the water for danger. The answer must contain, *go* for help, or *stay* for all is well.

Tyne nodded a greeting. "Miss Emerald. I'd love to chat, but I must go to the powder room. Mr. Caffey?"

The deputy shifted forward in eagerness to be away from Miss Emerald. He unlocked the cuff and led her down the narrow hallway. To Tyne's delight, her old friend followed, complimenting Mr. Caffey on his competency and the efficiency of train travel. Tyne gratefully navigated into the small water closet and cringed at the hopper toilet. Outside, she could hear Rose giggling and apologizing.

Tyne looked down at her hands, already chaffed from the cuffs. The door cracked open only a moment and something small dropped to the floor. Oh. The cuff keys. Rose had somehow gotten her hands on them. The voices in the hallway grew fainter. Had she somehow lured the deputy away?

She snatched the keys from the floor. It took several angles and drops of the keys to finally get the first cuff unlocked. With a sigh she quickly managed the other one. After tossing both the cuffs and keys down the hopper, Tyne stepped to the door and cracked it open. Rose had Mr. Caffey pushed against the wall, trailing a finger down his cheek. Then the daring woman shot Tyne a quick wink before going in for a snuggle.

Mr. Caffey shifted his back toward her to avoid Rose's advances. It was now or never. Tyne scooted from the facilities and turned the opposite way. Already the conductor shouted the all aboard signal. If only she could get off the train before Mr. Caffey knew she was missing.

Tyne bustled past the uniformed man and clomped down the two steps. Fresh evening air met her face. She fled into the crowd and ran for all she was worth.

Tyne had no idea where she was going. She only pounded her feet faster and faster into the ground, dodging people and wagons, heading for some place to hide. She cut right on a side street and, in the growing darkness, nearly plunged into a wagon with a covered load. Glancing desperately around, she lurched into the wagon and crept under the canvas. Underneath her hands met with what appeared to be bits of furniture. Wedging herself beneath a chair, she covered her mouth with her hands to ease the noise of heaving for breath.

The wagon below her jolted and pitched her forward as it took off. She caught herself against the rough floorboards. She'd escaped. She'd actually managed to escape. As her breath slowed to normal, a dread covered her like a sweat sheen of hard work.

Had she escaped? Or had she just abandoned everything that had ever mattered?

Roxie Hadasher plopped her carpetbag to the wooden platform. She righted the jeweled owl pin centered in the ruffles frothing the front of her blouse and adjusted the lapels of her jacket. My, the heaviness of the traveling ensemble made her wish for the coolness of her cook's uniform. But, there was no helping that. She'd had the urgent discernment that Tyne and Daisy were in trouble. And she never ignored her burning intuition. Why to do so would be to ignore God's divine direction in her life.

But my, it was hot. She hustled toward the train station window, where a thin, tall man sold tickets, his good nature on display for each customer. This was the man with the information. She stepped up with a determined tilt to her chin.

"Good afternoon, sir. I'm trying to locate Clementyne Bowlanders. She may be known as Tyne."

216

The cheer on the balding man's open face dried up like a prune in the summer sun. His handlebar mustache twitched in agitation.

"Why would you want anything to do with that rascal? Ma'am, I have no time to help anyone connected to criminals."

Roxie convulsed her body into a rigid stance. "I beg your pardon?"

"I don't have time to fill you in on the local gossip. Check in with the newspaper office. The whole story is on display. Next customer."

There was little Roxie could do but step aside. With a pat to her graying bun poof, she headed in the direction of downtown. The newspaper's office it would be. And she'd get some answers, for the Lord was pressing urgency on her heart like nobody's business.

Zeph leaned back against the train's worn velvet seat as the engine reached full steam. The jolt indicated they'd soon be at their next station. A figure dashed past the station. He jerked up and leaned to the window. If he wasn't mistaken, he'd recognized that dark brown skirt and matching bonnet. But surely he was mistaken.

He rose and steadied himself against the motion of the train and waddled toward the necessaries. In the dark narrow hallway, Miss Emerald all but lay wrapped about Mr. Caffey like brown paper to a side of beef. And the deputy didn't seem to be protesting near enough.

"Where's my wife?"

This demand seemed to spring Mr. Caffey from his fleshy constraint. "What? Oh, the Missus. She's in the hopper."

Miss Emerald Cluford turned her sultry smile to him. "Why, Mr. Rowley. Lovely you could join us. But, as you can see, Mr. Caffey and I are…"

Zeph shoved his face close to hers. "Where is she?"

Her charcoal brow lifted and a smirk tightened her face. Zeph spun and shoved the women's facility door open. Empty as school in summer. Nothing but the whoosh of the air beneath the hopper's open chute.

"You've let her go," Zeph growled at the gaping deputy. Then he rushed to the nearest ticket collector. "Did a woman get off at the last station?"

The older man nodded. "Yes, sir. Seemed to be in a right hurry, too."

Without bothering to thank him, Zeph rushed to the closed door and shoved it open. The ground sped past by this point as the train had built up some speed. Zeph glanced ahead in the growing dusk, and seeing a smooth grassy patch ahead, he timed his jump.

He landed with a heavy grunt and rolled several times before landing flat on his back. Another groan escaped his throat as he stared at the few stars struggling to find their way in the night sky. More scuffles near him brought Zeph to a painful sitting position. Mr. Caffey, minus the ivy-climber Miss Emerald Cluford, lay some twenty feet down the tracks. Zeph rose and limped toward him.

A low moan met his ears, and from the grimace on the deputy's face, his landing had not gone well.

"My gut." Mr. Caffey ran a hand across his side and gave a shudder. Still the man made an effort to rise. Zeph offered a hand, but the deputy chose a slower approach.

"You gonna make it? We need to track her now."

Mr. Caffey nodded and stumbled after Zeph who set up a stiff pace. It was hard to know just how far out of town they were, though they couldn't be more than a few miles. They'd just taken off not five minutes ago. Scratch that, ten minutes. Or fifteen? Ugh the more he thought about it, the more his muscles ached. Blast the time. He'd just keep jogging until he made it back to town.

Night had settled in for a long stay by the time they both reached the edge of town. Poor Mr. Caffey staggered several yards back, still holding his side.

"Wait, man," he puffed. "I…I'm not sure I can keep this up."

Mr. Caffey came abreast and leaned over to gasp air into his lungs. At this rate, they'd never find Tyne. The woman could be at the Mexican border before Mr. Caffey took another step. Zeph left the tracks and jogged to the nearest road to hail an approaching wagon.

"Stop. Please. We need help."

A wizened man pulled back on the reins, halting the pair of mules. A younger version of himself sat shotgun. "What's yer story?"

"I've an injured man. A deputy. We need to get back to

town, to the sheriff's office."

"Cain't hep ya there. We're heading out."

Mr. Caffey came huffing up. "I'll make it worth your time."

With that, the deputy held up a ten dollar gold coin. The man's weathered eyes leaped with interest.

"Reckon we can turn back." The old man jerked his head. "Get in the back."

With the load packed in the back and covered with a tarp, there was just enough room to sit on the tailgate. Zeph helped Caffey aboard and jumped up himself. He threw out both arms as the wagon jerked into motion in an effort to keep both of them from pitching out onto the dirt road.

What a mess. Even when they reached the sheriff's office, what would they do? Caffey was in a bad spot with his injuries, but he was in an even worse spot. His wife was gone and how in the world would he find her in such a huge city? One thing he did have, he supposed was Daisy. Tyne wouldn't leave the girl for good. If nothing else, he could return to Glennis Bluff and wait for her to show up. But then, what would he really have when she did?

A woman who didn't want him.

Chapter Twenty-One

It had taken a few moments to lock on the voices. But now she was certain. Deputy Caffey and her husband sat mere inches from her on the back of the very wagon she rode in. Tyne squeezed her eyes shut. Of all that was good and holy, could she not even run away properly? Her husband's voice interrupted her self-admonishing thoughts.

"Where do you think she is?"

Mr. Caffey grunted. Pain stitched his voice tight. "Who knows? Maybe she's involved with some kind of ring."

"What are you talking about?" Zeph sounded irritated.

"Obviously, she had help to escape. Miss Emeral...I mean, Miss Cluford or rather Yates aided your wife's escape by trying to garner my attention. Who knows how many there are protecting one another?"

221

"You are done touched in the head. And you didn't seem very reluctant with Miss Emerald," Zeph said. "But to get back to your crazy notion, my wife isn't involved in any...ring of outlaws. She's just—"

"A prostitute and a murderer," Caffey all but spat out his words.

"You best shut your trap before I throw you from this wagon. That's my wife you're badmouthing."

A shiver danced through Tyne. Hearing him defend her made her feel all mushy inside. She would've thought he'd only jump in to defend Daisy. But, apparently, she fell into the same category of needing protection, like...like some child.

She tried to work up some anger for his arrogant boast of protection, but she couldn't. Being all independent and hard to the world had taken a huge toll on her. Truth was, it'd simply shredded her insides. Her throat filled with tears. Besides, the man stayed with her through all the vile accusations. He'd defended her even. It was all she could do not to tear down the canvas and leap into his lap sobbing her gratefulness.

"And let's talk about this Miss Emerald, or whatever her name is," her husband continued in a low, decisive voice. "You sure seem to know her pretty well. And she ain't no fresh violet."

A throat cleared which was probably Mr. Caffey because he spoke next. "We'll not discuss it."

"You bet we won't. One more word about Tyne and I'll bust ya. All I wanted to know was how you'd planned to find her."

Silence stretched. The wagon bumped along. Tyne's muscles

ached from being crammed into a small ball between the chair legs. Finally, the deputy spoke.

"A woman like her won't want to be found. I reckon we'll rustle up a posse."

"A posse? That'll take too much time. We need to get a move on right away. Every minute takes her farther from us."

A deep breath sounded. "It's the best option. We have no way of knowing which direction she headed. Having a group of locals will speed the search."

As the wagon jolted, Tyne's resolve firmed. She'd married Zephaniah Rowley. He'd treated Daisy kindly, stayed when he should have left, and defended her even though she'd let him down. She deserved her lot for the things she'd done. But her husband, he'd only been…good. *He was* a good man, a truly good man.

Her heart thumped. Had she ever had someone who'd embraced her, faults and all? No, never. She'd always been alone, except for Roxie and her aunt, of course. But she'd never had a…good man by her side.

Suddenly, she knew what she must do.

When the wagon drew to a stop, Tyne pushed the tarp from her head and scuffled forward. Literally Zeph's mouth dropped. The two men stood on the dirt road in front of the sheriff's office. The last thing they'd expected, she dared to think, was her popping forth from the very wagon they hitched a ride in.

"You're under arrest. Grab her," Mr. Caffey wheezed while

fumbling with the extra set of cuffs at his waist.

Tyne rolled her eyes. "Keep your shirt on. I'm not going anywhere. Can't you see I'm turning myself in?"

Still Zeph stared at her. "How in the world did you get in that wagon?"

She shrugged. "I jumped in after I ran from the train."

Her husband stepped forward but didn't latch onto her as she expected. "So, my next question is why? Why did you not stay hidden? You could've gotten away."

"Are you daft, man?" Mr. Caffey grimaced and swiped a cuff toward her arm. But Zeph merely shoved it away.

"Hold on a minute." Zeph leaned forward and lowered his voice. "Answer me. Why didn't you run when you had the chance?"

Tyne swiped a tongue over her parched lips. She had no choice but to bare her soul. "Because...there's nothing to run to. Everything that is important to me is here."

Zeph nodded slowly with perhaps an admiring gleam in his eye? "Daisy would be hard to leave."

Tyne cleared her throat, ignoring Mr. Caffey who sputtered and then waddled toward the door of the sheriff's office. "Yes, Daisy. And maybe...you."

A small smile quirked on his lips and Zeph's eyebrow lifted. Then he gathered her hand in his. "Is that so?"

She nodded, unable to part from his warm gaze.

He squeezed her hand. "I'll do everything I can to protect you."

"You can't protect me from my past." For the oddest reason, moisture filled her eyes. She stepped forward to lean her head against his chest. His arm encircled her. It was the best feeling in the world. Warm, comforting...tender.

She felt his lips on the top of her head. This man. How would she ever understand him? His compassion, his heart. Somehow, she knew this moment was the beginning of that. The beginning of them.

Something yanked at her wrist and cold metal snapped around it. The warmth of her husband's embrace slackened, and she clenched her other fist in Zeph's cotton shirt.

"Stop."

Zeph's voice froze her, but he was staring down Mr. Caffey and a new gentleman, tall and lithe with a bit of age in the crinkles at his eyes. "My wife is willing to go where you need her to. These handcuffs are unnecessary."

Mr. Caffey screwed up one eye. "Might I remind you that she shucked out on us when she had handcuffs on before? And, here's a little bit of information. She's my prisoner."

"Take them off."

The tall man stepped forward with a bit of swagger. "Now, you gents don't need to get into fisticuffs over this. We can make accommodations for the lady. And, I think we can do better than hog-tying her. The keys?"

Zeph kept hold of Tyne's hand as the elder man took control of freeing her other. Once released, Tyne stepped closer to the sturdy build of her husband.

"Now, like civilized folks we'll march on in to my office and talk this out. Then, I'm going home to the good wife for a meal. Shall we?" The sheriff swiped a hand toward the boardwalk steps.

♥～♥

Once the explaining was done, the sheriff, Mr. Simon Platt, who had a penchant for propriety, had them fixed up in the closest hotel with a deputy at the door. Mr. Caffey took a quick trip to the doctor to see about his injuries, and then he, too, boarded in the room across the hall.

Meanwhile, Zeph stood staring at his wife across the dark room. Neither had bothered to light the candle on the table near the door. Mr. Platt had been very specific in keeping a gentle watch over the lady, whether accused of violent crimes or not. Yet, at this very moment, Zeph wondered if this arrangement were wise. He didn't feel much like a guardsman. He felt more like a husband with his wife.

"I like you," Tyne mumbled. "A lot."

"Here, let me light the candle."

"No, please. It's easier to talk in the dark."

Zeph nodded. He supposed it might make things a tad easier for her. "Okay. Shoot."

From the shadow of the last vestiges of light coming through the window, her silhouette showed her in a rigid stance, her arms locked tight at her chest.

"Like I said, I like you."

"A lot. Don't forget that." He wanted to chuckle at his reminder, but the air felt so charged, he wouldn't dare. And he didn't want her to stop talking. "I think it'd be fair to say I like you as well. A lot."

Her outline nodded. "I don't have anything to offer you. But you already know that. Even so…I might like you more than just…like."

He cocked his head at this unexpected confession. Instinctively, Zeph took a step forward but stopped. Any change might ruin the moment. Well, no time like the present to be honest. "I also might just like you more than…like."

Tyne exhaled a long breath. "I don't deserve a man like you."

This time a puff of a laugh exited his mouth. Not one of cheer, but derision. "You think I'm perfect or something? I assure you I'm not."

A few moments ticked by. A slight breeze rustled the lace curtain at the window behind her.

"You seem…perfect."

This had to stop. If only the woman knew the misery of his existence since Noreen's death. There was one way to halt her belief in his mythical virtue. "You remember Mrs. Hutchens? The lady's house I dropped you at on your first day in town?"

Her head bobbed.

"I was married to her daughter and she died under my care. Her name was Noreen. She wasn't like you, strong and independent. You're fierce. A fighter. She was…fragile and helpless on the Texas soil. She didn't last long. And that's why Mrs. Hutchens hates me. That's why I couldn't stay on her doorstep."

"Did you shoot her? Your wife, I mean."

"Wha—no." How could she ask such a question?

"Stab her?"

Now Zeph stomped right up to her and grabbed her arms. "Of course not. Now listen here. She died after a long sickness—"

"Then why do you think you killed her?"

He sucked in a long breath and gentled his hands upon her. She felt good, warm, soft, and Heavens…even pliant. He recalled holding her in the street as she'd leaned against him. It'd awakened so many emotions he'd thought long dead. Even now, she stepped closer. He closed his eyes and dropped his hands.

"It was my fault."

Her hands slid around his waist. "No. It wasn't. God…chooses the time of our deaths. Even though some people may choose to hasten that moment."

His hands couldn't resist her. His fingers slid to her lower back, and he stood for several minutes, just holding her. It felt so unbelievably right to just soak in the comfort of her body, of her shared understanding of loss. It charged his soul, made him hope for brighter days. Her closeness drenched his dry heart in a shower of budding faith. My, how lonely he'd been.

He didn't know when the kissing started. Only it did. And it flared up to a fevered passion in a burst. Perhaps they had only one night to get to know each other, to solidify their…more than like. And he knew as he pulled her closer, this had nothing to do with "like."

This…was love.

སྐ

Zeph's fingers on Tyne's back buttons drew a shiver. The night before had been like no other she'd experienced. It had felt like…love. That word she'd been so reluctant to use now warmed her heart. He'd been everything she'd thought—tender, loving, ardent. But more than that, he'd been gentle and…good. He'd held her through the night as she slept, keeping her tears upon his chest. If she had no other time with him, at least she had this lovely memory of the short time they'd spent together. He spun her, but she couldn't look him in the eye.

After all, she was on her way to revealing all the secret dirtiness of her world. How would he ever be able to look at her again without loathing her? At least Daisy would have a father with a deep-set goodness in him. He would take care of her, Tyne was sure. And for that gift of raising and loving her daughter into adulthood, Tyne would weather the lifetime of squalid jail time. She deserved it, after all.

Fingers grazed her chin and lifted, and without thought, her eyes drifted from the second button on Zeph's shirt to his eyes. Such a deep, abiding emotion there, she couldn't look at him any longer. Her eyelids slammed closed.

"Tyne, look at me. Please."

Her throat closed, but she blinked her eyes open.

"No matter what, we're in this together, you and I."

Tyne started to shake her head, but his big hand gently

stilled it. "Yes," his baritone voice caused something to swell within her. "You shared wisdom with me about the death of my wife last night. Let me share some with you."

She chanced a tongue swipe across her top lip, diverting his gaze for a moment. "The past is…the past. We must forgive ourselves of our terrible choices. God—" Zeph jerked to a stop, his mouth tightened and released. "I thought He'd forgotten me. I thought He was punishing me. But He was there all along. I just chose not to see it."

"Zeph…" But the ache in her throat wouldn't allow any more words.

A small grin indented the side of his cheek. Then his face grew serious. "I like hearing my name on your lips. Listen, we've been put together. Given a new chance. The things your friend, Mrs. Jenks shared with me suddenly make a lot of sense. Let's not waste this kinship."

He stroked her cheek and lowered his head. The kiss was the sweetest, gentlest caress Tyne had ever experienced, and she sighed and leaned against him. Then he tucked her into his arms and held her.

Tears pricked her eyes. She could almost—almost—believe him. And for a moment, she wanted to dive head first into the water of cleansing and swim in the fairytale story of this golden opportunity. A fresh start, dunked in the healing love and adoration of her husband's promise sounded wonderful. But, once the vile ugliness of what she'd done surfaced, Tyne was sure of one thing. It wasn't a promise he proposed.

It was a fable.

Chapter Twenty-Two

Zeph gripped the bars above his head and leaned forward. The Cairo sheriff didn't share the same warm sentiments of coddling a lady prisoner. Though Tyne's cell was somewhat isolated toward the back from the others, it was dark and dank and afforded little comfort.

"Hey, purdy lady," one of the cellmates called out.

"Shut that foul mouth, Hummel. You'll be losing your supper." The sheriff tapped one of the cell doors with a stick as he strolled past. "Dang lawbreakers. Ain't got no kind of manners."

Zeph looked up as the paunchy bearded man settled in front of Tyne's cell. "Well, Miss Sapphire. Long time, no see."

The chuckle from the man's purplish lips made Zeph's fist itched to connect with the man's jaw. He slid his hands down the bars but gripped them hard instead of swinging a punch.

"Reckon this trial won't last long." The sheriff winked at Zeph. "If you know what I mean."

"This is my wife, Sheriff."

"Oh," the sheriff's hued lips sputtered a few saliva speckles to his mustache. "My condolences."

Zeph's anger simmered closer to the surface. If he wasn't careful, he'd end up in jail himself for assaulting an officer. The sheriff rapped his stick on the bars at Tyne's cell.

"Supper be by in a few." He spun and whistled, twirling the baton. Then he stopped and tossed over his shoulder, "Visiting hours are over."

Small hands covered his clenched white fists on the jail bars. Her voice came on a whisper. "Don't anger him. I'll be fine."

With a grunt, Zeph swung his head to lock gazes with the woman who was now very much his wife. Those green eyes shimmered with both resolution and uncertainty. How he hated to leave her. What he wouldn't give for a little of Sheriff Platt's leniency.

"It's not right. You shouldn't be in this place."

A tiny smile touched her lips. "I've been in much worse."

He tried not to let his jaw clamp, but it did. Just thinking about her...well, he couldn't entertain those thoughts, and he certainly couldn't keep his misery from showing on his face.

"You can still get out, you know. Of this...marriage."

The woman didn't miss a trick. "I don't want out. It just pains me, that's all, to think of you..." He cleared his throat and searched her face.

To his surprise, moisture gathered in her eyes and a small tear trickled out. She swiped the drop away with an impatient hand before it crested. "I wish I had met you before…"

Her unfinished sentence was clear as the sky on a sunny day. He just nodded. Suddenly he wished it too.

"You better go."

"All right. I'll be back early in the morning."

She breathed an audible breath and for a moment he wished he could press his lips to hers. Just for a moment.

"I hope so."

"I will."

Zeph turned while he could and walked the short hall. Tyne had nothing to fear. He'd be here at first light even if he had to tear the jail office door to splinters.

৩৵৻৻

A noise snapped Tyne's eyes open. It had taken forever to drift off and now, something had awakened her. Before she could tease her mind to total wakefulness, a gag was thrust into her mouth and a bag jammed over her head.

Tyne came alive and bucked and punched for all she was worth. But it was in vain, for after a male grunt, two very strong arms yanked her hands together and tied them. Two other hands secured her feet. Then, like a sack of last year's potatoes, she was hoisted to a brawny shoulder and whisked from the cell.

She didn't float along for long. If her four other senses could be trusted, she'd just been pressed into a large container. Tyne tried to scream, but all she could do was gag against the wad of cloth in her mouth. Kicking only met with something soft, perhaps a pillow? A clunk and every sound became distant. Dear heavens. She was locked in a trunk.

Her world tilted and slid and became silent. A muffled hoot of a train departing clued Tyne where she might be, especially when the jerks and rocking sent her swaying against the soft packing around her. She'd been loaded aboard a train like so much baggage.

Daisy. Would she ever see Daisy again? And...Zeph, the man her hardened heart had betrayed her for? He'd never know what happened to her. Forced to leave the jail, all he'd ever know was she'd disappeared. Forever, he'd wonder if she'd escaped and left them both.

Escape? Surely Zeph could not conclude that, for she could've never freed herself from that thick prison cell. Spasmodic sobs rippled up her windpipe with little outlet. Debating her husband's conclusions of her disappearance was of little consequence now. She was nearly without breath. Would she die in this wooden cavern, trussed and gagged? Sweat trickled across her forehead as she envisioned a horrible death of suffocation. Just the thought of it sent tears to her eyes and energy to her bound limbs. She had to get out and get out now.

But thrashing against the padding about her did nothing but exhaust her and make it harder to breathe. No, she needed to calm herself and rest. For the next time the lid opened, she'd fight for her life.

❧

"Oliver Hendricks, Ma'am?" The scruffy young newspaper man eyed Roxie over the tall, scuffed desk. Behind him, the working of the press rolled on, fed by one older man. Another younger version, stood at the typesetter's desk, pulling letters from a wooden tray.

"Yes, yes. That's the name, I'm sure of it."

The blond boy, because really, he wasn't much more than that, leaned back, cocked his head, and hollered, "Oliver Hendricks?"

The mustached man at the table looked up over a pair of circular glasses. "Old man Ollie. West of town."

The boy adjusted himself on the stool. "There you go."

Then he leaned over and grabbed a stack of newspapers and began counting. Humph. Roxie would not be dismissed in such a manner from such a whippersnapper.

"Young man. I need transportation to this man's house immediately. Perhaps I need to talk to your superior."

The boy finished fingering out the allotted amount of papers, not pausing a moment at her demand, and then looked up. "Ma'am, we're a newspaper. Not a transportation service."

"Well, I never." Roxie spun and strode from the establishment. How such a business maintained a subscriber's list with such horrendous customer service was behind her. Well, she didn't need them the find her way about. She hailed a wagon, but it drove right past. My, what a backwards little town.

Her second attempt brought a young family to a halt. The pickle-face woman merely stared at her.

"I need a ride to Oliver Hendricks's farm. I'm willing to pay for transportation." When the thin woman turned to stare at the husband, Roxie added, "please."

He thumbed her to load into the back portion of the wagon and Roxie, nearly about to faint from lack of manners, made her way to the rear. There, five children stared at her from the straw-covered bed.

"Please, sir. A little assistance?"

Only at her pleading did the man jump down from the wagon seat. He dropped the end gate and hefted her aboard, much to her indignation. Imagine, bumping along, hanging on for dear life. But she swallowed her protest about the time the wagon pitched forward. Only by the grace of God did she keep her seat.

Roxie would endure all this hardship and this lack of decorum for her dear Tyne and sweet little Daisy. Hopefully, once she arrived, she'd find the small family happy and well cared for in their new home.

But even as she thought it, she knew it would not be so.

Turning her neck to attempt to assess their progress only made her precarious perch even more unstable. Therefore, she huffed and settled for the scenery they left behind. After some time, the wagon came to a stop. Roxie waited for the surly man to assist her from her seat, but he merely jumped down from his seat and stood with an outstretched hand.

Roxie fumbled in her reticule, feeling a slow burn rise. What poor manners the man displayed. She slapped a few coins in his hand and then wiggled herself down from the end gate herself, nearly planting herself in the dust.

With little more than a grunt, the man spun, swung up into the wagon, and left nothing but the dry earth to cloud the air around her. She tugged a hanky from her sleeve and waved it about before bringing it to her nose to catch a sneeze. Another sneeze gripped her, and when she'd come about herself, nose wiped and air cleared, she gasped.

Before her was the most run-down shack she'd ever had the misadventure to see. Roxie shot a desperate glance toward the distant wagon. But there was no going back. The folks aboard the wagon little cared what situation she found herself in.

Fine. She tugged down the tails of her jacket and straightened her shoulders. A determined mask fell over her face. If Tyne and little Daisy lived within, it was certain her presence was needed. Pursing her lips, she advanced on the ramshackle cabin, parting the hens and shooting a long perusal at the pigs sleeping under the overgrown wagon.

Once to the porch, she contemplated the sturdiness of the floorboards. Now, she knew she was not rail thin, but she'd have to be touched in the head to tread across such a swayed floor.

"Hello?" she tentatively called out. "Tyne? Daisy? Anyone?"

A shadow appeared at the screen door. "Get on with ya. Ain't got no need for niceties."

This town was fast turning into the rudest she'd ever encountered. And had that old man been Mr. Hendricks? Swayed or not, Roxie mounted the stairs and rumbled across the bouncy floor. She pressed her nose to the screen.

"Now, you listen here. I want to see Tyne...Bowlanders and her daughter Daisy. Right this instant."

The grizzled man reappeared through the screen. "Ain't seen nobody. Go away."

Roxie grabbed the door handle and yanked it open. "I'm not leaving until I get some answers. Are Tyne and Daisy here or not?"

Even as the man sat in a rickety chair by the open window, and she, insistent as she could be, couldn't ignore the absolute mess in the room. It was as if the place had never been cleaned. Why, she wasn't even sure if there was a wood floor beneath the layer of dirt. Broken chairs littered one corner, a mountain of dirty dishes with flies buzzing covered the table, and tools occupied the huge hearth overloaded with spent ashes. Finally she could stand it no longer.

"What in heaven's name is happening in here? Glory!"

Roxie snatched up a half-eaten broom and started swinging. It wasn't long until she'd stirred up a fine mess of dusty air, but she also found bare wood beneath the dirt. The more she swept the better it looked. Mr. Hendricks didn't move. He kept his gaze out the window.

The closer she came to his chair, the more she wanted to know what he stared at. She stood, fifth dust pan full of dirt and followed his line of sight. A lone cross stood at the edge of the woods. Roxie let go a sigh. Mr. Hendricks had a mess of sorrow in his heart.

She spun and finished the floor. Then Roxie yanked a bucket

from near the door. An hour later she laid the last dish on the table, now wiped and clean. Then she took up a towel and started drying. Her eyes caught sight of a couple of potatoes wedged in a bin. Maybe if she filled the man's belly, he'd be more inclined to talk. Roxie whipped off her jacket and pressed it to the back of the only other unbroken chair. The way to a man's inmost secrets could be his belly.

∽

"She done disappeared."

"But how? Where?" Zeph knew he was repeating himself, but he couldn't help it. There'd been no break-ins, no tunnels, no gunpoint kidnapping. Tyne was simply gone, as if someone with a key had come in the middle of the night and removed her. Either Zeph had the misfortune of meeting up with some of the most inept lawmen ever, or he was just lucky, or unlucky in this case, because Tyne had disappeared twice. *Twice*.

The sheriff spun, mumbling about folks disappearing into thin air. Zeph trailed him from the hall of cells. No one else seemed missing. The same prisoners with their hands stuck between the bars populated the jail. Only Tyne was missing.

Zeph entered the main office area just as Sheriff Conner slapped his wide rear end in the wooden desk chair. "Aren't you going to do anything?"

The uniformed man looked up, smoothing a mustache more than a bit too long. "Am doing something. Writing a report."

A growl escaped Zeph, and he strode to thump his hands on the desk top. "Now, listen here. My wife is missing. I want a search party organized. I want a—"

"Don't matter what you want. I got my protocol."

For a couple of moments, Zeph just inhaled and exhaled. This was getting him nowhere fast. And soon, if he wasn't careful, he'd be in the same cell his wife had occupied and no closer to finding his wife.

"Fine. You protocol. I'll look for my wife." Zeph spun and stepped to the door.

"Now, don't you go impeding this case. You've got no authorit—"

Zeph slammed the door shut on the sheriff's last syllable. Nope, he didn't have any authority. But he knew one thing. Tyne had been let out or kidnapped by someone with a key. And the only person he knew in this town who might know about how to get someone out of a tight spot was...

Miss Emerald.

Wild **Daisies** Bloom

Chapter Twenty-Three

Somehow, Tyne had managed to doze off, probably from pure exhaustion. She'd had no idea how long she'd been in the box, but it had definitely been hours. The clunk of being set down had startled her awake. *Please Lord, let the lid open.* That short desperate prayer was all her clouded brain could muster.

And then, like a miracle of water in the desert, the latches were thrown and the creak of the lid let Tyne know that she was closer to freedom than ever before. Dim light made Tyne blink at the canvas covering her face. She squirmed and mumbled about the cloth across her face. A startled cry stilled her movements.

"Oh!"

The young female voice threw Tyne for a loop. That was the last thing she expected. Summoning all her breath, she screamed.

But the muted sound must have set the person in motion for she felt the bag around her head being untied. Then, with much struggle, the fabric came free. Tyne turned her head. The girl, or perhaps woman, hovering over her with a lantern brought more questions.

Her rescuer took several short gasps and then her fingers worked to untie the gag and the restraints on Tyne's hands and feet. With a groan, Tyne sat up and took several long breaths, blinking away dust. Then she worked her sore body to a stand. It was then that she squared off with her captor. But it was all she could do not to gasp in shock.

The woman was small in stature, almost like a child. But that wasn't what caught Tyne's attention. Her skin gleamed so white that it was almost translucent, and her hair shimmered as white as the silver rays of moonlight. Even her lashes and her brows were startlingly white. But her eyes arrested Tyne more than anything. They were the purest blue with pink overtones.

Tyne sucked in a full breath, scrambled from the trunk, and back pedaled. Disoriented, she stumbled and fell to her rear on what appeared to be a porch. Tyne blinked, taking in the lantern-lit darkness, the crickets chirruping. The girl stepped forward, and Tyne scooted further away.

"It's all right. I won't hurt you."

The girl's gentle voice hushed Tyne's overwhelmed thoughts. "Where...where am I?"

"Depends on who you ask, I suppose."

Tyne eyed her as she stood. What an odd thing to say. "Well, just so you know, I've been stolen away."

"That much is obvious."

Tyne and the pale girl eyed one another. "It was Kerth, wasn't it?"

Pale brows descended. "Kerth?"

"You know who I mean. That sweaty bull of a man."

With a shake of her head, the woman motioned to the door. "Let's go inside. We can talk there."

Tyne eyed her up and down, and then studied the porch area with its stout supports, the shadowed trees in front of the house. "Is this still...Cairo?"

Her captor mounted the steps. The door creaked open and the pale girl-like woman stood waiting. "Let's get some tea."

Tyne ventured in and gave a start at the bonging of a grandfather's clock. Four strikes? She spun. "It's almost morning?"

But her unwanted host wandered into the kitchen where she pumped the teapot full of water. The candle on the large oak table revealed a large room equipped with rows and rows of glass jars, some filled some emptied. On other shelves lay crocks and baskets. Everything was perfectly organized. Several bowls covered with towels rested on a side board. Tyne dared a glance beneath.

"Apples. My next task." The girl placed the teapot on a low burning stove and turned to remove an infuser from a canister. "And yes, it's nearly sunrise, and no, this is not Cairo."

Tyne's hand dropped the cheesecloth against the plump fruit, spun, and parked her hands on her hips. "Tell me what is going on. Now."

The girl dropped the tea infuser. "I don't know what's going on."

Tyne's brows lowered and she crossed her arms. "So you are used to early morning drops of trunks filled with people inside on a regular basis?"

A thready laugh met Tyne's ears. "Actually, no. Usually the fruit comes in crates. So, I must admit, I was a bit taken back."

"You thought I was fruit?"

She blinked at Tyne. "Well, that is what I deal with."

With a groan of frustration, Tyne stomped to the table, pulled out a chair, and plopped down. "Let's start at the beginning."

Her host slipped into the chair across from her. "I think that's wise."

"What town is this?"

"Well, I live in the country, but the closest town is Fort Madison."

Tyne puckered her face. Already she was lost. "Fort Madison? Is that in Illinois?"

"Of course not. It's in Iowa. But Illinois is just across the Mississippi."

"Iowa?" Tyne's mouth fell open.

The pale woman nodded.

Tyne was in Iowa? That was so...far. She took a few short huffs and then stood. Tyne lifted her hands to cover her mouth and wandered to a nearby window. How would she ever get back? "I…I can't believe this."

The teapot whistled which set the woman behind her in motion.

But Tyne was frozen in dismay. She had no money, no idea exactly where she was, and more distressing, no one knew her location.

No amount of tea would fix this situation.

Zeph blew out a long breath and his fist froze in a knot. Knocking on this door could have lots of consequences, but it was where he'd been directed after two hours of hanging out in the bar that fronted this building. With a deep breath, he thumped on the wood.

He glanced back up the alcove that hid the door from the street. How convenient hiding the door behind the block wall. More discreet…more sinister.

He spun back to the door and thumped again. But nothing moved. No sound indicated a presence. Zeph grabbed the door knob and rattled it—locked. He shot away from the door and stepped into the alleyway. Here he looked up at the three-story building towering straight up. But at the back, a sloping roofline started near the second story. If there were a way to get up to that point, he might be able to shimmy through a window.

After circling the block and dodging down a dark alley, Zeph located a stairway and a back door camouflaged in the maze of back doorways. But, it was locked up tight. That only left him climbing. He scaled the porch railing which wobbled beneath his boot, and then wedged his way between the rooftops to reach his destination. He took a deep breath as he stood, getting a grip on his elevated position.

The sloping roof to his left gave him three window options. He plowed up the roof slope to the first window. The sash wouldn't budge. Neither did the second. But the third allowed him to get a few fingers under the window frame.

Zeph gritted his teeth and yanked. The window slid open enough for him to wriggle through. But he knew as soon as he landed, belly first with a grunt, that his determination to enter the property may have been useless, for the room was empty. Empty of everything but dust which danced on the shafts of moonlight coming through the sheer curtains. He muscled to a stand and went directly to the door. The long hallway looked much like the empty room—abandoned. This couldn't be right. Tyne had been here a few years ago. Miss Emerald had appeared, real as sunshine and rain, on the train.

He opened each door down the hallway. No people, no furniture. Nothing. He climbed the stairs at the end of the hall. But it was as he suspected, empty. He rattled down the two stairways to the bottom floor. Here he found open rooms. The main entry off the hidden entrance showed only a tall counter and shelves behind. The kitchen boasted only a stove. Everyone and everything had vanished.

And so had his leads to find Tyne.

He quickly retraced his steps. The last thing he needed was

to be found inside the empty Fleabag Saloon. He stepped through the window and tugged it closed. Then he stepped across the slope of the roof and shimmied down the porch pole to the elevated landing. A man stood at the bottom of the long line of stairs. Great, he'd been caught. Zeph took a deep breath and navigated the stairway.

But as he came closer to the bottom, he realized he recognized this man. And he wasn't one of the sheriff's deputies. It was Wylen Jenks, the quiet, somber husband of Pansy Jo. Zeph stepped down the last few stairs.

"Wylen." Zeph nodded his head.

"My wife can help."

The man didn't waste any time on how-do-you-do's. "Help?"

"Find your wife."

Wylen turned and wove his way through the back of the buildings to the alleyway. Zeph followed. Once the street opened up, Zeph strode alongside. "But how are you both even here? How did you know?"

"Pansy Jo was summoned by the court. To testify."

"But how did you know Tyne was gone?"

"Pansy Jo done been to the jail."

Hope rose in Zeph's chest. "And she knows where she's at?"

They strode a couple of strides before his answer. "Maybe."

Well, maybe was all Zeph had, so he would take it.

They arrived in front of a small house adjacent to a brick church and Wylen turned up the walk. Without bothering to knock, the man walked right in, motioning him to do the same. The inside was neat and filled with crocheted doilies, one on every surface as a matter of fact. But it was homey and warm. Pansy Jo appeared in the doorway across the room.

"Thank the Lord Wylen found you!" Pansy Jo rushed forward and hugged Zeph. "You must be in such a state, you poor fella. Here, let's get you settled. Gracie…"

Pansy Jo scurried toward the way she'd come. "We need some tea in here."

Zeph sat on the navy camelback settee and Wylen settled next to him. Then the woman spun, parked her hands on her hips, and set her face into a scrunch. "Did you find her?"

Zeph shook his head. "No."

Pansy Jo sank into a nearby chair and leaned forward. "They're all gone, aren't they?"

He nodded.

The woman chewed her lip for a moment. "Just what I suspected. I'd heard rumors, so I'll share them. But bear in mind, they are just rumors."

She stood and paced. "Apparently, the owner of the Fleabag was shot. And while it was deemed an accident, the new prosecutor has been investigating. The word is that Kerth shot him in cold blood to take over the place. But his plans of an accidental shooting didn't quite work."

"Kerth?"

Pansy Jo waved a hand. "Kerth Ebron. He's the muscle. But he was also the clean-up man. The night Tyne saved me, he was there. He's always there. Or was. And he always helped himself..." she cleared her throat, "suffice it to say he was a brute."

Zeph truly hoped she was on her way to telling him where Tyne might be. For the more she paced, the more agitated she seemed to be. Plus, imparting the interworkings of the bawdy house where his wife had once worked gnawed a raw spot in his soul.

"Anyway, everyone is saying he cleaned out the place and disappeared. Word on the street says he's bought a new place in Texarkana to escape the heat here. Of course, that's all conjecture—"

"Wait." Zeph stood. "We met Miss Emerald Cluford on the train. In Texarkana."

"Cluford?" A dark shadow seemed to flutter over Pansy Jo's face. "She said her name was Cluford? That makes sense. It's an old code to check on a person's safety. But her real name is Rose Yates. Miss Emerald is her...her...other name. But it proves what I've been saying."

"Yes, so where is Tyne?"

An older woman came through the doorway holding a large tray. Wylen scurried forward and took it from her and set it on a low table.

"Oh, this is Gracie Neil. She's Pastor Neil's wife. They were kind enough to let us stay here during this messy trial business."

"Which won't happen until we find Tyne." Zeph shoved his hands into his pockets.

"Please," the elder woman said. "Let's all sit and pray first. Tyne is in God's hands and we have to trust that. Then, we'll have tea and try to resolve her whereabouts."

As much as pounded within him to choke the rest of the information from Pansy Jo and hightail it out of town, the woman had a point.

"Let's join hands." The woman reached out to Pansy Jo and Wylen. Zeph just outright refused to hold hands with another man, so he parked his hand on Wylen's shoulder. "Jesus above, hear our prayer of protection for Tyne. We must find her, Lord. Please protect her and return her to her loving husband. We also ask you clear her name and protect all of us from the evil intentions of those who need you so desperately, Lord. Let your love pour into all of our hearts. Amen."

The women bustled about pouring tea and Zeph had no option but to sit. Mrs. Neil was right. A few more minutes certainly wasn't going to make much of a difference. He found himself praying, asking that Tyne would indeed be found.

And as he sipped the tea, he contemplated how far he'd come in such a short while. Here he sat, dressed well, shaved, and full of determination versus waking up in a dusty bed cursing the sunlight.

Yes, Tyne was missing. Yes, a trial awaited. Yes, Daisy was left to friends miles away in Texas. But…his heart was different. So different. This…love, for he couldn't call it "like" anymore, he held for Tyne had transformed him. He sent up a thankful prayer. Somehow, God had done it. He'd healed him. Now, all he wanted to do was get Tyne back, return home to Daisy, and start life fresh with his family.

"Now, back to our conversation." Pansy Jo sipped her tea. "If they are in cahoots, they will be trying to hide Tyne, I suspect. And I do know Rose, or rather, Miss Emerald, and she has a daughter. And she lives in Iowa…"

"All I know is some slip of a woman came out here, had a little spitfire girl with her. Young Zephaniah Rowley brought her here in his wagon. Then, they loaded up and disappeared. That's all I know."

The cantankerous Oliver Hendricks went back to shoveling in the fried potatoes Roxie had rustled together. The way he ate, the old man hadn't seen decent food for a good long while. "Was she small? The woman, I mean."

"Shore."

Understanding dawned on her. Of all that was holy. "You ran her off, didn't you?"

Chapter Twenty-Four

Oliver Hendricks stopped dead in his devouring state. "Mighta."

"She'd come to marry you."

"Blast. I weren't onto marrying nobody." He went back to his potatoes. "Cain't even take care of myself, why would I take on a slip of a girl with a child?"

Why, indeed? Roxie stood and busied herself with cleanup. Now, she was at a quandary. She buzzed about, organizing and wiping. The place looked decent almost. It just needed some love and care.

Roxie squinted at the man seated at the table. He wasn't terrible looking. He just needed a good shave and a haircut and maybe some new threads. Her friend, the real Clementine Bowlanders, Tyne's aunt, would've been happy here, living on the outskirts of town in her own house. And this man, who'd faithfully penned loving letters, had some sort of genteel quality, though as he gulped down the fried tators, it was hard to see.

"I knew Clemmy. She shared her letters with me."

"Huh?" Oliver raised his head. "What letters?"

"Letters from you."

He stared at her. "I cain't even write."

Roxie blinked. What kind of nonsensical answer was that? "I read them. Every one."

Oliver forked the last bite into his mouth and leaned back in the unsteady chair. "Ma'am, I cain't write no letters if'n I cain't cypher no letters."

Dear heavens. What had she sent Tyne and Daisy into? She'd come to another dead end. "Then we're finding out who did. Get your hat. We're going to town."

"I ain't going nowhere."

Roxie stomped to the table. "You get your suspenders outa that chair, get your hat, and prepare a wagon. We're going to town."

With a series of mumbles, he rose and waddled to the back door.

"And bring your money, because you're getting a haircut and shave today. And clothes."

Goodness. She had to mother everyone, even strangers. "Lord Jesus, help me."

Twenty minutes later, a very poor excuse for a horse and an even poorer excuse for a wagon pulled up in front of the house.

Somehow the man must have scared up a wheel. Roxie, who'd been sitting on the porch in the one sturdy chair, rose, jacket in place, and strolled to the wagon. "Really, Mr. Hendricks. This outfit needs repairs. What could you be thinking? Will it even transport us into town?"

"Shore, shore. It's sturdier than it looks. Just needs a little paint." He leaped down, seemingly a bit more spry with a mess of potatoes in his belly. He trailed her around the wagon and assisted her to her perch on the seat, his hands hairy and gnarly, but surprisingly strong.

Roxie sent up a prayer that Mr. Hendricks was indeed correct about the sturdiness of the wagon. She had to find Tyne and Daisy, and she would start at the sheriff's office. Why hadn't she thought of that before she'd come traipsing out here to this old wizened relic? The man turned to her and gave a half smile. Although he was growing on her, Lord knew he'd needed help. Well, Roxie would do what she could.

Once in town, Roxie gave a sigh of relief. The wagon's wobbling and creaking had her nerves in a state. "Now, you go on over to the barber and get a shave and haircut, you hear me?" At his solemn nod she continued, "Then get this rig over to the blacksmith and have him check it over. And buy some food for that poor nag."

Mr. Hendricks fell all over himself getting out to assist her down. "Yes' um, I'll do all that and more. Maybe you cook again for me?"

She looked straight into his face, for he only was an inch or two taller. "Perhaps."

He nodded and winked at her. Then he hopped aboard the rig and urged the skinny nag to continue down the street. Roxie pointed her nose toward the sheriff's office, all the while praying that God would somehow send Tyne and Daisy to her.

It didn't take long to learn the whole story from Sheriff Elwood where Tyne was. The woman was so far out of reach that Roxie felt tears shine her eyes. The trouble that Tyne had tried to avoid had caught up with her. Well, at least the girl knew how to pray. Roxie had taught her that.

"What about Daisy? Where is that poor child? Surely they didn't take her on such a journey. A journey that might end in her mother's incarceration?"

"No, ma'am. But I'm not at liberty to say where she is." The sheriff lowered himself to his desk chair and pulled out some paperwork.

Surely he didn't think he would just carry on with his day without telling her where Daisy was? Roxie plopped down in the wooden chair. "That's fine. I'll just sit here until I find out where that sweet child is. After all, I'm practically her grandmother."

The sheriff raised his eyes. "But you are not her grandmother."

"Humph. What you know. I've taken care of them for years. Protecting, guiding, doing my best by Tyne's aunt to pick up the slack of mothering that poor child and her babe. And now you say I can't see Daisy? That's preposterous. Now, Sheriff, I see it's time for me to go into complete details of my close relationship

with Tyne and Daisy. It's past four years ago when they arrived—
"

The door burst open behind them. There stood Daisy holding the hand of an older woman almost the same age as Roxie herself. As if the Lord himself had dropped the girl from the sky, the child froze, eyes widening, mouth dropping open.

"Miss Roxie?"

Roxie sucked in a breath. "Daisy."

The child tore from the woman and launched herself into Roxie's lap, her little arms nearly strangling her.

"I neber thought I see you again." The child began to cry. "Mama's gone. She went far away."

"I know, pet. I know. But Roxie's here now. All will be well."

☙❧

Tyne glanced up from the apples she peeled, the smell of cinnamon permeating the air. Poor Roose. Her host rushed about the kitchen setting out one pie crust after another. Thirty pies were expected by nine. And they'd been up since three a.m. sorting, peeling, mixing, preparing. The girl never stopped. This was apparently her life. Tyne shook her head and resumed her peeling.

Perhaps it was odd that Tyne had fallen in with the woman who reigned in fruit. The shack the girl lived in, that had become Tyne's home the last several days, was small by any standards, but the kitchen took up a large portion of the entire house. It was the hub. Shelves and bins filled with flour and sugar occupied every empty space. And it was easy to see why. Roose went through a great deal of supplies meeting her demands.

The table occupied the small space in the center of the room. No settee or comfortable chair of any kind existed in the shack. They'd slept in the attic nestled in quilts, their heads just a few feet from the roof.

The place was thrust deep in the back of an orchard that boasted endless rows of apples, peaches, plums, apricots, pears and whatever else. And that's what concerned Tyne. Why was it hidden away? And why was she dumped here? The trunk Tyne had arrived in just disappeared by the next day as if by magic with no other explanation.

Roose seemed as much in the dark as she. But the woman had taken her surprise guest in with gusto. Perhaps her lonely existence made her happy for any interloper that happened along. Tyne's bevy of questions were mostly answered with puzzlement, for the albino girl hardly ever left the shack.

"Will it be the same wagon that has come the last three days?"

Roose didn't bother to look up from crimping the edge of a pie. "Yes. It's the same every day."

"And these are all for the Hotel Alexander?"

Roose nodded.

There were so many questions circling Tyne's mind. "How did you start this?"

The girl went back to the low table and threw out more dough. "I don't know. Honestly, Tyne, I just grew up with the orchard caretaker's family. When the wife passed away unexpectedly, my…well, you just might as well know it, but it's kept quiet. My great uncle owns the hotel."

"Oh."

Roose blew up her pale bangs. "Anyway, I was put out here when I was thirteen and—"

"Thirteen? That's impossible. You were just a child."

The rolling pin clinked as Roose rolled out the dough. "I suppose. But, I welcomed it. Being…well, you know, albino, I preferred to be alone even at thirteen."

Tyne added the rest of the apples to the pot and carried it to the stove. She swiped a sleeve across her forehead. It had to be over a hundred degrees in this kitchen. "So, do you ever go to the hotel?"

With skilled hands, Roose laid out the fifteenth pie pan. "No. Never. I don't go anywhere."

Tyne spun from the stove. "Ever?"

Roose's body grew still, and she turned to face Tyne. "I know it's hard to understand, but it's dangerous for me to be out and about. There are those who like to find…unusual people and put them on display."

"You mean like in a circus?"

The girl's eyes grew round, fear live in those unusual blue eyes. "Yes."

Roose drew near to the stove and stirred the boiling apples, poking one to test for doneness. "So, you see, my Uncle Ansel—I mean, Mr. Alexander is protecting me. He's keeping me safe."

Was he keeping her safe or keeping her imprisoned in this kitchen to slave away on his hotel's desserts? Tyne decided not to say anymore. "Well, I'm going to follow the wagon back to town today. It's been lovely staying here, getting to know you, and helping you in your chores. But, I have to find my husband. I have to get back."

The forlorn expression on Roose's face saddened Tyne's heart. "Oh."

"You could come with me."

Roose's eyes flared wide. "I can't go into town!"

Tyne's brows crinkled. "Why?"

"It's safer to stay here." Roose tapped the spoon on the edge of the pot to remove the sticky sweetness clinging there. "I prefer not to show my face at all. And you…shouldn't either."

Prickles broke out on Tyne's skin. Did Roose know more about her kidnapping than she let on?

"Exactly why is my presence here a secret?"

The intricate rose patterns on the top crust flattened on one side and Roose pulled her hands free and shook them. Then she closed her eyes. "Because—" Roose stopped abruptly and puckered her lips closed to concentrate on the crust.

"Do you know something about who brought me here? Please. I need to know."

The girl blinked her eyes and then gave her a long measured look before turning to remove the heavy pot from the stove's eye. Tyne rushed over with a towel and grabbed one end. "Let me help."

With a clank, they plopped the cast iron pot on the long table scarred with many batches of pies.

"I wish…" Roose's sentence stopped so suddenly that Tyne froze. The girl's pale eyes bore into Tyne's. "I wish you could stay."

The longing was live in Roose's eyes. The loneliness, the pain of being alone, of being a virtual slave of Hotel Alexander and never living a life of her own showed clearly on the girl's face. Yet, would Roose hide the circumstances of her kidnapping to keep her here longer?

"But, you know…I can't stay. You understand that I have to figure out how to get back, right?"

Roose dropped her gaze. "Yes," she whispered and then gave a heavy sigh. "I suppose I should tell you. That place you mentioned, Cairo, Illinois? Something about it seems…familiar."

Tyne handed her a pie shell and Roose spooned in the gooey apple goodness.

"Do you know anyone from there?"

"No."

"Have you ever been there?"

"Not that I am aware of. I've never been anywhere, really."

"Strange." Tyne passed another pie pan from the line. "Where did you first hear about it?"

"When I was little, living in the caretaker's cottage."

As she arranged the filled pies, Tyne grabbed another empty shell. Then she paused to study the lithe woman, so adept in her baking skills. It was obvious Roose had been making such desserts for a long time.

Roose turned to her. "You know if I had any money, I'd be glad to give it to you."

The girl's voice rang so sincere, Tyne felt a prick of consciousness by not quite believing her. "How long have you been here? In this house?"

"Ummm. Seems like forever. But it's only been five years."

Almost an eon ago as far as Tyne was concerned. Even before Daisy was born. A sharp ache pierced Tyne's heart. *Daisy.* How she yearned for her. To hold her in her arms, smell the little child's sweet scent. How Tyne yearned to be back in Texas, this mess—her current one and the one she'd been kidnapped from— were nothing but a bad dream.

Wouldn't it be lovely to wipe away the old and embrace a new start with Zeph? Tears pricked her eyes. That happily-ever-after fable was always haunting her.

"Tyne, you never told me your full name." Roose expertly wove the crust strips into intricate designs atop the next filled pie.

Fascinated, Tyne watched the girl's nimble fingers create eight small roses that would grace each slice when cut. Yet, Tyne also felt a reluctance to impart more information. If Roose was involved in her kidnapping...what was Tyne thinking? If the girl was involved, she probably already knew everything and everyone involved.

"My whole name is Clementyne..." The pause was real, her married name still so unfamiliar, "Rowley."

But Tyne's hesitation brought Roose's attention. Tyne

shrugged and cut another long strip of pie dough. "I just got married."

The look of pure pity crossed Roose's ivory features. "Oh. I'm...sorry. I mean, congratulations."

Tyne chewed her lip, Zeph's handsome face crossing her mind for the hundredth time this morning. "It can't be helped, I suppose. Anyway, what about yours? Your full name?"

Now it was Roose's time for hesitation that stretched into several moments. "Sorry, I don't usually get to share anything about me. It's Jerusa. Roose for short."

As if standing in front of a large audience, the girl cleared her throat and stood a little taller. Giving utterance of her full name, seemed to make Roose realize her worth, her dignity as a human. "Yes, I'm Jerusa. Jerusa Rose Yates."

Tyne caught her breath. Rose Yates? The infamous Miss Emerald? Suddenly Roose's connection to Cairo, Illinois became clear as crystal.

Chapter Twenty-Five

Roxie couldn't believe her eyes or her ears. Daisy, in tones much too mature to grace the child's lips, entranced the entire congregation. It was beyond comprehension, as was Tyne's extradition to Cairo for murder. *Murder.*

Roxie tipped up her chin and refused to think further on it. Instead, she whispered a prayer and settled herself back against the pew bench. Oliver Hendricks, all spit shined, sat on her left while Ovie Musgrove occupied the seat on her right. If only that m-word, *murder*, could be struck from reality, for what a fine community this would be for Tyne to set down roots.

And from the tales Ovie had imparted the last few days, Tyne had already found herself a right fine young man and done married him. Not that Mr. Hendricks wasn't fine in his own right.

He just wasn't a good match for a budding woman like Tyne. Perhaps, Oliver, Ollie for short, might be better suited for an...older lass. One who could cook. Ollie could use some fattening up.

Daisy finished her song and pranced up the aisle. With a pert grin, the child launched herself into Roxie's lap. Roxie gladly wrapped the tot in her arms, pressing a kiss against Daisy's forehead.

My, a woman could surely cotton up to a place like this—a warm town, a handsome man, Daisy cared for and treasured, and Tyne happily hitched to her new significant other. Why, Roxie couldn't think of a better way to spend her declining years.

Roxie spent the remainder of the sermon storming the gates of heaven, pleading with God to take care of that m-word. She prayed fervently that Tyne and her husband might be on the next train to Glennis Bluff, right that very moment.

After the closing prayer, Daisy slid from Roxie's lap and tiptoed to Ovie. The woman adjusted Daisy's white collar and planted her hand in the little girl's. Then Ovie leaned over.

"Mr. Hendricks? We'd be right glad for you to join us and Roxie for lunch."

"I'd be much obliged." Ollie nodded, sneaking in a wink for Roxie's eyes only.

Roxie nodded at him, letting a small smile slip across her face. The man was shaved and suited in his new threads. He looked very handsome. Roxie's neck heated, even at her age. She couldn't wait to gaze at him across the pastor's table. Who'd thought at her age she'd be interested in a gentleman?

"So, you're Mrs. Rowley's friend."

A cutting voice drew Roxie's attention from Ollie who stood outside the pew with his elbow ajar. But it was the emphasis on Mrs. Rowley that had Roxie lowering her brows before she connected gazes with a dried-up prune of a woman. Her face was drawn up, the skin liberally lined, her pure white hair scraped in a bun, and her hands clutched a crocheted shawl about her shoulders.

"I am. I'm Roxie Hadasher."

"Humph." The woman's white brows shot up. "Best say goodbye to her now. That is, if she returns to town. Zephaniah Rowley is a curse."

"Excuse me?" Roxie's jowl gave a twitch at the jerk of her head. But the woman had already melted into the crowd. But Roxie could just make out that powder white head. "Let me through, Ollie."

By the time Roxie made the door, shook hands with the good pastor, and smiled a quick acknowledgement at those who greeted her, that ghost of a woman was hiking down the sidewalk. She spun and accosted the first woman near her.

"Hello, yes. Could you tell me who that woman is?" She was ashamed to point, but she had no other option.

"Oh," the gray-headed lady started at her abruptness. But she dutifully turned her weathered eyes on the thin woman some distance down the street. "I believe that is Annabelle Hutchens. She runs a boarding house north of town."

"Thank you so much. And I do apologize for my rudeness. I'm Roxie Hadasher."

After the standard introductory chat with Millie Smithe, hoping to still any rumors of Roxie's curiosity, she reunited with Ollie and Ovie Musgrove near the church's front steps. She'd bide her time today and enjoy a nice Sunday lunch with Pastor, Ovie, and Ollie.

Then, she would pay a visit to Annabelle Hutchens.

Nothing like following a shot in the dark. Zeph glanced out the train window as it slowed. The wooden depot came into view and Zeph grabbed his bag. Now the big question was where to start? He dodged as many people as he could and headed straight through the structure to the front. A bit of an evening breeze met him as he chugged through the door.

With very few wagons and buggies on the road, Zeph jogged across the street railway in the middle of Front Street and scanned the business. To the left, Hotel Alexander was well marked with a large, block-printed sign gleaming yellow with gas lights. Zeph headed that way in a more sedate walk.

Inside, he scanned the interior, very well equipped and a bit swanky to Zeph's way of thinking. With a floral carpet covering shiny tiles, and ornate pillars leading him to the check-in counter, he nearly did an about face. To his left a large dining hall with white tablecloths and well-dressed patrons did nothing to encourage him to stay. He glanced around to locate a clock. Zeph glanced between the chandeliers hanging from the ornate ceilings.

When he shifted his gaze down, he finally caught sight of a large grandfather clock situated beside a gleaming grand piano.

Nearing nine explained the sparse crowd at the dining tables. He stuck his hand in his pocket. Tonight he would stay in this gentleman's inn, but tomorrow, he would search out a more economical option. But right now, he was tired. The daylong rattles from the train were still echoing in his spine. All he wanted now was a long drink of water and fresh sheets.

Tomorrow he would organize a new plan of action. Hopefully, he could locate Tyne in quick order and return to Cairo. How he wished he could say return to Texas. But he had to think through one problem at a time.

Once he parted with a chunk of his coins, he stood at the window of his room. However, his heart sank. Lights appeared to stretch forever in each direction. While not a huge city, Fort Madison was still sizable. He closed his eyes. How had he ever ended up here, looking for his wife, a murderer, and trollop? This had to be God's last joke on him.

He spun. No. He wouldn't wallow in that ditch. Instead, he knelt at the bedside and bowed his head because he knew he needed a miracle. As dire as the present circumstances were, there was still One he knew who could deliver Tyne.

In more ways than one, his wife needed deliverance.

When the morning rays awakened him, Zeph groaned and climbed from the mattress. He grabbed his pants and dressed with efficient movements. Leaving his carpet bag, he made his way down the gleaming white stairway. The dining hall was bursting with patrons. The mumble of many voices interspersed with the clink of silverware met his ears. The scrape in his belly made Zeph take one step toward the arched doorway.

"May I show you a table, sir?" The sharp-dressed lad at the dining hall door stepped forward.

Zeph held up a hand. There was no time for breakfast. He had to get started. "No. I have other business to attend."

He hit the door before the engaging lad could coerce him to part with his coin. First things first. A livery, a horse, and a lot of divine guidance were the immediate necessities.

But, by lunch, Zeph, grumpy, hot, and hungry enough to eat a bear, pulled his substandard mount to a halt in front of the hotel. No one had heard of Tyne. No one had seen anyone new. And the city was just too doggone big to cover much area. With a bit of frustration, he stomped in and headed for the dining hall.

The young man, impeccable in his burgundy uniform, led him to a table near the window. Zeph sat with his back to the crowd. He ordered the lunch special and stared out the lace-paneled window to think about his next move.

Once Pansy Jo had told him Rose Yates's connection to Kerth, general consensus had assumed they'd conspired against Tyne. And Pansy Jo knew Fort Madison is where Rose's only daughter lived. It seemed the most likely explanation as to where Tyne might be. But now, after hours of searching, Zeph had strong doubts.

No one had heard of Rose Yates, or any woman with the name Yates. He'd even checked the bawdy houses, no happy task was that, but no one had any connection or knew of anyone with a connection to Rose Yates or Cairo.

He was stuck.

Zeph polished off the fried chicken as the waiter brought a dessert plate. "Dessert too? Quite a feast for lunch."

The somber waiter, dressed in white with a spotless towel across his arm, straightened, causing the dark lock of hair to flop to his forehead. "Hotel Alexander is known worldwide for its exquisite dessert tray. This is our Rose-lattice Molasses Apple Pie with hand whipped sugar cream topping."

The fruity delight was quite the presentation. The brown crinkled rose stood curled in the center of the slice, the delicate lattice pie crust extending out across the darkened filling, the whipped white cream encircling the triangular slice like a bit of frothy cloud. Zeph inhaled the intoxicating smell. Surely it was breeze straight from heaven.

"You must have some kind of fancy chef buried back there in the kitchen. I can see why this place is known for its desserts."

The slender man shook his head, setting the lock free to bounce about his forehead. He flipped it back into place. "Actually, our desserts are handled off-site. Indeed, it's quite a mystery where they come from."

Zeph forked a sliver from the decadent pastry but paused. "A mystery? How could baking a pie be a mystery?"

The waiter bent slightly, his dark eyes taking in the busy dining hall before he lowered his voice. "Many believe our desserts are made by a conjurer of confections who whips a bit of bewitchment into each slice."

A bolt of laughter burst from Zeph. "That's quite a tale. It, no doubt, helps sell a lot of desserts."

The man stiffened, his brows descending. "Oh, it's no tale. She's real. Well, as real as any ghost might be. She's known as the Fruit Phantom."

Zeph forked in a bite of the pie. Glory, it melted like apple butter and crisped like the lightest pastry he'd ever tasted. If any dessert was bewitched, surely it was this one. At least, it was a good slogan to draw in customers. What a gimmick. The whole tall tale was probably memorized by each worker. Zeph swallowed and turned a smile at the hard-sell waiter.

"Indeed, give my regards to the...Fruit Phantom. It's delicious."

The waiter nodded and spun to march toward the kitchen. Zeph chuckled to himself. At least it gave him something to laugh about. It gave a nice break from the burden of finding Tyne. He polished off his pie and stood. There was nothing more to do but to get back to searching. Perhaps he'd stay another night in this overpriced hotel just to sample the next dessert.

He needed something to cheer him if he came up empty again.

◈

"You know a woman named Rose Yates?"

Tyne nodded.

Roose blinked those pale eyelashes and then shook her head. "I suppose there could be another woman with my middle and last name. Right?"

The girl's earnest face dug at Tyne's heart. Yes, she supposed so, but unlikely. "Perhaps."

With quick steps, Roose hurried to the scarred table and sat opposite her. "Tell me about her. This woman."

"Well, she's…" Tyne took a deep breath. What could she tell her? That the woman who could possibly have ties to her was a prostitute? That she'd worked for years entertaining vile men? "…tall. With green eyes."

"Is she…" Roose covered her cheeks with her hands, "albino?"

"No. But I do know she had a daughter. Before…I knew her."

Poor Roose. She looked absolutely thunderstruck. She took slow breaths and blinked. "I don't understand."

She rose and took a few steps to the kitchen window. Then she spun. "I was told my mother was dead."

Whoa, whoa. Tyne rose and approached her. "Wait a minute. This woman might be some relation to you, but we have no way of knowing."

But Roose stood panting, hand to her chest. "I was named for my mother. I know that much. And I know Cairo. I've heard that word. Many times. Perhaps…perhaps it is my birthplace."

Tyne licked her lips and grabbed a sticky pot. "Shouldn't we get back to work?"

Roose stepped forward, her hands on Tyne's arm. "Please tell me. How do you know her?"

Inwardly Tyne groaned. It had been the one subject she'd hoped to avoid. "We're...friends, of a sort."

The grip on Tyne's arm tightened. "What are you hiding from me?"

"Some things are better left unsaid."

With a yank, Roose tugged the pot from Tyne and tossed it to the metal tub of soap suds. Water splashed the wall behind the dry sink. Then her unique eyes drilled into Tyne's. "I want to know."

"Then we ought to sit down."

The next twenty minutes Roose didn't move at all. The poor girl only absorbed the horrid tale of a person who could very probably be her mother. Afterward, Tyne had never seen anyone clean a kitchen faster. The girl had scrubbed as if possessed. It was nigh to midnight before they settled in the attic. Roose hadn't spoken a word. Tyne could only imagine the thoughts buzzing through the woman's head.

With a shiver, Tyne's mind turned to Daisy. Would she, too, someday learn all of her mother's sordid life? Would she sit speechless with the idea of how vile she was? An ache started behind Tyne's eyeballs as she disrobed for bed. Roose snuggled into the quilt with nothing but a light sheet covering her chemise-clad body. She faced the rafters, a clear message she didn't want to talk.

"Roose, are you...all right?"

A long silence stretched. And then she whispered. "I will be. Someday."

Sadness shivered into Tyne's belly. So, they were both trapped in an unfair world that steals the innocence from young women. Tyne let a sigh exit as she blew the flame from the candle.

Yet, Tyne couldn't let Roose's vulnerability imprison her here. There had to be a way that Tyne could follow that wagon without being seen. Yet, she had to think of Roose's protection as well as her own. Who knew who'd brought her here and through much questioning, it was obvious Roose was in the dark as well. The poor girl just seemed to roll with whatever presented itself on her porch, no questions asked.

Not even when her delivery was a woman.

Yes, tomorrow Tyne would find a way to get into town. And then, she would come up with a way to get back where she belonged.

Chapter Twenty-Six

"He's a rake. Dallied with my Noreen and now she's cold and dead in the grave. That's the facts. Good day."

Mrs. Hutchens, in her powdered anger, went to slam the door on Roxie. That would never do. Roxie stuck her foot in. The door bounced open.

"Well, I never!"

"Well, you will. Now, we're not done discussing Mr. Rowley. I'm afraid I'll need more information."

The woman fairly sparked with agitation, but stiffly gathered the white shawl at her neck. "This is simply preposterous. You can't barge in here. I won't have it."

Roxie sidestepped her and settled into a bedraggled rose-colored armchair. "And here I'll sit until I get some answers. Care to join me?"

Mrs. Hutchens, her lips puckered in an angry rosebud, stood by the door and tapped her foot for a few moments. Finally she huffed toward the adjacent wing chair, equally tattered as the one in which Roxie sat.

"Fine."

Roxie nodded. "Now, you have to understand, Tyne is like a daughter to me, Daisy a granddaughter. And if there is something vile in Mr. Rowley, I need to know."

A strange twitching set up on Mrs. Hutchens's left cheek and then she began to visibly tremble. A bit of moisture collected in the hollow of her eye. She opened her mouth to speak but only managed a few twitches of her lips. Was the woman about to keel over?

Roxie hefted her weight to a standing position. "Are you quite all right?"

Her weathered eyes shifted to Roxie's. "It wasn't supposed to be like this."

"Like what?"

"She wasn't supposed to die."

"Who?"

Tears pooled beneath Mrs. Hutchens's haunted eyes. "My daughter."

With a quick yank, Roxie pulled the rickety armchair close enough to sit, yet hold Mrs. Hutchens's shaking hands.

With a deep breath, Roxie rubbed the woman's hands. "Why don't you tell me all about it?"

And that's what Mrs. Hutchens's did. The poor dear poured out the whole heartbreaking tale in between sobs and bouts of crying. Her plans to wed Noreen to a well-to-do business man back in Chicago. Yet Noreen fell in love with Mr. Rowley, a ne'er-to-do farmer. It hadn't taken long for sickness to overcome her. And while Roxie certainly could sympathize with the sorrowful account of Mrs. Hutchens's only daughter, it became clear to Roxie that no blame could be assigned to Mr. Rowley. Equally clear was the fact that Mrs. Hutchens bitterly blamed him for the whole sad mess.

When Mrs. Hutchens's wound down, Roxie rose. "Let me just go fix some tea for you, you poor thing."

She left the woman sniffing into her hanky as Roxie headed for what could only be the kitchen door. The room lay hushed in meticulous order, and it took no time to locate the tea and get the pot boiling.

Roxie returned to the living room and dragged the armchair across the floor and maneuvered it through the front door. She situated it on the far side of the small porch and then returned to fetch a small round pedestal table.

"Come now, let's just refresh ourselves on the porch."

She led the meek woman to the chair and returned to the kitchen. Once she'd chipped some ice from the icebox, she added sugar to the tea and poured it over the ice-filled glasses.

The second chair was a bit more reluctant to wedge through the door, but Roxie managed it. Then she presented Mrs. Hutchens's with her iced tea and some shortbread cookies she'd found in the cabinet. Roxie wiped sweat from her forehead with her lace hanky and collapsed into the her seat. The woman who'd declared doom upon Tyne seemed much calmer as she sipped her tea.

"I've never thought of putting chairs out here. It's so much cooler."

With a grin Roxie gulped a swallow of the cold drink and set her gaze to the weathered picket fence covered with red rose blooms. "I agree."

"You know," Mrs. Hutchens nibbled on a cookie, "Zephaniah Rowley is not really of a bad sort."

A smile creased Roxie's face. "Exactly what I was thinking."

༺∾༻

Another day of searching had Zeph exhausted, trudging up the hotel's white marble steps at a slow pace. On the second floor he passed by a cracked door where employees sorted the linens. A young lad had his fingers in the door, whispering to the girl as she folded.

"…of course I never laid eyes on her. I just get the desserts and I'm off."

For some reason Zeph paused as he passed the door, making sure the staff didn't see him.

"By jeebers, you better not. She's cursed some say."

"Och, that's just dining hall jibberish and you know it. Hundreds of folks eat those desserts without any hocus pocus. I ain't in no danger. 'Sides, I saw someone else."

The girl's voice answered quickly. "In the house? With…the

Fruit Phantom?"

"Shhhh…I said so, didn't I? And she followed me."

"Who? The Fruit—"

"No. The other woman."

Zeph noticed all had become still, no noises indicating the linen folding and piling continued.

"Oh, Lawd, she done vexed you, didn't she? She doubled herself into a doppelganger and—"

A grunt stopped the girl's words. "Don't act like no idjit. The second woman didn't look at all like the phantom. She looked like a regular person."

"How far did she follow?"

"A ways."

Someone mounted the steps back down the hallway and the door snapped shut. Zeph took a breath and continued down the hallway. An unknown woman appeared at the Fruit Phantom's house? It sounded like some far-fetched plot of classical opera. Zeph inserted the key into the lock and walked into the room he should've given up long ago.

Wait a minute.

An unknown woman just showed up out of the blue? Could it be? Could it actually be Tyne? He spun and strode to the door and whipped it open. With purposeful steps, he made his way back to the linen room and grabbed the door handle. But it was now locked. He hammered on the sturdy panel. Nothing stirred. Were they still there? Or had they continued their little tryst and now merely hid inside, fearful of discovery?

He pressed his head against the door and waited. No sound echoed from within the small room. A glance down indicated no light spilled beneath the door. Zeph let out a growl. While he'd stood ruminating in his overpriced room, they'd slipped out.

The waiter. Maybe he knew something.

Zeph rattled down the gleaming stairs, but his heart sank as he descended the last few steps. The arched doorway of the dining hall was dark. It must be later than he thought. He paused on the last step and pounded his fist on the square marble newel.

Then another idea formed in his head. He headed for the check-in desk. The dour man behind the desk sorted papers at a low desk and stood when he saw Zeph approach.

"Good evening, sir. How may I help you?"

"Yes." Zeph cleared his throat a bit in frustration and a bit in a stall tactic to think how to go about getting the information he needed. "Where do you get your apples?"

The older man's eyebrows rose. "Apples?"

"The hotel apples, to make the desserts."

Dawning registered on the man's long face. "Ah, you've sampled our desserts I wager. All of our apples are grown right here in the local area."

"Uh-huh, sure. But where?"

At this prompt, only one bushy brow rose and a dash of trepidation entered the man's brown weathered eyes. "Sir?"

"I mean, which orchard?"

The clerk, spiffy in a pressed navy vest folded his hands on the counter. "I'm not sure what you are asking."

"I need to know the exact orchard where your pies come from."

"Do you wish to buy apples at this hour?"

Zeph hesitated. He was getting nowhere fast. "No…tomorrow."

The man sniffed. "I believe the orchard is northeast. But I'm afraid I have no knowledge of the exact location."

The clerk wasn't exactly a fountain of knowledge. "Is there more than one orchard northeast of the city?"

"I believe several."

He took a moment to assess the older man. Zeph wanted to throttle the information from him, but, of course, it was possible the man didn't know. So, Zeph nodded and thanked the man and spun on his heel to head for the door. He was just too antsy now. He had to search. A glance at the regal clock told him it was much too late to wander out into the night.

Zeph jogged down the street toward the livery. The double stable door was closed, so he headed for the smaller one. Inside was dark except for a low lantern light on the last stall. A low murmur of voices drifted toward him. As he swung around the low stall wall, the very two people he'd overheard in the hotel were wrapped around each other.

At his approach, they sprang apart.

"What's the meaning?" the young gent demanded, stepping forward, still encased in his rumpled hotel suit coat.

"This woman's virtue, no doubt." Durn, that shouldn't have been the first words out of Zeph's mouth.

"I've got it well in hand, sir." The pock-marked lad stepped forward, pulling up the waist band of his trousers.

Zeph's eyes traveled over the dark-headed girl, still dressed in her gray hotel staff dress. She avoided his gaze, but bothered not to speak for herself.

"Hotel Alexander might be interested in your after-hour activity given you're still attired as employees."

He hated to threaten them but Zeph had little time to find Tyne. The pallor that settled on their features let Zeph know he'd hit a mark.

The thin-faced lad narrowed his eyes. "What do you want? Money? Because we have none, and that's for sure."

"Not money. Information."

"About?"

The girl stepped forward. "Stephen, we canna—"

"Hush, woman." The boy swiped his face, bristled with a shadow of stubble. "What sort of information?"

"Where is the Fruit Phantom?"

The man's eyes flared, and he gripped the stall door to peer through the slats. "Who sent you?"

"No one. I'm looking for my wife."

The girl's gasp caught Zeph's gaze. The lad frowned. "The Fruit Phantom is your wife?"

"No. But I overheard you say there was an extra woman there."

"See!" the girl hissed as she scurried to the back of the empty stall. "I done said it was dangerous to talk of that haunt."

"Quiet." The lad pointed at the woman and swung to stare at Zeph. Then a twitch jerked his left cheek. "How much is it worth to you?"

Typical answer—it always came down to money. "Your jobs."

The kid's Adam's apple bobbed. Maybe now Zeph would get some answers.

❦

Tyne huffed a deep breath. The dark around her not only made her unsure of what direction she should go but seemed to also squeeze the breath from her. She stared down one way of the dirt road intersection and then the other. Then she looked forward. Crops and weeds made each path like an ominous tunnel. Which way? A few spasmodic sobs rose. She. Was. In. A. Hopeless. Situation.

"Daisy," her voice broke as she whispered her daughter's name. And then after a few beats, she huffed out, "Zeph."

But they weren't here. They weren't even close. Daisy was hundreds of miles away. Zeph, who knew where he was? And here she was, stranded with no money in a place she knew nothing of. Tyne had absolutely no way of getting anywhere she needed to go.

Her mind raced, as it always did. But there were no answers. Roose was more than likely Rose's daughter. What that meant was curious. Why would she be dropped at Rose's daughter's secluded house?

After much thought, Tyne thought she may have heard

Kerth's voice while inside the trunk. If that were so, he'd kidnapped her. Why, she could only guess that her testimony might indict him in the murder of Ervy Gumpers.

And then, why had Rose been on the train? Why had she helped her only to dump Tyne here with no way of leaving? Were Rose and Kerth working together? Thinking all of these thoughts for the hundredth time exhausted her. All it did was present more questions.

She spun around. Which way had she come from? Following the wagon had only gotten her to this point before she feared forgetting the way back. Should she attempt to retrace her steps and continue to stay at Roose's? Or should she try to press on?

Over the tassels of corn slight glow reflected in the sky. That must be the city of Fort Madison. But even if she managed to find her way there, what would she do then? She possessed no money, no lodging, no protection in a city at night. A groan snuck past her lips. She had to turn back and try to make it back to Roose's house. At least there she had a bed and safety.

In the distance, soft clomps of a horse at a good trot caught her attention. Tyne glanced about, looking for a place to hide before the rider caught sight of her, or rather, caught any sound of her. She quickly stepped through the weeds into a cornfield. Tyne dropped low to peer between the stout corn stalks.

Not much time went by before the horse approached and turned on the same road where she'd hesitated. The horse trotted by and Tyne caught just a glimpse of the figure riding. Hat in place, the man rode as if comfortable in the saddle. And then, he was beyond her, the soft plodding of the horse's feet growing fainter.

She didn't dare move from the scratchy corn until the sounds of the traveler disappeared. Then she stepped from the field and scurried down the dirt track, praying she'd chosen the right way back.

The dark kept Tyne guessing all the way. It wiped out all visual cues as to where she might be. So when the shadowed rows of low growing trees made their appearance, she gave a sigh of thankfulness. The dead raccoon she'd marked in her brain when she'd left, signaled the orchard next to Roose's house. Thank the Lord. Tyne was very near.

Yet the glow of a campfire not far in the distance made her pause. Whoever settled in for the night had chosen a rather odd place, close to the road. Even from this distance, she could see a horse, shed of its saddle and blanket, munching with its muzzle in a feedbag. The man worked about his fire, setting up camp, rolling out a blanket. She would have to pass by him or take a noisy journey through the fields to reach the shack.

Yet…something struck her as she stood indecisive. The way he moved, adjusted his hat, murmured to the horse. It was…familiar. She licked her lips and took a step closer. Pretty soon, her choice of staying or leaving would be over. He'd catch sight of her presence.

The man removed his hat and parked it on the saddle. Then his head turned and his profile cut a sure shape against the small flame of fire. Her breath snagged in her throat.

Dear heavens. It looked like…Zeph.

Chapter Twenty-Seven

A warmth bloomed in Tyne's chest, and she took a few more steps closer, clutching her hands at her heart. Indeed she saw his strong shoulders, his sure hands tending the fire.

Zephaniah Rowley had come. He'd come to find her.

Her hesitant steps became more confident as she approached the campfire. The man jumped up and spun, his hand going to the holster outlined on his hip.

"Who's there?" his gruff voice demanded.

That man, whose gravelly voice had become so familiar that she'd dreamed of it every night she'd been away, was here. She stumbled to a stop on the dirt road. "Zeph...it's me."

And then, Zeph's arms wrapped about her, his lips kissing her like she'd never been kissed before, and then his murmurs of disbelief, his hands roving her in a firm sort of roughness as if he couldn't quite believe she stood bodily against him.

Finally, he just stilled, breathing audibly, pressing her securely against him. She huffed out a small laugh and squeezed him tighter.

"You came," her voice breathed a soft whisper.

His lips found hers again. Then he pulled his head back and gazed at her in the low firelight. "How could I not? After all, I more than like you, Tyne Rowley. I...love you."

A coo escaped Tyne's lips and tears bit her eyes. "I love you, too."

His hand swept her cheek in a soft caress. "We're in this together." He seemed to shake himself. "I've got a hotel room in town. We can go back and in the morning—"

"No." Tyne didn't like the way he pushed her out to arm's length. She craved being back in his arms. "Not yet. I've been staying with...a friend."

After a short explanation, Zeph readied the horse, smothered the fire, and assisted her aboard his horse. Tyne pointed the way, reveling in his strong body behind hers. Zeph maneuvered the animal to the small trail leading back to the shack. All was dark in the small dwelling. Roose probably still lay asleep upstairs the same as when Tyne had snuck out.

They drew into the yard. A gun cocked. Zeph halted the horse. Tyne could feel Zeph's body grow tense.

"You been busy, Miss Sapphire."

A shiver ran through her. That caustic voice she would've

recognized anywhere, especially in her nightmares. Kerth.

She sucked in a few puffs of air. "I knew it was you."

Deep, rancorous laughter floated from the dark porch. "Sure you did. Now, you and your friend get off the horse. Nice and easy."

Something sliced through the air. With a sickening thump, Zeph slumped sideways and slid from the saddle. The horse danced away from Zeph's still body crumpled on the ground.

"Zeph!" Tyne shimmied down the animal and crawled to him. He was out cold. She glanced desperately around, trying to find out how many thugs Kerth had in the shadows. "Are you insane? You could have killed him."

Kerth's harsh chuckle floated through the dark again. "Good work Deevers. Drag him up here."

Suddenly, hands seized her and she fought like the dickens. She kicked, punched, scratched. But it did no good. She only received a few irritated grunts for all her exertions. Two men she could barely see soon wrapped her arms behind her and securely tied her feet together. Then, between the two of them, they carried her into the shack.

Guided by the moon, the men slammed her into a straight kitchen chair. Despite all her attempts to maim them, they managed to secure her. She sat huffing, trying to collect her thoughts when the men stumbled through the doorway again, hauling an unconscious, but much larger Zeph. They merely dropped him to the hardwood floor beside Roose's shelves filled with jars of preserved fruit.

A match scraped and the kitchen came into view. One of Kerth's heavies lifted the hurricane glass on the lantern and touched the flame to the wick.

"Hello?"

Roose's voice, soft and tremulous floated across the room from the attic opening.

Kerth muttered a string of obscenities. "Shut it, ghost. Get back upstairs."

A gasp and a flutter of feet told Tyne that Roose had wasted no time obeying Kerth's barked command. There would be no help from the timorous girl. Tyne let her eyes slide shut.

Her hopeless situation had just nosedived into the fire.

Roxie's eyes fluttered open. The room was dark. Something roiled within her. Had she had a bad dream? She rolled herself to the edge of the mattress and peered through the darkness toward the window. No light indicated it must be somewhere in the dead of night. She turned and checked on the sleeping child next to her. Dear, dear Daisy. She'd snoozed happily, oblivious to the world, just as it should be.

Tyne.

Like a whispered word, the name washed over her in a dreaded flooding wave. Roxie grabbed her robe and yanked it on her arms. Then she tied the sash as she stomped toward the door. She clicked it closed behind her and hurried to the other bedroom door. With a bit of soft hammering and calling out their names, Pastor Howe appeared at the door, shirt buttoned akimbo over his nightshirt. Ovie, in a robe, waddled up next to her husband.

"What is it?"

"Tyne. We gotta pray and pray now."

Pastor Howe reached up and scratched his head. "Now?"

"Surely." Roxie spun and led the way to the settee and maneuvered her chunky body to her knees. Ovie settled her stiff body next to hers and the pastor did the same on the other side. Without waiting, Roxie began.

"Oh, Jesus. My soul is in turmoil over my precious one, Tyne. I know she's in dire straits. I can feel it, Lord." Roxie pressed her head into the patterned material of the settee and clenched her joined hands tighter. "She needs your help, this minute, Lord, your deliverance. Please protect her and keep her safe. Bring her back to us. To Daisy. We need your help so badly, Lord. Please, please…"

She drifted off, but heard the other two praying as well and it eased the pain in her heart. Then a small arm slipped around her shoulders. Roxie pulled back. Tiny Daisy stood there, rubbing her eye with one hand. With a stifled cry of anguish, Roxie pulled the beloved child into her embrace and felt tears dampen her cheeks. "Oh, Lord for this one. Grant our petitions for this sweet angel."

"Don't crwy, Roxie. Don't crwy." Daisy snuggled into her arms.

A fresh onslaught of tears washed down Roxie's face. Oh, this child. How she touched Roxie's heart. More arms suddenly surrounded them as Pastor and Ovie added their support.

Wherever Tyne was, she was covered in the most sincere

prayers.

❧

Bringing a hand to his head, Zeph grimaced at the pain this movement produced. He shifted on the plank floor and slid up to a seated position. Everything spun. While the world righted itself, he leaned forward and closed his eyes.

"I...have some...water."

The spoken words made his eyes slice open. But he blinked for a few seconds before he raised his head. What met his eyes seemed nothing more than a strange dream brought on by too much food and not enough sleep or when he'd drunk too much. A slight girl, women perhaps, pale as the rays of moonlight and dressed in a drab, ratty housecoat, held out a chipped glass.

"Where am I?" His brain pondered whether what he was seeing was real.

"Uh...my home."

Deciding it might be best to verify if this apparition were authentic or not, he held out his hand and gripped the glass. It did indeed feel real as did the water that splashed against his hand. He turned the glass up and chugged, ignoring the shadow of unconsciousness that threatened to take him back. In just a few moments, he could feel the water reviving his mental state.

He'd been clubbed right off his horse. Tyne...a groan came from his lips. They probably had her. And as far as where he was, this must be the infamous Fruit Phantom the hotel lad had told him of. And from the looks of her, she was scared of her own shadow.

With pain stabbing through his head, he struggled to stand and then swayed. This drew a small cry of concern from the young woman. "I'm fine," though his voice, husky and halting, didn't quite show that.

"Perhaps you should...sit."

He nodded at the girl's invitation and slid into the nearest kitchen chair. Another fresh glass of water plopped in front of him. Then the strange ghost of a woman scurried to the other side of the table.

He took another long swig of water. Then he assessed his companion. "You must be Roose."

She nodded.

"The Fruit Phantom?"

Pure misery twitched across the muscles of the woman's features. "Just Roose...please."

Zeph nodded. "What happened? Did they take her?"

Again the apparition nodded.

He groaned and rubbed his forehead. "Just when I'd managed to find her."

"Texarkana."

With one last swipe across his weary face, Zeph turned his burning eyes on the girl. "What?"

"I...listened. And I heard them say...Texarkana."

Zeph blinked. "That's where they're taking her?"

The girl bobbed her head. Lord, help him, he must have been knocked cold by Kerth Ebron, the very man Pansy Jo had spoken of. And hadn't she mentioned Texarkana as the very place Kerth had gone to hide and begin again?

Begin again? With Tyne?

A terrible urgency gripped him. "Are you absolutely sure you heard this?

"Yes."

Zeph stumbled to a standing position.

"But they took all the horses."

Great. Zeph ran a hand through his hair, wincing when he hit a large lump. He was in for a long jog into town. But that wouldn't stop him. Nothing would.

The only way Tyne would be forced into her old occupation was over his cold, dead body.

❧

"Excuse me. My wife is ill."

Tyne registered the words but couldn't quite comprehend them. She tried to open her eyes, but they seemed weighted. She only caught a glimpse of light flickering in between her fluttering lids. Was she with Zeph? Near Texas? Hadn't she heard some kind of announcement to this effect or had it been her own blurry imagination? Perhaps she would soon see Daisy...

"Get her on the other side, moron."

Arms supported her on each side and she felt herself being shuffled along on her feet. Her toes pattered the ground that was more air than solid surface. But the voice, dark and demanding, was what she studied on. It wasn't...Zeph. She huffed a deep breath. No. It was—her brain skittered off into oblivion. She moaned as she forced herself to somehow awaken and think. The voice. Yes. Not Zeph. It was…

Kerth.

But the frightening realization faded into unconsciousness…

Tyne blinked rapidly, trying to rouse herself fully. But it was no use. Her head lolled about, and her brain skedaddled off into a white haze. Then, she took a deep breath. The haze had come and gone. How long had it been? Tyne opened her eyes, but only met the ceiling with peeling wallpaper. Her hands felt the soft stitched lines of a quilt below her. She…must be in bed.

A moan escaped as Tyne struggled to a sitting position on the mattress. The room whirled about her. She clenched her eyes closed and licked her dry lips, waiting for both the roiling of her surroundings and her own stomach to calm. Finally, when the nausea settled and the room righted, she fluttered her eyes open and attempted to peer around.

Small room. Red, patterned walls. Armoire. Dressing table, chair. Her eyes settled on the hair brushes, the combs, the various perfume bottles. Then her gaze found the cracked mirror, held together by only the wooden backing. It'd broken on the very night she'd earned her first black eye—her tumbled thoughts came to an abrupt stop.

She was in a brothel room.

Tyne gasped and jumped to her feet. It wasn't the same room, but it was undoubtedly a room for…service. Panic rose to choke her. She needed to get out. Tyne spun and rushed toward the window but found it nailed shut.

The scraping sound of a key in a lock made her whirl to face the door. The wooden panel swung open and in stepped Kerth. In the ample light, she noticed he'd grown fatter since she'd partnered with him to stage Ervy Gumpers's suicide on that bed so long ago. But that evil grin with his strangely pointed teeth and the lure in his eye were the same.

"Welcome back, Miss Sapphire."

Tyne's breath came in spasmodic huffs. "I'm...not...back."

His grin made her skin crawl. "Oh, yes you are. Do you think you don't have to pay for leaving me holding the bag in Cairo?"

"You can't force me—""

His laugh cut her off. "There's plenty of tonics downstairs to make you mind."

"Kerth, I demand you let me—"

The man laughed and drew a very familiar gun from the back waistband of his pants. "Demand? Ha." A spew of expletives made Tyne want to cover her ears. She hadn't missed hearing the vile words that seemed to hover inside such a place. But her attention focused on the gun he held.

"Ah, so you recognize this?" Kerth waved the weapon as if it were a posy picked from a field. "You should. You fired it before. With good aim, I might add."

Tyne's face chilled and the dizziness returned. She hugged herself tight as if her clenched arms would keep the bad memories from surfacing again.

"Now you behave. I'm sure I'll have ya a customer right soon."

As she struggled to breathe, the evil man stepped out the door. The sickening click sealed her fate.

She was locked in a brothel with customers on the way.

❦

Zeph awoke as the train's whistle sounded again. *Tyne.* How far behind her was he? His waking thoughts only continued the nightmare he'd envisioned with his head bouncing against the cool window. It was as if finding her plagued him not only in conscious hours, but in unconsciousness as well.

His scrambled brain fought to place time. Was it morning? It appeared so, from the weak easterly light through the window. A porter passed and Zeph reached out a hand and grabbed his navy jacket. The startled man spun.

"Sir?"

"What time is it?" The pain in Zeph's head made politeness a stranger.

The porter tugged a timepiece from his vest. "Ten o'clock."

"Morning or night?" Not the best question since he'd seen the sunlight, and the judgmental look the porter gave him left no doubt what he thought of Zeph.

"Morning. Now, sir, if you would unhand me, I'll—"

But Zeph tightened his grip. He didn't care if the man thought him drunk, he had to know. "How much longer to Texarkana?"

"An hour." The porter pulled away and continued up the aisle.

Good. And Sheriff Platt better be there. Zeph wouldn't waste a single moment.

He had to find Tyne.

Chapter Twenty-Eight

"Well, here's the problem with your plan." Sheriff Simon Platt leaned back in his chair. "Texarkana is filled with such places, on both sides of the Texas and the Arkansas line. It might be immoral to set up a bawdy house, but it ain't against the law."

"She's been kidnapped," Zeph tried to rein in some of his impatient ire. "And as far as I know, that's still illegal."

"All I can promise is that we'll check into it. I'll get a few deputies on it and we'll—"

"By that time it will be too late."

Sheriff Platt rose and palmed the hat onto his head. "We can't go knocking on every sporting house in town. After all, as unsavory as these places are, they aren't illegal. Yet. But I'll check around for news of," he paused here as his hand ran down a list on a sheet of paper, "Kerth Ebron and/or Rose Yates. I'm afraid that's the best we can do, son."

Zeph lowered his head as he leaned forward over Sheriff Platt's large, scarred desk. All he could do was draw a deep breath. Who knew how much lead Kerth and his lackeys had on him? And every minute that passed ticked toward an assurance that Tyne was not only unsafe, but possibly in grave danger. He didn't want to think beyond that.

He pushed away from the desk and strode toward the door. There, he paused and looked back at the man he'd thought would be a deliverance for both Tyne and him. "You may not have time to knock on every suspect door. But I do." He shut the door with a bit of force and jogged toward his horse tied at the hitch. With a skip, he slung his leg over the saddle and nudged the reins toward the nearest bar.

"Mr. Rowley."

The sheriff's call fell on deaf ears as Zeph spurred his horse to a canter. No sense wasting time on a man who'd merely fill him with dire warnings of impeding police work and hassling the anything-but-fine citizens of this town. He'd try his durndest to find Tyne himself. And the best place to do that was down in the red light district near the tracks.

He directed his horse down State Line Avenue and turned left onto Front Street, treading now on Arkansas soil. The Union Depot, flooded with passengers both coming and going, made the road quite crowded as people, attempting to cross the street, dodged the traffic. A woman in a satin green dress caught his eye.

As he drew near he knew why. It was none other than Mrs. Pansy Jo Jenks, swinging her carpet bag determinedly while ignoring a few wolf whistles. What was the woman doing here?

"Mrs. Jenks." Zeph raised a hand to hail her, but given the distance between them, she neither heard nor saw him. He gritted his teeth, dug his heels into his mount, and zigzagged between the carriages, buggies, and riders, drawing a few thunderous gazes and angry words from the drivers.

Mrs. Jenks scurried to the far side of the road in front of Huckins House, a four-story hotel. He urged his horse on and met her on the porch of the establishment, drawing gasps from the patrons attempting to sashay through the front door.

"I beg your pardon, sir," one puffed-up mustachioed man grunted. "This is quite irregular."

"Zeph." Mrs. Jenks didn't stand on formality but rushed forward with a huge smile on her face. "I thought it'd take hours to locate you. But here you are."

"Here he is indeed," the man huffed as he held the door for a dour woman that accompanied him.

By now, Zeph had dismounted and ushered his horse to the side of the road. Mrs. Jenks followed him. He lost no time. "Why are you here?"

"To rescue Tyne, of course." She glanced about. "She rescued me and I'm not about to let her down."

"You didn't waste any time getting here."

"When we got your telegram about Kerth attacking you and kidnapping Tyne," she closed her eyes and shook her head, "I

301

knew I just couldn't abandon her. Wylen went home to be with the kids, and I continued on here. And it's absolutely God's doing that I met right up with you. What did the sheriff say? Are they organizing a posse?"

Zeph let go a long breath. "There's no help coming from there."

Mrs. Jenks's brow puckered. Then she waved it off. "Well, it's just as well. We may have to do this a little...underhanded-like."

"I don't think—"

But the woman gave him no time to finish. "Let's talk about this after I check in. Time is of the essence. Darkness is not our friend."

The woman scurried into the hotel, leaving Zeph wondering what the woman had in mind. Ten minutes later she charged from the building, a look of iron determination on her face. That, and a lot of makeup. Zeph raised his brows. She flapped a hand at him.

"I know, I know. But if I have to infiltrate this horrible world of men buying flesh, I have to look the part."

The farther down the street, the shoddier the buildings became. The distant sound of tinny music seemed to draw Mrs. Jenks to a particular establishment. The Crow's Nest sported batwings and a plethora of men in dusty duds.

"Follow my lead."

The woman didn't pause at the leering looks she received near the door, but barged right through. Inside, the place was packed. The mirrors behind the shelving at the bar showed off the alcoholic selections while men jawed at every table. A slender man with garters encircling both biceps pounded on the upright.

"Go to the bar till I need you."

The hissed command set him in motion. He sat on the end, hoping to be able to keep an eye on the entire room. Though, if Mrs. Jenks set off too many men, he'd be in a heap of hurt.

The woman waltzed forward, swaying and toying with a gaudy necklace, toward a crowded table situated in the back. He settled on the perfect stool, completely flush with his line of sight. She smiled, arched her brows, cooed at the men leaning on the table, and touched a shoulder. Zeph adjusted himself on the stool, glad Wylen wasn't here to watch his wife in action.

But when a man rose, hiking up his pants, Mrs. Jenks beckoned him with a jerk of her head. Zeph nearly leapt from the stool to charge to her line of defense.

"...of course, but first you should speak with my...associate,"

Mrs. Jenks's voice came to him more clearly as he approached. The man beside her, a flushed-face compact man, stuck his chin out and assessed Zeph. The first thought was to greet him, but instead, Zeph nodded, letting his eyes narrow just a bit.

"You see, I'm looking for a dear friend. She's lost. And she's with a man new to the area." Mrs. Jenks's voice was velvet.

"Like you?"

A burly bearded man seated at the table jerked his head at them, bringing down equally burly eyebrows that nearly hid his eyes. Zeph felt himself bristle, but Mrs. Jenks continued on as smooth as ice in January.

"Exactly. But, you see, it'll be worth your...help," she nudged Zeph before continuing, "cause we're most eager to...recover her."

Zeph took her hint and dug deep in his pocket. He extracted a Morgan silver dollar and snapped it to the tabletop. The ruddy man standing next to Mrs. Jenks fluttered his eyes as his mouth dropped open. He eased back into his seat.

"That's it?" Burly beard pulled a fat cigar from his mouth. "Bit of spare change, ain't it, boys?"

Most of the men around the table wore bored yet watchful expressions. Zeph had no option but to fish the next coin from his pocket. When the second dollar plunked to the table, the rough characters leaned in toward the table top, their hungry eyes on the coins.

"Yes. For a bit of...spare change," Mrs. Jenks's silky voice enticed her audience. "All we need is information about a Kerth Ebron, Rose Yates, Miss Emerald, or Miss Sapphire. Or even someone named Clementyne or Tyne?"

One man actually licked his thick lips as his shifty gaze twitched from the money to the others surrounding the table, then back to Mrs. Jenks.

"Don't know no one by those names." Burly beard grabbed the deck of cards. "But why don't you and your...associate sit on down and join the game?"

The squirrely man on the far side of the table jumped up. "I might know something."

"Sit down, Farsten," the fat man beside him bellowed.

"I ain't got no cause to," Farsten fired back, shoving up his sleeves.

Chair legs squeaked against the floor as the fat man and several others jumped to their feet.

The fat man's chest bumped Farsten. "It ain't our business."

"That coin on the table makes it my business."

Where it all started, Zeph wasn't sure. Perhaps Farsten had tried to shove the fat man, maybe Burly beard took advantage of the distraction and lunged for the two silver dollars. All Zeph knew was that the room exploded into a fist fight. A small hand swooped up the coins and all he heard amongst the brawling noise was Mrs. Jenks's voice yelling, "Run!"

Zeph swooped her up and nearly carried her to the door as chairs flew across the room behind him and bottles crashed against the wall. He swept her down the steps and tossed her aboard his horse. Then he set his foot in the stirrup and swung up while urging his horse to skedaddle. He'd barely had time to connect with horseflesh before the animal took to full gallop.

Well, that hadn't gone well. And the bad thing was, they were no closer to finding Tyne than before.

Tyne crept beneath the bed. The dust and spider webs nearly ran her straight back out, but she sneezed and wiped away the offending filaments. Better a million spider bites than one customer through that door. She huddled against the wall as far away from the foot of the bed as possible. Silly to hide beneath a bed like a frightened toddler. But maybe, just maybe, she could throw Kerth off for just a few seconds and head for the open door.

The strategy was ridiculous, of course. By the time she scrambled from beneath the bed he'd be on to her and her plan. Still, it kept a shred of hope alive that she could escape. Footsteps echoed in the hallway. She could almost feel the boards beneath her give with the weight. Wherever she was, this building was none too sturdy. But what a silly thought. The place was obviously sturdy enough to hold her prisoner.

A jiggle in the lock froze Tyne. The door squeaked open then clicked closed.

"Tyne?"

Rose?

"If you're hiding under the bed, that's pretty pathetic."

Tyne hissed an impatient sigh and wiggled out, stood, and brushed the cobwebs from her skirt. There stood Rose Yates, or rather Miss Emerald, just as Tyne had suspected. Tyne crossed her arms in a tight knot. "Guess you had me fooled. Rescuing me on the train? Ha. You'd think I'd be smarter than to think you really cared."

Rose stepped closer, dressed in a somewhat modest lilac dress. "You saw her, didn't you?"

Tyne tightened her face. If the woman thought they might chitchat about their experiences along the way to this moment, she had another thing coming. "I don't know what you're talking about and I don't care."

"Roose."

With a long breath, Tyne narrowed her eyes. "What of it?"

Rose stepped closer, leaning against the brass rail at the end of the bed. Her face looked sallow, her eyes huge. "Was she well? Was she...happy?"

With a sniff, Tyne spun and strode to the barred window. Then she pirouetted back. "Why would I tell you anything? You are obviously working with Kerth to kidnap me."

"I'm not. I know it appears that way, but I'm really just avoiding the heat in Cairo." She eased to the edge of the bed.

"Then get me out."

There was a moment of silence as Rose stared at the far wall. "I just hoped that she was doing well. He promised me he'd look after her."

A shred of compassion worked its way into Tyne's heart. "Well, she's...surviving."

Rose's head snapped her direction. "Surviving? What's that mean?" She stood. "Is she in trouble?"

Tyne ran her hands over her face. "Listen, Rose. I'd love to chat. But as you can see, I am being held prisoner."

The woman whom Tyne had always known as a tough old bird nervously fingered the cameo at her throat. "Is she suffering?"

"No." Tyne took a deep breath. "She's living in a hidden shack, if you must know."

Rose nodded, sinking back to the mattress. "I knew it'd be...difficult for a girl like her. She's, you know, different."

"She's your daughter, isn't she?"

A slow bob was Tyne's only answer. "She thought you were dead."

That brought a quick look. Rose hummed a sad note. "I suppose it'd be best if she thought so."

"I told her otherwise."

The bed creaked as she swiftly rose and paced the small room. Then she halted. "What was her reaction?"

Thoughts of Roose's silent shock as she lay in her attic pallet rolled through Tyne's mind. And as Tyne had contemplated escaping, Roose had sniffed her way through the comprehension of her heritage. Yet Tyne, for some strange reason, decided to ease Rose's mind. "She was…excited to learn her mother might be alive."

"And when she found out what I…am?"

A long breath exited Tyne's parted lips. Rose lifted her green eyes, the wrinkles in her face looking so very defined. "Much as you would expect."

"Yes. I see." Rose nodded and trod toward the door. With her back to Tyne, head bowed, she whispered. "I will do what I can to get you out."

Then she slipped through and locked the door before Tyne could manage to move.

Chapter Twenty-Nine

The scrape of a key in the lock jerked Tyne awake. She yanked the quilt up to her neck and scrambled to the floor, shimmying beneath the bed. In the pale moonlight, large boots shadowed the floor in front of the door. How could she have fallen asleep? The very situation she found herself in should alone keep her wide awake. But, the weariness of continued apprehension and being hauled across the country had taken its toll. And now she'd be trapped with a vile customer.

Well, he wouldn't know what hit him. She automatically reached for the knife that usually rested in the fold of her skirt. But it wasn't there, of course. She'd been stripped of any weapon when Deputy Caffey had taken her into custody. It didn't matter. This man had never seen a she-devil in action. But he was about to.

"Tyne? Are you here?"

Her breath snagged in her throat. The deep baritone strummed a comfort in her heart like she'd never known. She scrambled from beneath the bed and stood. Zephaniah Rowley's shadow stood there.

"Is it really you?" she squeaked.

A low chuckle met her ears about the same time his muscular arms embraced her. With a coo of thankfulness and joy, she slapped her hands about him, squeezing him to her as she wept against him.

With relief, with thankfulness, with complete wonder, she wept. She couldn't speak for several minutes. Rather, she absorbed his warmth, his scent, his pure solace that filled her with hope. His lips pressed to the crown of her head, and it only brought more tears.

"It's all right. You're safe."

The rumbling words that she heard both from his lips and through his chest brought a smile. It seemed it was always all right when he was around, always safe.

"Hhh...how?" was all she could manage.

"Miss Emerald. She found me, rather us."

She nodded against him, content to let him block out the world and calm her soul.

"As much as I enjoy this," he chuckled against her hair, "we must get out the door before Kerth comes back."

Those words sent her into a flurry. She pulled from him and

searched the room. But nothing there was hers. "I...."

Zeph grabbed her hand and led her to the door. With a bit of stealth, he led her out, through a dark hallway, and down a set of narrow stairs. At the back door, a shadow made Tyne flinch. But it was Rose clutching a carpet bag.

"Quickly," Rose hissed.

She unlocked the door and they slid through. Rose wasted no time scurrying away down the alley and disappearing.

"Come on," Zeph pulled her in the opposite direction. "We've got to meet a friend."

∽∾

"Pansy Jo!" Tyne bolted from Zeph to engulf her friend in an almost painful bear hug. Tears clogged her throat as she sobbed against her friend. Never in all her born days had she ever cried so much. Thankfully, the dark alley hid them from any type of audience.

"Here, here now, such a fuss," Pansy Jo softly teased.

Tyne pulled back and swiped her face. Zeph handed her his handkerchief which almost made her collapse in another puddle of tears. To actually have someone who cared enough to hand her his handkerchief made her heart swell. "You came. Just to find me?"

Her friend gave a short laugh and then gave Tyne's shoulders a shake. "In a minute and sixty times more in an hour. Don't you remember what you did for me? You saved me, Clementyne Rowley. *Saved me*. Without you, I'd have been...well, I'm not going to think on it. I only knew one thing after Zeph boarded the train. I had to come too."

A snuff shimmied up Tyne's throat. "Thank you. So much."

"Uh, ladies," Zeph cleared his throat, "Not that I'm against all this reunion stuff. It's just that it's pretty late and we're still in a dangerous part of town."

"Oh, he's right." Pansy Jo grabbed Tyne's hand. "And there's the little problem with the bar fight we started."

"Huh?"

Pansy Jo laughed. "Never mind, I'll explain later."

Zeph disappeared for a moment and came back leading a horse. After a quick peck to her cheek, he helped Tyne mount and then assisted Pansy Jo behind her in the saddle. Then he took the reins and led the horse out into the darkened street.

"Time to find a place for the night."

"Yes." Pansy Jo agreed. "A nice respectable place like the Huckins House."

Tyne couldn't agree more.

ৡঌ

Zeph snugged his wife closer. The bed was small, sure, but he didn't mind. The woman he'd yearned for was here, safe. Though she was quiet, which concerned him, she was safe and unharmed. He was more than happy to tuck Mrs. Jenks in a room by herself and take this room for just Tyne and him. It felt good not to be missing a good portion of himself.

"You okay?"

"Mmm."

He pressed his lips to her temple. "That a good mmm or a

bad mmm?"

His wife's small body expanded with a deep breath. "Both I guess."

"Huh?"

"You know. The trial. Missing Daisy. But then...you. All rescuey and faithful."

He chuckled softly. "Rescuey?"

"Yes. You didn't give up on me," she sniffed.

Zeph stroked a tendril from her cheek. "That's right. You're my wife and I more than like you. I love you."

He felt her nod against him. "I love you, too. But, Zeph...I shot him. I shot Ervy Gumpers.

"You saved Pansy Jo."

A huff of sorrow met his ears. Her words came soft and broken. "True...and...I'd do it all over again. But I...took his life, Zeph. He was...a person who had...family and friends."

He tightened his arms around her and let her cry softly, praying this woman could overcome all the bad that had happened in her short life. "I know you're hurting. What you had to do was awful. But I want you to know that God understands and that his forgiveness is just a prayer away—"

"Oh, yes, Jesus, please forgive me. I regret pulling the trigger Lord. The agony of that memory will haunt me forever. But I don't regret protecting Pansy Jo, Lord Jesus. Please forgive me of taking this man's life, please. And somehow...let me face the punishment of my crime. Somehow."

The anguish in Tyne's voice stabbed at Zeph's heart. "Tyne—"

"And God, please bless this man, my husband. If you've prepared for me to be imprisoned, Lord, he'll have to carry on alone and so will my dear, dear Daisy. I just beg you to uplift them when times are low and keep my hope alive that I might be with my family. Oh, Jesus…"

Tyne buried her head against Zeph. He gulped down a lump and sent up his own prayer. For if he had to do life without Tyne, it would be torturous, and seeing her in prison would undo him for sure. All he could do was hold onto his wife and pray for mercy.

The next morning Zeph sensed the solemn determination of his small group. He saw it in the upward tilt of Tyne's chin and the firm set of Mrs. Jenks's jaw. He also felt it in his tense grip on the carpetbags.

Even as they boarded, he knew Sheriff Platt and his deputies at this moment were probably storming the rundown two-story house where Zeph found Tyne. He was pretty sure they wouldn't allow Kerth and his pals to escort themselves to Cairo as they were doing.

They boarded and found two facing seats. He and Tyne sat together while Mrs. Jenks sat across from them. She reached across and squeezed Tyne's hand, giving an encouraging smile.

"It's all gonna be fine. I just feel it."

Zeph certainly hoped so, but as he watched the scenery speed up outside the window, he wondered if Mrs. Jenks and her prophetic slant wasn't a little off this time.

༶

"Then he yanked me by the hair into the downstairs bedroom. I cried out but no one came."

Mrs. Jenks's voice was clear and firm, hard to argue with, but not impossible as the prosecuting attorney proved with his next question, or rather, accusation.

"But you were well acquainted with the place, correct?"

The well-dressed weasel, Artimus Folston by name, dressed in his plaid suit, held his wooden face a stiff, hardened mask, his dark eyes glittering with caustic brilliance. He breezed across the gleaming courtroom floor and stopped to lean an elbow on the corner post cap of the witness box. Zeph sat behind the guardrail beside Pastor and Mrs. Neil. Tyne's thin frame sat in front of him, slightly to his left. He could only see an angled view of her face which was pale as a bleached sheet.

"I worked there once, sir. But no more. And that has nothing to do with this man's intentions—"

"But you'd welcomed his intentions before," he cut in. "Isn't that so?"

"Mr. Gumpers was NOT my husband." Mrs. Jenks's jaw solidified into granite.

"You entertained a number of men that were not your husband, didn't you, Mrs. Jenks?"

The silver-haired man sitting next to Tyne stood. "Objection, Your Honor. Mrs. Jenks is not on trial here."

The smooth-tongued prosecutor didn't miss a step. "I'm

merely trying to establish if Mrs. Jenks," the sneer on her title was barely disguised, "were about business as usual, and if so, defending her was moot."

The elder judge, long jowls slack in almost boredom, nodded. "Sustained."

Mr. Folston sauntered back to his prey and centered an ominous stance in front of the box. Mrs. Jenks's eyes narrowed. "Did you or did you not, carnally entertain numerous men at the Fleabag Saloon?"

"Yes, but not during that—"

"No more questions, Your Honor."

Mrs. Jenks had to be beyond wishing she'd scooted on home to Missouri. Her loyalty to Tyne was admirable, but surely she'd had enough of these very biased leading questions. The slap of a hand on wood brought everyone's attention back to Mrs. Jenks.

"No! That man would have raped me had Tyne not shot him." Mrs. Jenks jumped to her feet and spun to the judge at her side who'd swiped up his gavel. "Are we to finding the truth or not, sir? Because that is the truth I was prevented from giving."

"Order, order." The judge pounded the gavel. "Strike the last statement from the record. Be seated, Mrs. Jenks."

With a huff, she complied.

"Your witness, Mr. Rutherford."

Tyne's attorney stood and addressed Mrs. Jenks from behind the table. "Mrs. Jenks, were you working at the Fleabag Saloon as a courtesan during the time of the shooting?"

"No."

"And why were you there?"

"I'd arrived late on the train. I needed to overnight with my friend, Tyne."

Mr. Rutherford nodded. "But not to entertain men?"

"No. I am reformed. And, I'm a married woman and a mother as well."

Mr. Folston stood. "Objection. This information is irrelevant."

One of the judge's furry eyebrows rose as he parked his fingers into his droopy facial flesh and leaned against his elbow. His sharp eyes perused Mr. Rutherford.

"I wish to establish that Mrs. Jenks no longer welcomed these types of interactions and that she, indeed, was in need of assistance."

"Sustained." The judge adjusted his portly frame in the big padded chair.

Perhaps this was just another day in the life of the judge, but Zeph felt every answer like a blade in his gut.

"And did you intend to entertain Mr. Ervy Gumpers?"

Mrs. Jenks took a steadying breath. "No."

Mr. Rutherford swung his tall frame out from behind the table and stuck a hand into his pocket. "Mrs. Jenks, tell the court if Mr. Gumpers's attentions were unwanted."

A tear trickled from the corner of Mrs. Jenks's eye. "Most unwanted."

"And do you feel he would've continued if Clementyne Rowley had not intervened?"

"Most…certainly." The woman swiped away the tear.

"No more questions."

Mrs. Jenks unsteadily rose and the bailiff graciously offered a hand as she exited the box. She shot Tyne a nod as she strode by.

The court calls Clementyne Daisy Ciders Rowley to the stand.

If Zeph thought Mrs. Jenks's testimony had been difficult to bear, it'd be pie next to watching his wife endure the harsh questioning, not to mention the pain of the truth.

Chapter Thirty

Tyne stood on legs made of melted wax and made her way across to the enclosed box. Once there, she raised her eyes. She gulped down a lump to find an entire gallery of local people staring at her. Oh, dear. The entire world would soon know every sin and misstep she'd taken in the last several years.

She answered the first several questions that simply established who she was and where she'd been. The judge had to remind her to speak loudly enough to be heard. Then Mr. Folston got down to business.

"Were you, Mrs. Rowley, prostituting in the Fleabag Saloon on the night in question?"

Hearing it put in such a plain and sordid way made Tyne want to melt through the floor. She didn't dare look at her husband. What the man must be thinking, she could only imagine. She licked her lips and scrubbed at the raw spot on her thumb.

"Answer the question, Mrs. Rowley," the judge prodded.

She nodded.

"In words, please, Ma'am."

"Yes."

"Did you shoot Mr. Ervy Gumpers with a .41 caliber Remington Derringer?"

"I don't...know."

"You don't know if it was Ervy Gumpers or you don't know the type of gun?"

"I'm unsure of the gun."

Mr. Folston approached, carrying the same white handled pocket gun she'd used. He plunked it on the cherry railing. "Examine this weapon and verify for the court if this was the gun you used."

With a sickening jolt, she reached for the weapon she'd last seen in Kerth's hand. How had they recovered it? Did they have Kerth in custody? There was no way of knowing until they escorted him into the courtroom.

Tyne ran her fingers over the worn mother-of-pearl handle inserts and the cold silver barrel of a gun she knew too well. Its entirety was small enough to fit into the walnut cigar box that always rested on the alcove table at the bottom of the stairs. The small gouge at the front edge of the handle was too familiar. She'd rubbed her thumb against the sharp edge while facing off Gumpers. The cut of the memory made her almost toss the offending weapon to the railing.

"That's the gun."

"The gun with which you killed Ervy Gumpers."

Tyne swallowed and sucked in a shaky breath. "Yes."

"No further questions."

Mr. Rutherford stood and adjusted his suit jacket. "I think all we need to know, Mrs. Rowley, is what truly happened. The prosecutor can turn oranges into apples by his insinuating questions, but the fact remains that we have not established the reason why you held that gun."

"Objection." Mr. Folston said. "Conjecture."

The judge slammed down the gavel. "Overruled. Continue defense."

Again Tyne's attorney nodded, a certain satisfaction coming into his face. "Mrs. Rowley, if you would describe that night at the Fleabag Saloon."

For a moment, she allowed the courtroom to disappear. The memory flared alive, and she was there, at the Fleabag, feeling and seeing it all again as if time hadn't worn away any detail. "I was at the top of the stairs. I'd heard the back door open. It was very dark. And late. Past time for business. And then I saw them. Gumpers yanked Pansy Jo across the hallway floor into the downstairs bedroom. I knew it was him. I knew his shape. I recognized her voice. She was...pleading," a tear wet Tyne's cheek, "begging to be let go. She tussled but he was too strong. I tiptoed down the stairs to the cigar box in the alcove because that's where we kept the gun."

Tyne's throat felt tighter and tighter. "Just in case."

"In case of what?" Mr. Rutherford prodded.

"In case we needed protection."

He nodded and she continued. "I slipped into the room and stayed along the wall. Gumpers was on top of Pansy Jo on the bed. She struggled to get loose, begged him to stop. I knew Pansy Jo didn't belong there anymore. She'd gotten out. Free. And once you get out, you don't ever go back. Not ever. You don't get freed from hell only to turn around and step back in."

Tyne wiped a tear with a trembling hand. "I heard a rip of clothing, and I knew the man wouldn't stop. I lined up and raised the gun. When I cocked the hammer, they both froze. I fired high. Gumpers scrambled to the other side of the bed, and Pansy Jo came toward me. I think she was talking, not sure. I only saw Gumpers pull a gun and tuck behind the bed. He just kept saying horrible things. Stuff he wanted to do to Pansy Jo. To me. To both of us. Stuff he'd been doing…for years. And I knew. He was going to have his way or kill us trying. So—I fired."

A coldness like Tyne had never felt shivered through her. "I yelled at Pansy Jo to run. Kerth and I dumped him back on the bed. I wiped up the blood and ran for my room."

She took a deep breath to steady herself. "And then it became so clear what I had to do. I had to get out, too. I couldn't take another moment of that horrid place doing unspeakable things. I packed a few necessities and slipped out the window. I never looked back."

Tyne brought up her teary eyes and met Zeph's gaze. How

compassion and love could shine from that man's face, she'd never understand. But that's what she saw there. She snuffed as sobs took control. She shifted her eyes to the judge and then to Mr. Folston.

"So you can jail me. But I did what I had to do to save us. And don't think for one moment I that I don't regret taking a life. Cause I do. But I had to save Pansy Jo."

The rest of the trial passed in a blur after she stumbled from the witness box. Kerth and Rose were brought in separately, handcuffed, to testify. Then in came the sheriff and a few customers connected to the Fleabag Saloon.

But it didn't matter. She'd told the truth, bared her soul. There was no more running, no more hiding. Shivers danced down her arms. She was free. Even if she went to jail, she had peace, a peace so deep only God could've put it there. Everything would be all right, even if she ended up in prison.

And she realized something else through the blur of questions and conjectures. Tyne would find a way to be honest with Daisy when the time was right. She'd bare the truth with her daughter and help her understand and find her way through the muck that was their past.

The haze finally lifted several hours later when the presiding juror rose.

"We find the defendant, Clementyne Daisy Ciders Rowley, acted in self-defense and is not guilty of the murder of Ervy Gumpers."

Cheers went up around her, but all Tyne could do was sink

to her knees. Amid her sobs, she whispered a fervent prayer.

"Thank you, Jesus."

☙❧

"Mama, Mama. Hurry. Roxie's getting married today."

Daisy pounced on the bed, making Tyne wince and Zeph grunt. The girl wasted no time pulling the blankets from them, but Zeph growled and scooped her up to snuggle her between them. Daisy giggled as he tickled her.

Then they all grew still. Tears wet Tyne's lashes as she stroked Daisy's hair behind her ears and listened to the birds cheerily sending out their song of joy to wake the day. Zeph's hand caught Tyne's, and she glanced to him over Daisy's head. The love there in his face nearly took her breath. How had God done this? He'd brought her from a life of horror to a contented family unit. It was unthinkable, yet true.

"Baby brother," Daisy wiggled until her head rested against Tyne's swollen stomach. "Roxie's getting married today. Why don't you come out and see?"

Zeph chuckled, and Tyne smiled. "I'm afraid it's going to be a few more weeks before baby brother shows up."

Daisy jumped to her feet. "Well, okay, Mama. But Roxie needs us now. I gots to sing."

With that, the child bounced on the end of the bed with the expertise of many mornings, and bounded away.

"I suppose she's right. We need to get up."

Zeph's chuckle deepened as he drew her to him. "That woman don't get married till plumb after lunch. We got plenty of time."

He lowered his head and kissed her neck.

"Oh." Tyne gave a start and grabbed Zeph's hand and pressed it to her belly. "Feel him? I told you he'd come out kicking."

Her husband's face grew so solemn she squeezed his hand. "It will be fine. Don't worry."

He nodded but an uneasiness still crinkled his brow. Finally, he let a smile quirk the side of his mouth.

Tyne rose to a sitting position. The man wouldn't be settled fully until the baby arrived and all was well. She sent up a prayer for her husband, so haunted by what had happened in the past. If anyone could understand how the devil could use a person's past to cause distress and doubt, it was Tyne.

She slipped from the bed and pulled on a robe. Thankfully, Zeph would be too busy to notice his concern today.

❧

"I now pronounce you man and wife. You may kiss the bride."

Pastor Howe nodded as he cradled his Bible.

Old Ollie Hendricks, hair trimmed and slicked down, looking quite spiffy in a new suit and boots, leaned forward to plant his puckered lips on Roxie's. Her little giggle made Tyne smile. How life had come full circle. The very man Tyne had journeyed to Glennis Bluff to marry was now Roxie's husband. Ollie looked much improved since last year when Tyne had first encountered him. He was cleaned up, smiling, excited for every new day. Roxie's love had worked magic on the old man. Love did that. It transformed and shined up a person.

Daisy clapped her hands and giggled. "Grandpa Ollie kissed Grandma Roxie."

A wave of laughter rippled across the daisy-strewn church sanctuary, and Tyne smiled. Her girl had a special talent for blurting out the wonderful truth with such volume. What a blessing she was.

They all stood and watched the new couple walk the aisle to the door while Effie Lou pumped the organ to the "Wedding March." The congregants followed, filled with the joy of a new union. Daisy launched herself into Zeph's arms. Tyne stepped to follow her husband when a ripple of pain shot across her swollen belly. With a sharp breath, she pressed a hand to massage out the catch. But a warm squeezing sensation still remained. Thankfully, Zeph hadn't noticed. After a few breaths, Tyne managed to get outside into the spring sunshine.

Everyone had gone to the back of the church where tables had been set up for a potluck dinner in honor of the couple. And while the spasm concerned her, she was sure it was a passing thing.

Fried chicken, potato salad, and enough desserts to strangle a barn full of horses took Tyne's attention. Getting Daisy settled with a plate took a great deal of time since she was the belle of the ball. Everyone seemed to be fascinated with the gregarious girl.

But when Tyne stood face to face with a plate of food, she

realized she couldn't stomach anything. The warm squeezing had not ceased. It only grew stronger. She lifted her eyes to Zeph, who already had a questioning look on his face. Perhaps he'd noticed more than she'd thought.

"I...I don't feel well."

Zeph nodded and rose. In no time, he had Ovie escorting Daisy to her place beside Pastor, and the doctor alerted.

"Please," she whispered to Zeph as she rose, "I don't want to alarm Roxie."

They managed to circle the church on the opposite side and avoid most folks. Doc Henley, a pastoral sort, smiled and motioned inside the church. She lay on the back pew while he gave her a quick examination.

"What's the pain like?" he asked as he pressed the ear horn to her lower belly.

"I don't know. Warm? Squeezing. It just makes me nauseous."

He nodded and straightened, looking up at Zeph outlined in the doorway. "We've got a baby coming."

"What?" Tyne popped up and earned a shot of agony across her middle. She hissed and squinted her eyes closed until it passed. Thankfully, Zeph made the point she'd meant to.

"It's too early, isn't it?"

Tyne panted and cut a glance up to Doc Henley.

"It is. But the baby has other plans. We'll get her loaded into the wagon and over to my office. I don't have the best setup for delivery, but we'll make do."

A shadow darkened the door. "No. She can come to my house."

There stood Annabelle Hutchens, swathed in her white shawl looking positively grim but determined.

Zeph cleared his throat. "We couldn't possibly—"

"Of course you could. Why I'm practically...family." The woman, powder pale, lifted her chin and sniffed. "It's the least a...grandmother could do."

A lengthy silence stretched and only Tyne's coo of pain brought it to an abrupt end. Zeph hurried around the pew and helped her to stand.

"Annabelle, we appreciate your offer." He nodded to Doc. "We'll meet you at Annabelle's if that suits."

Doc Henley nodded. After informing Ovie of their destination, it was a rough ride to Mrs. Hutchens's house. Zeph carried her to the second floor where he deposited her in the very room she and Daisy had occupied when they stayed. The pains came harder now, and all Tyne could do was stare at the ceiling, breathe, and pray.

Pray that Zeph's hopes for the future would not crash once more.

ॐ

"Where's Tyne?" Roxie jumped to her feet. How had it escaped her notice that Tyne was no longer present? "Ollie, Ollie."

She yanked on the man's new suitcoat, in the middle of his entertaining the neighbors with some long tale from the Civil

War. "Huh?"

"Tyne. She's gone."

Roxie made a beeline for Ovie who was busy keeping Daisy from jiggling everyone on her side of the bench. "Where'd she go?"

Ovie didn't even hear the first time, but when she did, she didn't even pretend not to know who "she" was. "Annabelle's. They think she's laboring."

Roxie let out a humph and strode back to her husband. In a matter of minutes, she had the man helping her into their refurbished wagon. Tyne needed her, and even if this was her one and only wedding day, she wouldn't let that girl down.

Annabelle appeared solemn when they arrived but invited them right in. Soon, Ovie and Pastor Howe arrived too.

"Where's Daisy?" Roxie demanded.

"Don't fuss, dear," Ovie patted her shoulder. "The sheriff and his wife are taking good care of her."

It was a long agonizing wait. Zeph came downstairs a few times but preferred to keep a vigil next to his wife. Annabelle kept them all supplied with drinks and snacks. A few food items made their way up the stairway to an empty room to refresh the doctor and Zeph.

My, the waiting was pure torture for Roxie. She finally stood and paced, then stepped to the door to grab a few breaths of fresh air in the falling twilight. Her dear Ollie joined her, slipping his hand into hers. The man knew how to comfort her. It felt good to have a man beside her, loving her, supporting her. It was something she'd never had before. God was so wise. Two were better than one, for Ollie sure did lift her up.

The night grew longer after they'd returned inside on the settee. Ollie dozed against her, but her nervous energy wouldn't allow her to sleep. Yet, as the hours waxed on, she found herself snuffing awake a time or two.

Just as the pink light of dawn started to light the sky, a tiny squall roused her from semi-sleep to full wakefulness. "Ollie!"

Roxie jumped to her feet and hustled toward the foot of the stairs. Ollie woke much slower, stretching out his arms and legs. Pastor and Ovie also awakened from their cramped spots on the cushioned chairs. Annabelle appeared through the kitchen doorway wearing a floral wrap.

"I heard a cry," Roxie whispered. "Oh, why don't they tell us? Where's Zeph?"

A hand wrapped around her waist. Dear Ollie. "All will be well, wife. Just you wait."

≈

Zeph could barely believe what he held in his hands—his son. Daisy had been right. It was her baby brother. Dark pinkish-purple, he looked a much smaller, ruddier version of Ollie Hendricks. Like a little old man. A smile touched Zeph's lips. His...son.

Doc went to the door and soon had the three women up the stairs helping to clean and redress Tyne, contented but exhausted. They set her gently up on plumped pillows, and Tyne held out her hands. The woman looked exhausted, but the look of yearning was unmistakable.

Zeph took a step closer and lowered his precious bundle into her waiting arms. With a gentle sigh, she settled back against the pillows, gazing at her newborn son.

"He's beautiful."

Zeph nodded, but wanted to laugh. Truth be known, he was a little homely. But he'd never tell that to the woman who'd just spent the last twelve hours in hard labor to bring him into the world.

He spun and followed the doc into the hallway. "Is she okay?"

Doc nodded, adding his ear horn to the black bag on the chair. "She's doing exceptionally well."

"And the baby?"

The man turned and laid a hand on Zeph's shoulder. "You've no need to worry. They're both healthy and strong, even if your son did decide to show up early."

Zeph nodded, trying to believe the doc's words. "But they seem so…frail."

Doc laughed. "Of course. She's completely worn out. And he's so new, but he's sturdier than he looks. A very determined boy. Now," the man thumped him, "go enjoy what God has given. You've waited a long time for this."

An odd swelling shut off Zeph's breathing for just a moment as he turned and took in the sight of his wife nuzzling his child. And…Zeph felt the strangest thing—like something tangible in the air. Was it an assurance, maybe, or even a soft whisper? His son was here and all would be well.

At long last…all would be well.

⚭

Tyne stifled a giggle as she waved to Roxie and Ollie standing on the porch of their tidy little home. How love did transform a person, especially God's love. Tyne set her feet against the warming brick and snuggled Henry against her breast.

"Bye Grandma Roxie, bye Grandpa Ollie!" Daisy waved as the wagon jingled along and then the child buried herself in a cave of blankets in the back of the wagon. Daisy launched into a muffled rendition of "Silent Night." All six verses plus a German verse Ovie had taught her.

My, how that child had bloomed like a precious flower, like a precious daisy. And so had Tyne and her small family. A smile tugged at Tyne's mouth. She supposed she should include her extended family. For Roxie and Ollie had become the grandparents Tyne had always wished for her children. She rubbed her full stomach, a witness to the fullness of her new life.

As full as their bellies were, how would they ever manage another Christmas dinner? Tyne wasn't sure, but knew that Granny Annabelle, yet another grandparent in her children's lives, would be outdoing herself in that big house of hers. Nevertheless, Tyne would do her best to make this the best Christmas that Annabelle had ever had in several years. My, that woman was smitten with little Henry.

Tyne breathed in the crisp air and slid her hand across Zeph's thigh. He grinned and wagged an eyebrow at her.

"Happy?"

Tyne felt such a strong urge to crumble into a puddle of tears. If the man only knew. Instead, she blinked back the moisture and stiffened her trembling lip. "More than you'll ever know."

Zeph slipped his hand into hers, maintaining the reins in his other hand. "Me, too."

Daisy's voice grew quieter as she reached the end of the verses. And truer words were never lisped before.

Jesus, God's promise of peace,
Jesus, God's promise of peace.

Ransomed-Ever-After Fiction

Hello reader~

Thank you for reading *Wild Daisies Bloom!*

I pray you can use Tyne's journey as an inspiration for your own. If you've ever read my books before, you know I love to take characters at the end of their rope, at the bottom of the pit, in the worst possible circumstance and then allow them to be redeemed by Christ. Life is hard, crushing, and troublesome, true, BUT...Jesus. He brings you out of the miry clay of sin and circumstance.

Sometimes we as humans think we are beyond God's ability to save us from our sins. That we are so deprived, we could never entertain the idea of being cleansed of all unrighteousness and living eternally in heaven.

But that is just not true. King David had a man murdered to steal his wife. Yet, he was the man after God's own heart. Paul cheered the killing of Christians and went on with zeal to murder them by his own hand. But he became one of God's most dedicated followers and missionaries, giving his life to spread the gospel.

No one is beyond God's saving grace. Not even a soiled dove like Tyne. And that's her simple message.

You are not beyond saving.

You matter.

You are loved.

Still puzzled? Intrigued? Gripping your fingernails on the edge of unexplained horribleness? Go to my testimony page @https://www.peggytrotter.com. Finding God's saving grace is as is as easy as ABC, A—Admit you're a sinner, B—Believe in Jesus as the Son of God and His forgiveness, C—Confess your sins/Choose to follow Jesus, your Savior.

If the Son therefore shall make you free, ye shall be free

indeed.

John 8:36

Please find me all around the web and sign up for my newsletter:

peggytrotter.com

peggytrotter.blogspot.com

diamondsinfiction.blogspot.com

Twitter: https://twitter.com/Peggy_Trotter

Facebook: https://www.facebook.com/PeggyTrotterAuthor

Goodreads:

https://www.goodreads.com/author/show/13778873.Peggy_Trotte

r

Amazon Author's Profile Page:

amazon.com/author/peggytrotter.com

Instagram: https://www.instagram.com/peggy_trotter_author/

Pinterest: https://www.pinterest.com/PeggyTrotterAuthor/

LinkedIn: https://www.linkedin.com/in/peggy-trotter-44a29b95/

BookBub: https://www.bookbub.com/authors/peggy-trotter

MeWe: mewe.com/i/peggytrotter

Parler: https://parler.com/profile/PeggyTrotterAuthor

Usa.life: https://usa.life/PeggyTrotterAuthor

Gab: https://gab.com/PeggyTrotterAuthor

Soon to be released from the Up From the Miry Clay Series:

Chapter One

Fort Madison, Iowa—May, 1994

"You will do what I say, or I will contact Mr. Sterling."

Like a nail driven into soft wood, fear pierced Roose. Her trembling hand went to her throat and she stepped back. "Mr....Sterling?"

Her uncle, black eyes thinned with...hate? Anger? Roose wasn't sure which. Or maybe something more diabolical. Like greed.

"Yes," his smoke-roughened voice almost whispered in a hiss. "You remember Mr. Sterling, don't you?"

That deceptively gentle voice, placating at best, caused Roose to stumble backward again, colliding with the rugged side table. Glass jars tinkled behind her as the bit of furniture shifted.

She swallowed. Oh, she remembered Mr. Sterling. Even though it had been nearly three years ago now. Etched in her mind was how the compact man had run his fingers along her jaw, turning her head, inspecting every facial feature, gathering the expanse of her ghostly white hair in his hands, tipping her head back to examine her blue-pink eyes. Then, he'd turned to handling her body, her skin. She shuddered.

Her uncle gave a humorless laugh. "Ah, I see you do. He's hounding me, you know. Thinks adding you to his list of attractions would be quite beneficial."

For just a moment, Roose allowed herself to think of being nothing more than a circus attraction, gawked at, stared at, whispered about. Mr. Sterling, standing unnaturally straight, had promised her own enclosure to protect her from customers in her own tent. A place of safety, he'd said.

But all Roose could imagine was a cage. A large iron bird cage. And she with her pale-white skin, colorless hair, and blue-pink eyes would be on display for all to see. The hawkers in front of the red and white tent would yell, *come see the Iced Banshee, a colorless woman cursed for life for the horrible sins of her past! You can only see it here, folks, at Sterling's Traveling Circus and Spectacle.*

Uncle Ansel let his heavy lips widened into a smile as he slipped that horrible smelling cigar into the corner of his mouth. His dark spiny brows elevated. "He's willing to pay handsomely."

Roose wanted to close her eyes. Remove her uncle from her sight if only for a few seconds. But she didn't dare take her gaze from him. Instead she focused all her energy on breathing normally and not collapsing. "I will do it. I'll get it done."

Fat lips curled around the cigar in satisfaction, and Uncle leaned back in his woolen and silk roll-collared frock coat over his starched boiled shirt. Roose knew without looking he'd donned his gray trousers with the elegant side braid. Surely the man's entire closet consisted of multiples of these same garments, for he wore the ensemble every time she'd ever had the misfortune of seeing him. And those button boots would be shined to a blinding glare.

Instead of ruminating on his attire, Roose blinked. "I will, Uncle. I'll finish it all."

"Mr. Alexander will do, as you well know." His voice hardened over like his eyes of iron. "Not even in these confines will you address me so. Understood?"

Roose bobbed a shaky acknowledgement. Would she never learn? Her feeble mind thought bringing up the relationship would soften him. Make him more merciful. Again, wrong.

"After your trollop mother spawned you, she recognized you were nothing but an unfortunate freak of nature. If only she'd lived to bear your upbringing." He spun and strode toward the shack's door. Then he paused and looked back. His string of obscenities degraded her further. "But, now I am cursed to look upon you, a misbegotten mutant. Pay your expenses with my coin. And I will do so, one way or another. Even if that means auctioning you off to Mr. Sterling."

"Please, I—"

The screen door slapped her plea in half. Roose squeezed her eyes closed, rolled her lips into her mouth, and fisted her hands. Tension locked up her body. For a moment she did nothing but huff short breaths. Would Mr. Sterling come? Would her uncle really sell her like a bushel basket of fruit?

That brought her eyes open to assess the ten bushel baskets of strawberries strewn across the rough wooden floor. The fruit, red, very ripe, and tender demanded immediate attention. This overabundance had led Roose to plead for extra time to process the fruit into pies, jams, and jellies before it ruined. An impossible task.

This was her life. She was the...Fruit Phantom.

She let go a strangled cry. How she hated that name. Not that it mattered. One way or another, she was imprisoned. Forced to work until she dropped or exposed in a cage for customers' unadulterated amusement. She sucked in one last breath. At least she could work here hidden from lewd glances and lecherous innuendos. With a cry of despair, she grabbed up two large tubs. There would be no sleep tonight. Only work. Work until she collapsed. At the pump outside, she primed with the pitcher and yanked the handle until the water spilled forth.

Pies first, as always, then the preserves. Her mind switched automatically into practical matters. She had to get this done. Giving her uncle another reason to seek out Mr. Sterling just wouldn't do.

She would not let this round of rotting fruit be her downfall.

Sign up for my newsletter so you don't miss *Flawed Roses Flourish's* release! Sign up @https://www.peggytrotter.com/

Find all my books @https://www.amazon.com/Peggy-Trotter/e/B00V15P2LU